Ransleigh Rogues

***Where these notorious rakes go,
scandal always follows...***

Max, Will, Alastair and Dominic Ransleigh—cousins,
friends...and the most wickedly attractive men in
Regency London. Between war, betrayal
and scandal, love has never featured
in the Ransleighs' destinies—until now!

Don't miss this enthralling quartet
from Julia Justiss.

We met Max, Will and Alastair in

The Rake to Ruin Her

The Rake to Redeem Her

and

The Rake to Rescue Her

Now follow Dominic's adventures in

The Rake to Reveal Her

Author Note

When I first envisioned the Ransleigh cousins, I knew Dom was going to return from Waterloo with serious injuries and struggle to re-create his life—with the help of a remarkable woman (and in this case, her passel of orphans!). What I didn't know was how personal this story would become.

In August 2012, my husband, father-in-law and I were rear-ended by a vehicle traveling at high speed. My husband, riding in the backseat, had his pelvis fractured in eight places and broke the C-2 bone in his spine. For six weeks, he was totally paralyzed from the chin down. Slowly, over the next seven months of hospitalization, through extensive physical therapy and unrelenting effort, he gradually retrieved the use of his arms and legs. Today, he continues to work toward normalcy, fighting chronic pain with a smile.

Dom's injuries, fortunately, were less severe—but as they prevented him from resuming the occupation he'd always pursued, they were equally difficult to accept. But Dom, a hero like my husband, rejected self-pity and fought off depression. Persevering to find himself again, he responds to the unusual, unlikely heroine who reaches out to him, and leads them both to a happy future.

I hope you will enjoy their story.

Julia Justiss

The Rake
to Reveal Her

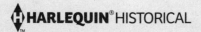
HARLEQUIN HISTORICAL

Recycling programs
for this product may
not exist in your area.

ISBN-13: 978-0-373-29832-7

The Rake to Reveal Her

Printed in U.S.A.

Julia Justiss wrote her first ideas for Nancy Drew stories in her third-grade notebook, and has been writing ever since. After publishing poetry in college, she turned to novels. Her Regency historicals have won or placed in contests by the Romance Writers of America, *RT Book Reviews* magazine, National Readers' Choice and Daphne du Maurier. She lives with her husband in Texas. For news and contests, visit juliajustiss.com.

Books by Julia Justiss

Harlequin Historical

Ransleigh Rogues

The Rake to Ruin Her
The Rake to Redeem Her
The Rake to Rescue Her
The Rake to Reveal Her

Silk & Scandal

The Smuggler and the Society Bride

Linked by Character

The Wedding Gamble
A Most Unconventional Match

Stand-Alone Novels

One Candlelit Christmas
"Christmas Wedding Wish"
From Waif to Gentleman's Wife
Society's Most Disreputable Gentleman

Visit the Author Profile page at Harlequin.com for more titles.

To my husband and hero:
Never give in.
Never give up.

Chapter One

Suffolk—spring 1816

His ears still ringing from the impact of the fall, Dominic Fitzallen Ransleigh levered himself to a sitting position in the muddy Suffolk lane. Air hissed in and out of his gritted teeth as he waited for the red wave of pain obscuring his vision to subside. Which it did, just in time for him to see that black devil, Diablo, trot around the corner and out of sight.

Headed back to the barn, probably, Dom thought. If horses could laugh, surely the bad-tempered varlet was laughing at him.

It was his own fault, always choosing the most difficult and high-spirited colts to train as hunters. Horses with the speed and heart to gallop across country, jumping with ease any obstacle in their paths, but needing two strong hands on the reins to control their headstrong, temperamental natures.

He looked down at his one remaining hand, still trembling from the strain of that wild ride. Flexing the wrist, he judged it sore but not broken. After years of tending himself from various injuries suffered during his service with the Sixteenth Dragoons, a gingerly bending of the arm informed him no bones were broken there, either.

His left shoulder still throbbed, but at least he hadn't fallen on the stump of his right arm. Had he done that, he'd probably still be unconscious from the agony.

Resigning himself to sit in the mud until his muzzy head cleared, Dom gazed down the lane after the fleeing horse. Though the doctors had warned him, he'd resisted accepting what he'd just proved: he'd not be able to control Diablo, or any of the other horses in his stable full of hunters, with a single good hand.

Sighing, Dom struggled to his feet. He might as well face the inevitable. As he'd never be able to ride Diablo or the others again, there was no sense hanging on to them. The bitter taste of defeat in his mouth, he told himself he would look into selling them off at Tattersall's while the horses were still in prime form and able to fetch a good price. Sell the four-horse carriages, too, since with one hand, he couldn't handle more than a pair.

Thereby severing one more link between the man he'd been before Waterloo, and now.

Jilting a fiancée, leaving the army, and now this. Nothing like changing his world completely in the space of a week.

Could he give it all up? he wondered as he set off down the lane. Following in his hunting-mad father's footsteps had been his goal since he'd joined his first chase, schooling hunters a talent he worked to perfect. Before the army and between Oxford terms, he'd spent all his time studying horses, looking for that perfect combination of bone, stamina and spirit that made a good hunter. Buying them, training them, then hunting and steeplechasing with the like-minded friends who called themselves 'Dom's Daredevils'.

Stripped of that occupation, the future stretched before him as a frightening void.

Though he'd never previously had a taste for solitude, within days of his return, he'd felt compelled to leave London. The prospect of visiting his clubs, attending a ball, mixing with the old crowd at Tatt's, inspecting the horses before a sale—all the activities in which he'd once delighted—now repelled him. Sending away even his cousin Will, who'd rescued him from the battlefield and tended him for months, he'd retreated to Bildenstone— the family estate he'd not seen in years, and hadn't even been sure was still habitable.

He'd sent Elizabeth away, too. A wave of grief and remorse swept through him as her lovely face surfaced in his mind. How could he have asked her to wait for him to recover, when the man he was now no longer fit into the world of hunts and balls they'd meant to share?

Ruthlessly he extinguished her image, everything about her and the hopes they once cherished too painful to contemplate. Best to concentrate on taking the next small step down the road ahead, small steps being all he could manage towards a future cloaked in a shifting mist of uncertainty.

Fighting the despair threatening to suck him down, he reminded himself again why he'd left friends, fiancée, and all that was familiar.

To find himself…whatever was left to find.

Wearily he picked up his pace, his rattled brain still righting itself. He traversed the sharp corner around which his horse had disappeared to find himself almost face to face with a young woman leading a mare.

They both started, the horsing rearing a little.

'Down, Starfire,' a feminine voice commanded. Looking up at him expectantly, the girl smiled and said, 'Sir, will you give me a hand? I was almost run down by a black beast of a stallion, which startled my mare. I'm afraid I wasn't paying enough attention, and lost my seat. I'll require help to remount.'

His mind still befuddled, Dom stared at her. Though tall enough that he didn't have to look down very far, his first impression was of a little brown wren—lovely pale complexion, big brown eyes, hair of indeterminate hue tucked under a tired-looking bonnet, and a worn brown habit years out of date.

The unknown miss didn't flinch at his eye patch, he had to give her that. Nor did her eyes stray to the pinned-up sleeve of his missing arm—the sleeve now liberally spattered with mud and decorated with leaf-bits, as was the rest of his clothing. Heavens, he must look like a vagrant who'd slept in the woods. It was a wonder she didn't run screaming in the opposite direction.

His lips curved into a whimsical smile at the thought as her pleasant expression faded. 'Sir, could you give me a hand, help me remount?' she all but shouted.

Dom flinched at the loud tones. *She must think me simple as well as dishevelled.* As his mind finally cleared and her request registered, his amusement vanished.

The images flashed into his head—all the girls he'd lifted in a dance, tossed into saddles…carried into bed. With two strong arms.

Anger coursed through him. 'That would be a bit of problem.' He gestured to his empty sleeve. 'Afraid I can't help you. Good day, miss.'

Her eyes widened as he began to walk past her. 'Can't help me?' she echoed. 'Can't—or won't?'

Fury mounting, he wheeled back to face her. 'Don't you see, idiot girl?' he spat out. 'I'm…impaired.'

Crippled would be a better description, but he couldn't get his mouth around the word. He turned to walk away again.

She hurried forward, the horse trailing on the reins

behind her, and blocked his path. 'What I see,' she said, her dark eyes flashing, 'is that you have one good arm, whether or not you choose to use it. Which is more than many of the soldiers who didn't survive Waterloo, including my father. *He* wouldn't have hesitated to give me a leg up, even with only one hand!'

Before he could respond, she shortened the lead on the horse's reins and snapped, 'Very well. I shall search for a more obliging log or tree stump. Good day, sir.'

Bemused, he watched the sway of her neat little bottom as she marched angrily away. With well-tended forest on either side of the lane—deadfall quickly removed to provide firewood for someone's hearth—he didn't think she was likely to find what she sought.

Turning back towards Bildenstone, he set off walking, wondering who the devil she was. Not that, having spent the last ten years either with the army, at his hunting box in Leicestershire or in London, he expected to recognise any of the locals. That girl would have been only a child the last time he'd been here, seven years ago.

He'd probably just insulted the daughter of some local worthy—though, given the shabby condition of her riding habit, not a man of great means. He meant to limit as much as possible any interaction with his neighbours, but in the restricted society of the country, he'd likely encounter her again. Perhaps by then, he'd be able to tender a sincere apology.

Stomping down the lane without encountering any objects suitable for use as a mounting block, Theodora Branwell felt her anger grow. After a fruitless ten-minute search, she conceded that she might have to walk all the way back to Thornfield Place before she could find a way to remount her horse.

Which meant she might as well abandon her purpose and try again tomorrow.

Not the least of her ire and frustration she directed at herself. If she'd not been so lost in rehearsing her arguments, she would have heard the approaching hoofbeats and had her mount well in hand before the stallion burst around the corner and flew past them. After all the obstacles they'd ridden over in India and on the Peninsula, how Papa would laugh to know she'd been unseated by so simple a device!

No sense bemoaning; she might as well accept that her lapse had ruined the timing for making a call on her prospective landlord today.

She had Charles to check on, she thought, her heart warming as she pictured the little boy she'd brought up. Then there were the rest of the children to settle, especially the two new little ones the Colonel had just sent her from Brussels. Though the manor's small nursery and adjoining bedchamber were becoming rather crowded, making settling the matter of the school and dormitory ever more urgent, Constancia and Jemmie would find them places. But she knew the thin boy and the pale, silent girl would feel better after a few sweetmeats, a reassuring hug, and a story to make them welcome.

How frightening and strange the English countryside must seem to a child, torn from the familiar if unstable life of travelling with an army across the dusty fields and valleys of Portugal and Spain. Especially after losing one's last parent.

It was a daunting enough prospect for her, and she was an adult.

The extra day would allow her to go over her arguments one more time. She liked Thornfield Place very much; she only had to convince Mr Ransleigh, her mostly absentee landlord who had now unaccountably taken up residence, that turning the neglected outbuilding on his property into a home and school for soldiers' orphans would cause no problem and was a noble thing to do.

A guilty pang struck her. She'd really been too hard on the one-armed, one-eyed man in the lane. Though he might have been injured in an accident, he had the unmistakable bearing of a soldier. Had he suffered his wounds at Waterloo? Recovering from such severe losses would be slow; frustration over his limitations might at times make him wonder if it would not have been better, had he never made it off the battlefield.

She knew it was. She'd have given anything, had Papa been found alive, whatever his condition. Or Marshall, dead these five years now.

The bitter anguish of her fiancé's loss scoured her again. How much different would her life be now, had he not fallen on that Spanish plain? They'd be long married, doubtless with children, her love returned and her place in society secure as his wife.

But it hadn't been fair to take out her desolation on that poor soldier. Wholly preoccupied with her own purpose, she only now recalled how thin his frame was, how dishevelled his rough clothing. When had he last eaten a good meal? Finding employment must be difficult for an ex-soldier with only one arm.

He'd not carried a pack, she remembered, so he must be a local resident. Country society comprised a small circle, she'd been told, much like the army. Which meant she'd probably encounter the man again. If she did, she would have to apologise. Perhaps in the interim, she might also think of some job she could hire him to perform at Thornfield Place.

Satisfied that she'd be able to atone for her rudeness, she dismissed him from her mind and trudged down the lane back towards Thornfield.

* * *

Nearly an hour later, Theo finally reached the stables and turned over her well-walked horse. Dismissing her irritation over an afternoon wasted, she entered through a back door, to have Franklin, her newly hired butler, inform her that a visitor awaited her.

Since she had no acquaintance in the county beyond the village solicitor she'd written to help her find staff, she couldn't imagine who might be calling. Curiosity speeding her step, she'd reached the parlour threshold before it struck her that, according to the dimly remembered rules of proper behaviour her long-dead mama had tried to instil in her, she ought to have gone upstairs to change into a presentable gown before receiving visitors.

But the identity of the lady awaiting her drove all such thoughts from her head. 'Aunt Amelia!' she cried in surprise and delight.

'My darling Theo! I'm so glad to have you home at last!' the lady declared, encircling her in a pair of plump, scented arms.

Theo's throat tightened as she returned the hug of her last remaining close relation. 'I'm so glad, too, Aunt Amelia. But what are you doing here? And how did you know I was at Thornfield Place?'

'I'd hoped you'd come to see me in London after you left Brussels. When you wrote you'd already consulted Richard's lawyer, found a suitable country manor, and wished to get settled there before you visited, I just couldn't wait.'

'I'm so glad you've come, although I fear you'll not find the establishment nearly up to your standards. I'm still hiring staff, and everything is at sixes and sevens.'

Pushing away, she surveyed the lady she'd not seen in over five years. 'How handsome you look in that cherry gown! In the first crack of fashion, I'd wager—not that I would know.'

'You're looking very well, too, my dear—though I can't in good conscience return the compliment about the habit.' After a grimace at the offending garment, she continued. 'Now that you're finally back in England, we must attend to that! One can understand the unfashionable dress, living in all the God-forsaken places my brother dragged you, but how have you managed to keep your complexion so fresh? I thought to find you thin and brown as a nut.'

'I've always been disgusting healthy, or so the English memsahibs used to tell Papa.'

'Unlike your poor mama, God rest her soul.' Sadness flitting across her face, she said, 'I still can't believe we've lost Richard, too.'

Steeling herself against the ever-present ache of loss, Theo said, 'I'm glad you've given up your blacks; the colour doesn't suit you.'

'You don't think it too soon? It's only nine months since…' Her voice trailed off.

'Since Papa fell at Waterloo,' Theo replied, making herself say the words matter of factly.

'It just doesn't seem fair,' Lady Amelia said, frowning. 'My brother surviving all those horrid battles, first in India, then on the Peninsula, only to be killed in the very last action of the war! But enough of that,' she said after a glance at Theo—who perhaps wasn't concealing her distress as well as she thought. 'Shall we have tea?'

'Of course. I'm devilish thirsty myself,' she said drily. 'I'll ring for Franklin.'

After instructing the butler to bring tea and refreshments, Theo joined her aunt on the sofa.

'How long can you stay? I'll have Reeves prepare you a room. It's a bit hectic with the children not settled yet, but I think we can make you comfortable.'

'Children?' her aunt repeated. 'So you still have them— Jemmie, the boy your father took in when his sergeant father died? And the little girl you wrote me about. Besides Charles, of course. How is the poor little orphan?'

'Doing well,' Theo said, her heart warming as she thought of him. 'A sturdy four-year-old now.'

'Goodness, that old already! His father's family never…'

'No. Lord Everly's commander, Colonel Vaughn, wrote to his father again when I returned with Charles after the birth, to inform him of the poor mother's death in childbed, but the marquess did not deign to reply.' She neglected mentioning how she'd rejoiced at learning she'd be able to keep the child. 'So, he's still with me. Indeed, I can't imagine being parted from him.'

'You're quite young enough to marry and have sons who truly *are* your own,' her aunt replied tartly. 'I suppose you had to do your Christian duty and accompany that unfortunate girl, *enceinte* and grieving, back to England after Everly was killed. I do wish you'd made it to London for the birth, though. How unfortunate to have his mama fall ill, stranding you at some isolated convent in the wilds of Portugal! Naturally, after her death, you felt obliged to take charge of the infant until he could be returned to his family. But with that family unwilling to accept the boy and Richard gone—are you sure you should continue caring for him? As for the others, would it not be better to put them into the custody of the parish? Under a colonel's guardianship, such an odd household might have been tolerated in the army overseas, but even with your papa present, such a ménage here in England would be considered very strange.' She sighed. 'You were ever wont to pick up the stray and injured, even as a child.'

'I'm sure you would have done the same, had you been there to see them, poor little creatures left on their own to beg or starve.'

'None the less, without Richard… It's just not fitting for a gently reared girl to have charge of…children like that.'

Theo laughed. 'After growing up in India and all those years following the drum, I don't believe I qualify as "gently reared".'

Her aunt gave her a fulminating look. 'You're still gently *born*, regardless of the unconventionality of your upbringing, and are as well, I understand, a considerable heiress. Despite your…unusual circumstances, I wouldn't despair of having you make a good match. Won't you come to me in London for the Season, let me find you a good man to take your father's place in your life?'

With a firm negative shake of her head, Theo said, 'I can't imagine a prospective suitor would look kindly on the idea of taking in a child not his own. Since I won't give up Charles, I doubt my fortune is large enough to tempt any man into marrying me. That is, any man I'd consider marrying.'

'You do yourself a disservice,' Lady Amelia protested. Giving Theo a quick inspection, she said, 'Your figure is fine, your complexion lovely, and those brown eyes quite luminous. I'm certain my maid could do wonders with that curly dark hair. You're a bit taller than is fashionable, but with the proper gowns, I think quite a number of eligible gentleman might come up to snuff. You are the grand-daughter of an earl, after all.'

Waving Theo to silence before she could protest again, Lady Amelia continued. 'If you love Charles as you say you do, you must know the best thing for him would be for you to marry! Give him a father to pattern himself after, someone who could teach him all those manly pursuits so important to gentleman, and introduce him to the clubs and societies he must frequent to be accepted by his peers. As for the other children… I don't wish to set your back up, but it really would be better for them to be placed in an institution where they can learn a vocation. You do them no favours, to raise them above their stations.'

Ignoring her aunt's words about Charles, which had the uncomfortable ring of truth about them, Theo said, 'I don't intend to raise the others above their stations. In fact, arranging for their proper care is the main reason I decided to come here. I have to admit, I'm looking forward to having a settled home again myself, something I've not had since we left India.'

She left unspoken her fear that making a life alone in England, the ancestral home in which she'd never lived, whose ways often seemed as strange to her as India's would to her aunt, might prove a daunting task.

No matter, she would master it. She must, for the children and for herself.

'I did wonder why you chose a manor in Suffolk. As I understand the provisions of the will, Richard left you numerous properties, along with your mama's considerable fortune. Why did you not settle on one of them?'

'The solicitor informed me that all the properties are let to long-term lessees, whom I wouldn't wish to displace. So I asked Mr Mitchell to find me a suitable country manor to rent, something with a sturdy outbuilding nearby of sufficient size to be turned into a dormitory and school. A place where the children can learn their letters and be taught a trade.'

Her aunt laughed. 'Goodness, that sounds like a great deal of trouble! Wouldn't it be simpler to send them off to the parish? It's only two children, after all.' At the look on Theo's face, she said, 'It is just the two?'

'Well, you see,' Theo explained, well aware of her aunt's probable reaction to the news, 'Colonel Vaughn told me before we left Brussels how much he appreciated what Papa and I had done for the orphans. After Waterloo, I… found two others, and in a reply I've just posted to his letter enquiring about the possibility, I assured him I would be happy to take in more.'

'Theo, no!' her aunt cried. 'You can't mean to bury yourself in the country and turn into some glorified—*orphanage matron*, looking after the children of who knows who!'

'Who else will look after them, if I don't? Should I just stand by and see the offspring of our valiant soldiers end up in a workhouse? Besides, I need something useful to do with my life, now that…now that I won't be running Papa's household any longer,' she finished, proud to have made it through that sentence without a tremble in her voice.

'My dear Theo, you're far too young to behave as if your life is over! I know you believe you buried your heart when Marshall fell at Fuentes de Oñoro. But I promise you, one can find love again—if you will only let yourself. I'm certain Lieutenant Hazlett wouldn't want you to dwindle away into an old maid, alone and grieving.'

'At seven-and-twenty, I imagine society already considers me at my last prayers,' she evaded. Though it had been more than five years now, she still couldn't speak of the horror of losing Marshall. Loving so intensely had led to intolerable pain, all she could endure. She had no intention of subjecting herself to that ever again.

Besides, she could never marry someone without telling him the truth—and she didn't dare risk that.

'I'll not argue the point—for now!' her aunt said. 'But I would like to persuade you to come to London. Though I perfectly understand why you felt it your duty to remain with Charles's mother during her Hour of Need, I was so disappointed when you didn't come stay with me as we'd planned. I've hoped since then we'd have another chance for me to spoil you a bit, after all the time you've spent in the wilds, billeted who knows where, never knowing where your next meal might come from, and with the worry of impending battle always weighing on you!'

'One never completely escaped the worry,' Theo admitted, 'but battle was the exception. Most of the time was spent training, moving between encampments, or billeted in winter quarters. Provisions were generally good, with game to supplement the soup pot. As for accommodations…' she chuckled, remembering '…Papa and I shared everything from a campaign tent to cots in a stable to the bedchamber of a *marquesa*'s palace! It was a grand adventure shared with marvellous companions, and I wouldn't have missed it for the world.'

It had also brought her Charles, and, she thought as a stab of grief gashed her, a fiery passion she didn't expect ever to experience again.

Which also reminded her that not all the companions had been marvellous. After the devastation of her fiancé's death, one officer who was no gentleman had sniffed at her skirts, certain she must eventually succumb to the blandishments of a man of his high birth and social position.

The only benefit of leaving the regiment was she'd never have to deal with Audley Tremaine again.

'Game in the soup pot and a cot in a stable!' her aunt cried, recalling her attention. 'Call me pudding-hearted, but I prefer a bed with my own linens under a sturdy roof, awakened by nothing more threatening than the shouts of milk-sellers.'

'Campaigning would not have been for you,' Theo agreed. 'But I must leave you now to check on the children. Constancia—you remember Constancia, the nursemaid I brought with me from the convent after Charles was born?—will show you to your room. I hope you'll make a long visit!'

'I am due back in London shortly, and you'll have much to do, getting your establishment put together. Unless I can dissuade you from this enterprise? Coax you to leave the children with those used to dealing with orphans, and concentrate on your own future?'

'Abandon them to a workhouse?' Theo's heart twisted as she thought of those innocents turned over to strange and uncaring hands. 'No, you cannot dissuade me.'

Lady Amelia sighed. 'I didn't think so. You're as head-strong as Richard when you get the bit between your teeth. The whole family tried to talk him out of going to India, but no one could prevail upon him to remain at home, tending his acres like a proper English gentleman, once he'd taken the idea in his head.'

'I do appreciate your wishing to secure a more suitable future for me,' Theo assured her. 'But having never lived in England and being so little acquainted with the society's rules, I fear I'd be an even greater disappointment than Papa, were you to try to foist me on the Marriage Mart.'

'A lovely, capable, intelligent girl like you? I don't believe it! Though I admire your desire to aid those poor unfortunates, I refuse to entirely cede my position. I still think marriage would be best for you *and* them, and I shall be searching for a way to make it happen!'

Theo laughed. 'Scheme, then, if it makes you happy.'

'It's your happiness I worry about, my dear. You're still so young! I want you to find joy again.'

Joy. She'd experienced its rapture—and paid its bitter price. She'd since decided she could make do with contentment, as long as Charles was safe and happy.

'I expect to be happy in my life, helping those "poor unfortunates",' she told her aunt firmly as she kissed her cheek.

So she must be, she thought as she walked out of the room. It was the only life left to her, a choice she'd sealed years ago when she left that Portuguese convent with a swaddled newborn in her arms.

Chapter Two

By the time Dom, beyond exhausted by the long walk home, arrived back at Bildenstone Hall, all he wanted was a glass of laudanum-laced brandy and something soft on to which he could become horizontal. Instead, he was met at the door by the elderly butler, Wilton, who informed him the Squire, Lady Wentworth and Miss Wentworth awaited him in the parlour—and had been waiting more than an hour.

'Send them away,' Dom ordered, limping past the man, desperate for that drink to ease the headache that was compounding the misery of his throbbing wrist and shoulder.

'But, Mr Ransleigh,' Wilton protested as he trailed after Dom, 'the Squire said the matter was urgent, and he would wait as long as necessary to see you today!'

The words trembled on Dom's lips to consign the lot of them—the Squire, Lady Whomever, the girl in the lane, Diablo and the butler—to hell and back. With difficulty, he swallowed them.

While Dom hoped to socialise as little as possible, he'd known that, once the Squire learned the owner of the most extensive property in the county had taken up residence, courtesy demanded he pay a call at Bildenstone Hall. Though his head pounded like an anvil upon which a blacksmith was hammering out horseshoes, he knew that it would be the height of incivility to send away sight unseen so distinguished a neighbour.

Unless he wished Wilton to tell that worthy and his party that, having fallen off a horse and been forced to walk home, Mr Ransleigh was in no fit state to receive them.

He might not have resided at Bildenstone Hall for years, but beyond doubt, every member of the gentry for miles around knew of 'Dandy Dom' and his exploits on the hunting field and in the army. Call it foolish pride, but even more than being branded as churlish, he dreaded being considered a weakling—a conclusion his injuries might make strangers all too quick to draw.

Dredging up from deep within the will that had kept him in the saddle through the fatigue and strain of many long campaigns, Dom said, 'Very well. Tell them I'm just back from…riding the fields and will need a few moments to make myself presentable.'

'Very good, Mr Ransleigh,' the butler said, obviously relieved not to have to deliver a message of dismissal to a man of the Squire's stature.

Hauling himself up the stairs, he rang for Henries. He had his mud-spattered garments removed by the time the batman arrived to help him into clean ones. Battle-ready within minutes, he squared his tired shoulders and headed for the stairs.

Though he ached for a soothing draught and a deep sleep, he figured he could stay upright for the length of a courtesy call. He was too tired to wonder why Lady Somebody and her daughter had accompanied the Squire.

A few moments later, he forced a smile to his lips and entered the drawing room.

'Squire Marlowe, how kind of you to call! And whom

do I have the honour of addressing?' He gestured to the ladies.

'So good to see you, too, Mr Ransleigh, after so many years!' the Squire replied. 'Lady Wentworth and Miss Wentworth, may I introduce to you our illustrious neighbour, Mr Dominic Ransleigh. A captain in the Sixteenth Light Dragoons who charged into the teeth of Napoleon's finest, one of the heroes of Waterloo!'

'Ladies, a pleasure,' Dom said as the callers curtsied to his bow.

'We've heard of your gallant deeds, of course, Mr Ransleigh,' Lady Wentworth said. 'Everyone in the county is so proud of you.'

'We were all of us delighted to learn you intended to take up residence at Bildenstone Hall again,' the Squire said. 'Your father and mother, God rest their souls, were sorely missed when they abandoned Suffolk to settle at Upton Park.'

Had the neighbourhood felt slighted by his father's removal to Quorn country? Dom wondered, trying to read the man's tone.

'When she learned I meant to call today,' the Squire continued, 'Lady Wentworth, head of the Improvement Society for Whitfield Parish, begged leave to accompany me. With her lovely daughter, Miss Wentworth, the ornament of our local society who, sadly, is soon to join her godmother for the Season in London.'

So that was why Lady Somebody had come, Dom thought, his mind clearing as he caught this last bit. As closely as news about his family was followed, he suspected that word of his broken engagement had already made it to Suffolk. The nephew of an earl with a tidy fortune and important family connections would be considered an attractive prospect by country gentry like Lady Wentworth, regardless of his physical shortcomings.

Equally obvious, the enthusiasm engendered in her mother by his matrimonial assets was not entirely shared by the daughter. Dom noted her gaze travelling from the pinned-up sleeve to his eye patch and back, her expression a mingling of awe and distaste.

First the girl in the lane scolding him for making excuse of his limitations, and now Miss Wentworth's fascinated disdain. As if he were the prime attraction in a raree-show.

He had the ignoble urge to sidle up to her and see if she would flinch away. When his continued attention finally alerted her that he'd caught her staring at him, she coloured and gave him what he supposed most men would consider an enticing smile.

With her pretty face and glossy blond locks, she was as lovely as the Squire had pronounced her—and he felt no attraction at all.

Perhaps he ought to relieve her anxiety by assuring her he was in no danger of falling for the charms of an *ingénue* who'd probably never set foot outside her home parish. Then, rebuking himself for his uncharitable thoughts, he turned his attention back to the mother, who was nattering on about her reasons for accompanying the squire.

'...take the liberty of accompanying Squire Marlowe, when in the strictest sense, I should not have called until my husband, Sir John, called first. However, there is a matter of urgency at hand. My society oversees the parish poorhouse, where honest folk in need are offered assistance. As I'm sure you'll agree, it's imperative that such unfortunates, their morals already weakened by low birth and squalid surroundings, not be made more vulnerable by exposure to additional corruption. As they certainly would be, were children of that sort allowed to reside here!'

'Children of that sort?' Dom echoed. 'Forgive me, Lady Wentworth, but I have no idea what you're talking about.'

'Have you not yet been informed of the matter?' the lady cried, indignation in her tones. 'Infamous!'

Resigning himself to the fact that, though Lady Wentworth's main purpose might be to show off her attractive daughter, her secondary one was not likely to be quickly accomplished, Dom said, 'Shall we be seated? I see Wilton already brought tea; can he refresh your cups?'

Resisting the devilish urge to seat himself close to Miss Wentworth, and see whether the inducements of his wealth and lineage won out over her distaste for his damaged person, he took a chair opposite the sofa.

After Wilton had served the guests, he turned to the Squire, hoping his explanation would prove briefer. 'Won't you acquaint me with the matter?'

'Certainly,' the Squire said. 'Two days ago, Mr Scarsdale, the solicitor in Hadwell, mentioned to me that Thornfield Place, which abuts your southern boundaries, had been let by a Theo Branwell. He then informed me that this man, already in residence, intends to approach you about renting the old stone barn your father once planned to turn into a cloth manufactory. For the purpose of setting up a *home for soldiers' orphans*.'

'A terrible prospect!' Lady Wentworth cried, seizing hold of the conversation. 'Having been with the army, Mr Ransleigh, you know better than we how rough a life it is! Lord Wellington himself referred to the common soldiery as "the dregs of the earth". Only consider the offspring of such persons, growing up around vulgarity, drunkenness, and the company of...' With a glance at her daughter, she leaned closer to whisper, *'Campfollowing women!'*

Settling herself back, she continued in normal tones. 'They could not help but have been corrupted since

birth. I'm sure you understand our horror at the prospect
that such children might be lodged nearby. Unthinkable
enough that gently raised folk be subjected to their presence! Only consider how much more injurious association with them would be for the orphaned poor, with their
innate bent to depravity. As head of a society devoted to
their well-being, I felt it my Duty to speak with you at once
about this nefarious scheme. Doubtless, this Mr Branwell
means to play upon your sympathies as a former soldier.
But as a gentleman of wit and discernment, I'm sure you
could not wish to lend yourself to such an enterprise.'

In truth, Dom didn't wish to lend himself to anything,
particularly not to the lady whose strident voice was intensifying the pounding in his head. Knowing that responding would encourage her to embellish, likely at enough
length that he got a good eyeful of her beauteous daughter's neatly turned ankles, he meant to give her no excuse
to prolong the interview.

'I understand your concern, Lady Wentworth, and
yours, Squire Marlowe. I assure you, when and if I'm approached by Mr Branwell, I will give the matter my most
careful consideration. After such a long wait, I'm sure
you must be pressed to return to other engagements. I
myself am overdue to consult with my steward,' he lied
smoothly. 'So you must excuse me, but do finish your tea
before you depart.'

He rose as he spoke, continuing quickly. 'Squire, a pleasure to see you again. Miss Wentworth, I wish you well
on your Season, and best of luck with your society, Lady
Wentworth.'

Deaf to their expressions of gratitude and protesta-
tions that they were in no hurry, Dom bowed and left
the parlour.

Retreating to his chamber with as much speed as he
could muster, he barely made it to the bed before his legs

crumpled under him. Bracing himself with his good arm, he sank face-down on to the blessedly soft, flat surface and fell instantly to sleep.

With dim memories of having awakened in the dark to glug down a glass of the laudanum-laced brandy at his bedside, Dom pulled himself from sleep late the next morning, groggy and aching. He took another quick swallow of the brandy, thinking as he sank back against the pillows that he'd not indulged in strong spirits before breakfast since his salad days at Oxford.

After a few moments, the liquor soothing the sharp edges off his ever-present pain, Dom felt human enough to ring for his batman. Hot coffee and a hot bath would dispel the grogginess, after which he could dress and ready himself…for what?

Once, he would have headed for the barns to check on his horses. How he'd prided himself on his reputation for finding the most spirited yearlings with jumping promise and bending the difficult horses to his will, schooling them to jump obstacles they'd rather avoid. Gloried in the excitement of sitting astride a ton of barely controlled wildness while galloping through woods, fields and meadows, jumping streams, brush and fences.

There'd be no more of that, as yesterday had demonstrated with painful clarity.

He should go to his study, check the London papers and the current prices for prime hunters at Tatt's. Or write to some hunting enthusiasts, asking if they were interested in purchasing any of his horses.

His spirits, already at a low ebb, sank even more at the prospect.

No, he couldn't face that today. He'd go poke about in the library, which was as respectably large and well filled a room as he remembered. The pleasure of reading, a pastime often indulged while in winter quarters on the Peninsula, had been restricted by the dearth of books available. The single bright spot in his decision to retreat to Bildenstone was having access to the wealth of volumes his grandfather had accumulated.

Finding something intriguing would distract him from his misfortunes and raise his spirits, he told himself. Maybe he'd wander outside to read, see if the gazebo in his mother's garden was still a pleasant place to sit.

He needed to start figuring out his future…but not yet. Once the additional aches of yesterday's disastrous episode faded, he'd be in a better frame of mind to move forward.

An hour later, fed, dressed and feeling marginally better, Dom walked towards the library. Encountering the butler on the way reminded him of the previous day's meeting, and he paused.

'Wilton, I don't wish to receive any more visitors. I mean *no one*, not even if God Himself turns up on my doorstep!'

Looking pained at that sacrilege, Wilton nodded. 'As you wish, Mr Ransleigh.'

'That's what I wish,' he muttered, and continued to the library.

After browsing through Caesar's *Commentaries*, lamenting his inattention during Latin studies, Dom settled on a volume of Herodotus. The day having turned cloudy, he abandoned thoughts of the garden and settled in a wing chair before a snug fire.

As he'd hoped, the discussion of the struggle between Xerxes and the Spartans soon absorbed his attention.

When Wilton bowed himself into the room later, he realised enough time had passed that he was hungry.

Unwilling to leave the comfortable chair, he said,

'Would you ask Cook to prepare some of the ham and cheese from last night, and bring it here to the library?'

'Of course, Mr Ransleigh. But first...' the butler hesitated, an anxious expression on his face '...I'm afraid I must tell you that...that a young lady has called. I explained that you weren't receiving anyone, under any circumstances, but she said the matter was urgent and she would not leave until she saw you.'

Yet *another* lady on an urgent errand that would not keep? Who might it be now?

Though he'd happily tilled his way through fields of accommodating beauties before getting himself engaged, he'd always been careful; he had no fears that some dimly remembered female stood on his doorstep with a *petit paquet* in arms.

Curiosity was soon submerged by a lingering irritation over yesterday's unwelcome visitors. 'You didn't admit her, did you?'

'No, sir. Following your instructions, I closed the door—in her face, as she refused to move, a thing I've never done in my life, sir!'

'Sounds like problem solved,' Dom said. 'Eventually, she'll tire of waiting and go home. Will you have that tray brought up, and some more coffee, please?'

The butler lingered, looking even more distressed. 'You see, sir, as the young lady arrived at just past eight this morning, while you were still abed, I felt no hesitation in refusing her. But it's now nearly two of the clock and... and she's still waiting.'

Annoyed as he was to have yet another person try to intrude upon his solitude, Dom felt a revival of curiosity which, as he reluctantly reviewed the situation, intensified.

He hadn't mingled with society here for years, and only a few knew he'd returned to Suffolk. He had no idea who the woman might be, or what matter could be compelling enough to prompt her to come alone and wait for hours to consult him.

Arguing with himself that he would do better to ignore the caller, and losing, he finally said, 'Who is it? Not the girl from yesterday, surely.'

'Oh, no, sir,' Wilton said, sounding scandalised. 'Miss Wentworth's mama would never allow her to call alone on a single gentleman. The Young Person didn't give me her name, saying it wouldn't be known to you anyway.'

It *would* be scandalous for an unmarried girl to call on him, Dom belatedly realised. He'd been out of England so long, he'd initially forgotten the strict rules governing the behaviour of gently born maidens.

Maybe she wasn't so gently born.

There might be possibilities here, he thought, his body now taking an interest. Not that he was sure he was yet healed enough that such pleasant exercise wouldn't cause him more agony than ecstasy. 'You called her a "young lady", though. Why, after such brazen behaviour?'

'Well, she is young, and in speech and dress, she appears to be a lady, however improper it might be for her to come here.'

'Alone, you said.'

'Yes, sir.'

'What has she been doing all this time?'

'When I last glanced out, she'd seated herself on the brick wall at the end of the courtyard. She appeared to be reading, sir.'

'She hasn't knocked again?'

'No, sir. I suppose, sitting where she is, she knows the household must be aware of her presence.'

So his unwelcome caller had been waiting for hours. Without trying a second time to force herself upon them.

Reading a book.

Persistence he understood, but he knew few men, and no females, that patient.

After an irresolute moment, that bedevilling curiosity overcame his body's urging that he remain seated. Dom rose from his chair and paced to the mullioned windows.

Glancing out, he could see, below to his left, the three-foot wall that set off the courtyard spanning the space between the two Tudor wings projecting from the main block of Bildenstone Hall. Sitting there, wrapped in a cloak, was a female, her figure so foreshortened by height and distance that he couldn't accurately estimate her shape or stature.

The day, already gloomy when he'd made his way to the library, had darkened further. As he gazed at her, a gust of wind rattled the window.

'It's going to rain shortly,' he said, after a soldier's inspection of the clouds. 'That should send her on her way. I'll have that tray now.'

'Yes, sir,' Wilton said, looking brighter. Apparently feeling that, having discharged his duty to the fairer sex by informing his master of the girl's presence, he could now absolve himself of responsibility for her welfare, he trotted off for the tray.

A responsibility he obviously felt he'd transferred to Dom. Though his will tried to tell his conscience he wouldn't accept the charge, within a few minutes of seating himself again, he felt compelled to return to the window.

The rain he'd predicted was pelting down from clouds that didn't look likely to dissipate for some time. The girl was still there, though she'd tucked the book away and huddled in upon herself, as if to provide the smallest possible target to the besieging rain.

Her choice, he told himself, returning to his chair.

But after a few more minutes of reading the same paragraph over and over without comprehending a syllable, he tossed down the book and returned to the window.

She sat as before, huddled on the wall.

Uttering a string of oaths, Dom stomped to the bell pull and yanked hard.

A few moments later, Wilton reappeared, panting. 'I came as fast as I could, sir!'

Dom walked back to window and stared down at the female, still sitting immobile as a gargoyle rainspout on a cathedral roof.

Probably didn't shed moisture as efficiently, though.

'Damn and blast!' he muttered before turning to Wilton. 'I suppose we'll have to admit her before she contracts a consumption of the lungs.'

'At once, sir!' Wilton said, sounding relieved. 'I'll show her to the small receiving room.'

'Better put some towelling down to protect the carpet. She must be drenched.'

Wondering when he was going to find the solitude he sought, angry—but more intrigued than he wanted to admit by the mysterious female—Dom exited the library and headed for the receiving room.

After entering, he took up a commanding position before the cold hearth—the lady might have won the first skirmish, but Dom had no intention of looking defeated—and awaited his uninvited visitor. Underscoring the caller's lack of pedigree, she was being conducted to a small back parlour, rather than the formal front room into which the Squire and his ladies had been shown yesterday.

Dom wondered if she'd recognise the subtle set-down.

He heard the murmur of approaching voices and his body tensed. To his surprise, he found himself looking forward to the encounter.

But then, this female had already shown herself a skilled campaigner. Using neither force nor threat nor any of the tears and tantrums upon which ladies, in his experience, normally relied to soften male resolve—relying instead on his own sense of honour and courtesy—she'd induced him to yield.

The female entered. He had only a quick impression of a tall girl in an attractive, if outdated, green gown before she bent her head and sank into a curtsy.

'Thank you for receiving me,' she said, her throaty voice holding no hint of the reproach he would have anticipated from someone subjected to so long and discourteous a wait.

His unwilling admiration deepened. Yet another good tactic—unsettle an opponent by not responding in the expected manner.

Noting she was not, in fact, dripping on the carpet, as she rose to face him, he said, 'I suppose I should apologise, but you seem no worse for a drenching, Miss…'

'No need to apologise. My sturdy cloak has protected me through many a…'

Her voice trailed off and her eyes widened as Dom's brain added together luminous brown eyes, pale skin, and slender form.

'You!' she cried at the same moment Dom realised he recognised his persistent visitor.

The girl from the lane.

Chapter Three

For a long moment, they simply stared at each other.

Recovering first, the girl sighed. 'Oh, dear, this is…unfortunate! I suppose I should start by apologising for being so judgemental and inconsiderate yesterday. I do beg your pardon, Mr Ransleigh.'

If she could be magnanimous, he supposed he should be, too. 'Only if you'll accept my apology in return. There was no excuse for my rudeness…even if I'd just had my limitations rather forcibly demonstrated.'

Her eyes narrowed. 'The stallion!' she said. '*You* were riding that black beast that nearly trampled me.'

No point in denying what, with impressive quickness, she'd already figured out. 'Until he dumped me off,' he admitted.

'I don't wonder he unseated you. I expect you'd need the hands of a prize fighter to keep that one under control.'

'True. But, oh, can he fly like the wind! And jump anything in his path,' Dom said wistfully, remembering.

'Waterloo?' she asked, pointing to his arm.

'Yes.'

'I'm sorry.'

He nodded an acknowledgement before the memory

surfaced. 'I seem to recall you saying your father fell there? My condolences on your loss.'

Anguish showed briefly on her face before she masked it. 'Thank you,' she said softly.

Watching, Dom felt her pain echo within him. It had been difficult, losing comrades with whom he'd ridden and fought, but he'd never lost anyone who was truly family. How much more agonising would it have been had some battle claimed one of his cousins—Will or Max or Alastair?

Recovering her composure, the girl said, 'Had I known you were recuperating, I should have asked first for your lady mother. That is, I imagine she is here, caring for you during your recovery?'

'I'm afraid I lost my mother years ago.'

'Ah. So who is here, assisting you? Surely your family didn't leave you to cope alone.'

She must have sensed his withdrawal, for before he could utter some blighting set-down, she said, 'Now I must beg your pardon again! I didn't mean to pry. I should confess at the outset that, never having resided in England, I have trouble remembering the rules governing polite society. I've spent my life in the compounds of India or in the army, where everyone knows everyone else's business. I'm afraid I'm deplorably plain speaking and have no sensibility at all, so if I say something you find intrusive or inappropriate, just slap me back into place, like Papa's sergeant-major always did when I was too inquisitive.'

Having just been given permission to ignore her question, he felt unaccountably more inclined to answer. Unlike his former hunting buddies and the society maidens who had spent the war safely in England, she'd evidently lived through it with the army. She understand hardship, danger—and loss.

'My cousin Will found me on the field after the battle,

had me removed to a private house and cared for, then stayed with me until I was able to be transported back to London, about a week ago. He urged me to accompany him to our cousin Alastair's home, so our aunt could tend me. But she would have cosseted me within an inch of my life, and I…I didn't think I could bear that.'

She nodded. 'Sometimes one must face the bleakest prospects in life alone.'

The truth of her words, uttered with the poignancy of experience, resonated within him. The death of her father and returning to an England she didn't know were certainly bleak enough.

'But here I am, taking up your time while you're probably wishing me at Jericho! Let me state my business and leave you in peace. I'm Theodora Branwell, by the way,' she said, holding out her hand. 'My father was Colonel Richard Branwell, of the Thirty-Third Foot.'

She offered the hand vertically, for shaking, rather than palm down, for a kiss. Amused, he grasped her fingers for a brisk shake—and felt an unexpected tingle dance up his arm.

Startled for an instant, he dismissed the odd effect. 'Dominic Ransleigh,' he replied. 'Though I suppose you already knew that.'

'Yes. I recently leased Thornfield Place, specifically because it abuts your property. Or rather, one particular part of your property.'

Suddenly the connection registered. 'Theodora—Theo!' he said with a laugh. 'I'd been told to expect a call. Except the folk hereabouts seem to think you're a man.'

A mischievous look sparkled in her eyes. 'Though I didn't deliberately try to create that impression, I might not have used my full name when I contacted the local solicitor. So, you've been told that I'd like to lease the stone building in your south pasture and convert it into a home and school for orphans?'

'I have. I must warn you, though, the neighbourhood isn't happy about the idea. To quote the head of the Improvement Society of Whitfield Parish, whom I had the misfortune of receiving yesterday, such children, growing up around "vulgarity, drunkenness, and the company of loose women" must have been "corrupted at birth" and could only be an affront to decent people and a deleterious influence upon the county's poor.'

Miss Branwell's eyes widened at that recitation. 'No wonder you didn't wish to receive anyone today.'

While Dom swallowed the laugh surprised out of him by that remark, she turned an earnest look on him. 'Surely you don't share that ridiculous opinion! You're a soldier, Mr Ransleigh! True, the conditions in the army were… rougher than those the children might have encountered in England. I would argue, though, that the hardships they've survived make them stronger and more resilient, rather than less suited for society.'

Like she was? he wondered. Stronger, perhaps. Suited for *polite* society—that might be another matter.

'Besides, what they become will be determined, not by the circumstances of their birth, but by how they are treated now,' she went on. 'The best way to avoid having them fall into vice is to make them literate and give them training in a proper trade. Do you not agree that is the least we can do for the orphans of the men whose valour and sacrifice freed Europe from Napoleon's menace?'

Though her words were stirring, Dom found himself more arrested by the lady delivering them. How could he have thought her a little brown wren?

Her cheeks flushed, her eyes sparkling, her enticing bosom rising and falling with every breath, her low, throaty voice vibrant with conviction…. As his skin prickled with awareness and his body tightened in arousal, he felt himself almost physically drawn to her.

Surely a woman so passionate in her defence of the orphans would bring that passion to every activity.

To her bed.

'What happened to Christian charity, to compassion for the innocent, to leaving judgements to God?' she was demanding.

Her reference to the Almighty a rebuke to his lust, he told himself to concentrate on the subject, rather than the allure of the lady. 'Abandoned for preconceived notions, probably,' he replied.

That brought her flight of oratory to a halt. Sighing, she said, 'You're probably right. But…*you* don't share such notions, surely?'

She gestured towards him as she spoke. He had to force himself to keep from taking her hand, now near his own. Tasting her lips, still parted in enquiry. So nearly tangible was the pull between them, surely she must feel it, too?

For a moment, she did nothing, simply standing with her hand outstretched. Just as he was concluding that his previously reliable instincts must have gone completely array, she raised her eyes to meet his gaze. Some *connection* pulsed between them, wordless, but eloquent as a sonnet.

Hastily, she retracted her hand and stepped back. 'I shouldn't harangue you—though I did warn you I'm deplorably outspoken! If allowing me to use your building would put you at odds with the neighbourhood, perhaps I should come up with another plan.'

Dom thought of yesterday's call by Lady Wentworth. How many other mothers of marriageable daughters lived within visiting distance of Bildenstone Hall? Finding himself at odds with his neighbours might not be a bad thing.

'What would you do if I refuse permission?' he asked, curious.

She shrugged. 'Break the lease on Thornfield and make enquiries about settling elsewhere.'

'Wouldn't that be a great deal of trouble? To say nothing of the disruption to the children.'

'Having known nothing but following the drum, they're used to disruption and trouble.'

Despite his automatic inclination to do the opposite of whatever the officious Lady Wentworth had urged, with his desire to be left in solitude, he had been leaning towards refusing, should the then-unknown Theo Branwell approach him about renting his property.

Now he wasn't so sure.

Apparently sensing his ambivalence, Miss Branwell's face brightened with new hope. '*Would* you consider it? I promise we shall not intrude on your peace! You needn't make a final decision now; let us stay on a provisional basis. If you find the school a disturbance, you can send us all packing!'

That sounded reasonable enough—and might have the added benefit of keeping the Lady Wentworths of the area at bay. 'Very well, I agree.'

'Splendid!'

The delight in her smile warmed him, and he couldn't help smiling back.

Though she'd claimed she would not cut up his peace, with that…*something* simmering between them, Dom wasn't so sure. With a little shock, he realised that for the first time since the urge for solitude had consumed him, the possibility of company didn't displease him.

'Do I have your permission to inspect the building at once, while the solicitors discuss terms?' she asked, pulling him from his thoughts.

'Certainly.'

'Thank you. I need to determine what materials and

supplies might be necessary to make it suitable. I shall cover all the costs of renovation, of course.'

'The building hasn't been inhabited for years,' Dom felt it necessary to warn her. 'My father constructed a second floor, intending to convert it into a weaving factory, but the rest of the work was never completed. Getting it into shape may be quite costly.'

'My father left me well provided for.'

Suddenly it occurred to him how odd it was for a girl of her age and situation to undertake such a project. 'It's one thing for a *Mr* Theo Branwell—doubtless an idealistic cleric of some sort—to open an orphanage. Why are *you* doing this?' he asked. 'If I have relations to cosset me, surely you have family in England to take you in—or find you a proper husband. Maybe a prospective fiancé waiting in the wings?'

He wasn't sure what imp had induced him to add that last, but at the stricken look on her face, he instantly regretted it.

'He fell at Fuentes de Oñoro,' she said quietly. 'For many months afterward, I wish I'd died, too. But the orphans needed someone. Now, with Papa gone, so do I. I've sufficient funds for the endeavour, and some of the children have already been with me for years. We're good for each other.'

So that explained why such a vibrant girl wasn't already riveted, mothering a quiverful of her own children. The odd notion struck him that though he *missed* Elizabeth, he'd never felt he would perish without her. Shaking off the thought, he returned to the topic at hand.

'I should probably go with you to inspect the building.'

'You needn't! I've just promised we wouldn't be any bother. Your estate agent can accompany me.'

Again, she'd offered him a graceful way to disengage—and again, he was curiously disinclined to take it.

'Not having seen the building in years, I've no idea what would be a suitable rent,' he countered.

'I have seen it—at least from the outside—and had a figure in mind,' she said, naming one that sounded quite generous to him.

'You are certainly…well organised,' he observed, substituting a more flattering adjective for the one that had initially come to mind.

'Managing, you mean,' she acknowledged with a smile. 'You're quite right. You see, I've overseen my father's household since I was the merest child. Then, on the Peninsula—well, you were there, you know how it is. Having to anticipate movements, preparing for every contingency! Water, or none. Provisions, or none. Shelter, or none. Having your gear and supplies ready to move at a moment's notice, should battle threaten or the army's plans change. Which,' she added with a chuckle, 'they always did. Which regiment were you in, by the way?'

Before he could answer, she waved her hand in a silencing gesture. 'There I go, prying again, after just assuring you I would not. Please excuse me.'

'It's not prying to ask about the experiences of a fellow campaigner,' he replied, surprised to discover he meant it. 'I was with the Sixteenth Light Dragoons.'

'Did you charge with the Union Brigade against D'Erlon's Corps at Waterloo? A magnificent effort, I was told.'

Dom shrugged, having never sorted out his feelings about the event that had so drastically altered his life. 'When the trumpet sounds, one goes.'

'Duty, in spite of fear or likelihood of success, Papa always said,' she murmured, grief veiling her face again.

'Duty,' he agreed, struggling himself with a familiar mixture of pride, sadness and bitter regret for what he had lost that day.

After a silent moment, both of them doubtless recalling what duty had cost them, Dom shook himself free of the memories. 'When do you want to inspect the property?'

'Now, if possible.'

'I appreciate that you don't mind the damp, but the weather is rather inclement. Are you sure you wouldn't prefer to wait until tomorrow?'

'Oh, no! I'm impatient to begin. Besides, the worst of the rain is over now. But truly, you needn't bother yourself to accompany me.'

'It won't be a bother. If I'm to reside here, I must know what's going on with the property. Did you come on horseback?'

'Yes, but as I recall, the building isn't too far from the manor. We could walk.'

Was she recalling his admission that he no longer possessed a horse he could ride? he wondered. 'If you'll wait until I get my coat, I'll escort you. By the way, in spite of what you saw me wearing yesterday, I do own a coat respectable enough that you needn't fear being seen with me.'

To his puzzlement, she gave a peal of laughter, quickly stifled.

'What?'

She shook with silent mirth, her eyes merry. 'It's nothing.'

'Come, you must tell me. Have pity on a man whose face now frightens children.'

That sobered her. 'You can't be serious! Don't you ever look in a glass? You must know you are quite handsome.'

It being obvious by now that Miss Branwell was incapable of toadying or flattery, he knew she spoke the truth as she saw it. His spirits, consigned to the lowest of dungeons after yesterday's ignominious ride, climbed several storeys at this verbal confirmation that the unusual girl who attracted him so strongly found him attractive, too.

As he gazed at her, their physical connection, simmering just below the level of consciousness, intensified again. Struggling to resist its pull, he said, 'Now, tell me what was so amusing.'

She remained silent for a long moment, her eyes locked on his. Then gasped and shook her head, as if breaking a spell.

That, he could understand. He felt a bit enchanted himself.

'What was amusing,' she repeated, as if trying to recover her place in the conversation. 'Well, you see, reflecting upon your appearance after parting from you yesterday, I concluded you must be a poor, unemployed ex-soldier. I'd decided to make up for my rudeness by hiring you to perform some tasks at Thornfield Place.' Another chuckle escaped. 'How ridiculous! Thinking I was doing a favour, offering odd jobs to a man who owns half the county!'

'Not so ridiculous, given how disreputable I looked,' he said, amused, but also touched by the compassion she'd felt for a chance-met stranger—and a surly one at that.

No wonder she had a heart for homeless orphans.

'You'll wait while I get my coat?'

'I really shouldn't task you with this…but if you are truly sure it wouldn't be an imposition, and I'm not keeping you from other matters?'

'It won't be, and you aren't.' He refrained from mentioning he had nothing on his calendar—now or any subsequent day. 'I consider it an opportunity to become better acquainted with my new neighbour.'

Which, though perfectly true, he thought as he left the room, was certainly singular, given his original intention not to mingle with any of them.

Chapter Four

Reviewing their conversation as he climbed the stairs, Dom marvelled at himself. Was the solitude he'd sought wearing on him already, that he felt such a lift at the prospect of inspecting some musty old building?

But thinking about London, or Leicestershire, or even Elizabeth, still brought an automatic shudder of distaste. Perhaps what he really sought was not so much solitude, but a world completely different from the society he'd once enjoyed and the company of those who'd known him there.

Miss Theodora Branwell was certainly different. Though his little brown wren had been more attractive today in a green gown that accentuated her graceful figure, made her skin glow and emphasised her lovely dark eyes, were the stunningly beautiful Lady Elizabeth to have entered the room, most men wouldn't have given Miss Branwell another glance.

Compared to Elizabeth, who'd been trained since her youth in the art of conversation designed to make her companion feel himself the most fascinating man in the room, Miss Branwell, with her frankness and total lack of subtlety, would be considered unpleasantly plain-spoken and offensively inquisitive.

And yet, though he'd always appreciated Elizabeth's

beauty and avidly anticipated the pleasures of the wedding bed, he didn't remember ever having the sort of immediate, visceral reaction he'd felt for Miss Branwell. Perhaps that response was intensified, coming as it did after Miss Wentworth's distaste and representing as it did the first time since his injuries that he'd felt a sense of his own masculine appeal. The first evidence as well that a woman who attracted him could find him desirable for who and what he was now, rather than as the damaged remains of the man he used to be.

But enough analysing. Like today's rain, Miss Branwell had blown a freshness into his life, lifting his spirits and imbuing him, for this moment, with a sense of lightness and anticipation he hadn't felt in months. He'd accept it as a gift from Heaven.

Recalling that the walk to the stone building was rather far, he took a swig of the laudanum-laced brandy at his bedside. He didn't want to end up so cross-eyed with pain by the time they arrived that he was incapable of accurately assessing the building. Or appreciating the company of the lady he was escorting.

Miss Branwell awaited him in the entry as he descended the stairs. 'I took the liberty of asking your butler if there was a pony trap we might use. He's having one sent up.'

'Afraid I might collapse on you?' he tossed back. And regretted the hasty words, as his mind jumped to other ways he might cover her that had his body immediately hardening in approval.

'…nursed enough soldiers to know,' she was saying by the time he got his thoughts back under control. 'You have the look of a soldier still recovering from his injuries. Did you suffer a lingering fever?'

'For months,' he confirmed, no longer surprised at how easy he found it to speak frankly to her. 'I wasn't well enough to leave Belgium until quite recently.'

She gave him a quick inspection that his body hoped was more than an assessment of his level of recovery. 'You're still rather thin. In my judgement, you should have more careful tending—but that's for you to decide, so I shall not mention it again. However—' She stopped herself with a sigh. 'No, excuse me, I shall say nothing.'

Dom shook his head with a chuckle as they walked out to the vehicle a groom had pulled up outside the entry. 'You shall have to tell me, you know.'

She looked back at him, smiling faintly as she shook her head. Remembering her rebuke of the previous day, he offered her a steadying hand as she climbed into the vehicle, savouring more than he should the touch of her gloved fingers.

She didn't turn to see if he had trouble climbing up himself. And though, army veteran that she was, she probably could drive the trap better than he, she made space for him on the bench seat and waited for him to take the reins with nary a solicitous look nor a concerned enquiry about whether he felt well enough to handle them. That, after just pronouncing her nurse's opinion that he was not fully recovered.

A tiny glow of satisfaction lit within the gloomy depths of his battered self-esteem. She assumed he was adjusting to his handicap, continuing with his life. Expected he would eventually master it.

As he would. Feeling better about his condition than he could remember since his wounding, Dom motioned for the stable lad to release the horse and jump up behind them.

After yesterday's fiasco with Diablo left him doubting his ability to do anything, his spirits rose further as he discovered he could handle the single horse and simple carriage with ease. The expertise honed through years of practice returned without thought, and as the trap rattled down the lane, he found himself relishing the business of driving.

As Miss Branwell had predicted, the rain had ceased, leaving the air cool and scrubbed clean. Dom exulted in the wind ruffling his hair, the scenery flashing by, the taut feel of the reins in his hand and the horse responding to his commands. With a rush of gratitude to the Almighty, he realised at least one of the pleasures of his former life wasn't totally lost to him.

Of course, this was only a pony trap, the nag pulling it far from a high-stepping carriage horse. But effortlessly controlling horse and vehicle felt…good. He told himself to stop equivocating and just enjoy it.

His mastery of the reins allowed him to enjoy watching Miss Branwell as well. After noting her chattiness at the house, he was encouraged to discover she could remain silent as well. Sitting relaxed, her hands resting on the rail to steady her over the bumps, she gazed from side to side, her eyes bright with interest. Trusting this one-armed soldier to drive her safely while she investigated her new surroundings, he thought, buoyed by her confidence.

The spring woods just coming into leaf were lovely, and so was his companion. Though, he noted in a reprise of the discriminating standards from his days as 'Dandy Dom', the battered-looking bonnet and well-used cloak would go, if he had the dressing of her.

Then again, he'd rather have the undressing of her.

Preoccupied by reining in that line of thought before it bolted into ever more inappropriate directions, he started when she cried out, 'Goodness, what is that, just ahead?'

Squinting in the direction of her pointing finger, he saw around the corner a stretch of lane bordered on both sides by an expanse of flowers. 'It's a bluebell wood,' he replied. Not having been at Bildenstone during the spring for years, he'd forgotten this part of the lane, less densely treed than the one they'd travelled yesterday, was home to thousands of the little bulbs.

'Can you slow down?'

'Of course,' he said, reining the horse to a stop.

She gazed around her in delight at the sea of blooms surrounding them. 'It's as if an ocean had been cast down under the trees! How beautiful!'

Looking at the expanse, he realised it *was* beautiful. And that, had she not been with him, he would have passed through it, preoccupied by his own problems, with scarcely a glance.

Turning back to him, she said, 'I can't get enough of gazing at the woodlands here, the tall trees with their leafy canopies. After the dry plains of India and the scrub of Portugal and Spain, I find them endlessly fascinating.'

He, too, would do well to appreciate every simple pleasure, instead of brooding on what he'd lost. To the attraction and interest she'd generated in him today, he added gratitude for bringing him to recognise that truth.

'We are fortunate in our forests,' Dom replied, clicking the horse back into motion, 'especially those lucky enough to possess a bluebell wood. Now, what was it you were going to tell me and decided not to?'

He laughed at the surprise on her face. 'Did you think I had forgotten? I must warn you, I have a mind like a poacher's trap. So…confess.'

'Very well, but as I had resolved to say nothing, you may not afterwards accuse me of interfering! It's just…I noticed that your butler is rather elderly. I expect, having been around him for years, you haven't marked the passing of time, but the truth is, he struggles to open that heavy door. Does he still bring in the tea tray? I imagine it's difficult for him. Of course, that's only my observation. It's really none of my business.'

Dom recalled Wilton carrying in the service to his

callers yesterday, lugging a tray full of victuals from the kitchen up to the library for him this afternoon.

'It's been more than seven years since I visited, and years before that since the family resided here,' he admitted. 'Beyond noting in a general way that Wilton had aged, I'm ashamed to say I never considered whether resuming duties he'd not had to perform for years would be hard on him.'

He'd come up from London in a laudanum haze that enabled him to bear the jolting of the journey, then shut himself in the master's chamber and, until yesterday, hadn't set foot out of the house. To his mortification, he hadn't given a thought to how his unexpected arrival must have upset the routine of the handful of servants who'd remained to oversee Bildenstone Hall during the family's long absence, or the strain on all of them required to extract the place from its holland covers and make it habitable.

'Even though I don't intend to entertain, I should probably hire more servants,' he admitted. 'While I'm at it, perhaps I will put Wilton out to pasture.'

'Oh, I don't think—' she began before closing her lips.

Dom laughed outright. 'You might as well tell me the whole. I promise not to accuse you of interfering.'

'Wilton has been long at Bildenstone Hall?'

'He's been butler since I was a lad.'

'Then I don't think I'd retire him—not immediately, after such a long absence, lest he feel you are dissatisfied with his service. Why not find someone to serve as under-butler, whom Wilton can train up as his eventual replacement? Then, after a suitable interval, you can offer him a cottage nearby and a generous settlement for his lifetime of loyalty. If the family hasn't resided here for some time, it probably would be wise to hire more staff, which will also earn you the good will of the neighbourhood—

paying jobs are always prized, especially now, with so many being let go from the army.'

'That sounds like excellent advice. If you have any other suggestions, pray offer them.'

She uttered a delightful gurgle of a laugh. 'As if you thought I could keep my opinions to myself! Goodness, though, your family must possess some magnificent properties, if they chose to leave the beauties of Bildenstone for another location.'

'It's worse than that—Papa actually had to purchase the other property. Having always loved hunting, both haring and fox, he happened to meet Hugh Meynell, now of Quorn Hall in Leicestershire.'

He paused, but as no hint of recognition dawned in her eyes, he continued. 'Meynell, another hunting enthusiast, believed there was no reason that hounds couldn't be bred for a good nose and for speed, which would allow fox hunting at any time of the day, not just early in the morning when the foxes, weary after a night of hunting, return to their dens too tired to outrun the slow hounds. My father thought it an intriguing idea, and along with Meynell and some others, experimented with producing fast-running hounds. So absorbed did he become in the project, he determined to obtain a property in Quorn country, where he could continue the breeding experiments and hunt with Meynell's pack.'

He paused, remembering. 'I'd just outgrown my first pony when we relocated to Upton Park. It took only one hunt to make me as keen about the chase as my father. So I can't say I regretted leaving Bildenstone, despite the beauties of its bluebell wood.'

'Appreciation for flowers isn't generally a trait possessed by young boys,' she replied. 'I don't wonder you found the excitement of Leicestershire much more to your liking. So you devoted yourself to the hunt?'

'Single-mindedly. Which reminds me,' he said, recalling her hours waiting on his wall. 'What would you have done if I'd not relented and admitted you today?'

Following the sudden change in topic without a blink, she said, 'Waited a bit longer, then tracked down your estate agent. When I first proposed to lease Thornfield, I was told your family hadn't occupied the property for years, so finding an owner in residence was an unwelcome surprise. If the agent thought you were indifferent to the use of the building, or were not planning to remain long at Bildenstone, I would have proceeded. Otherwise, I would have made plans to go elsewhere.'

He had to laugh. 'You really are resourceful!'

'Papa always said you can never count on the enemy to do what you expect; for a sound battle plan, one must devise alternates for every imaginable contingency.'

He smiled down at her. 'I hope you don't consider me the enemy.'

She gazed up into his eyes. 'No, I consider you…' Her words trailed off, her lips slightly parted as she stared at his face…his mouth.

Attraction crackled like heat lightning between them again, scorching his face, leaving his mouth tingling. Immobilised by its force, Dom wasn't able to tear his gaze from hers until the jolting of the vehicle over a particularly large bump forced him to return his attention to his driving.

Chapter Five

Patting her flaming cheeks with one hand, Theo took a deep breath, her heart thudding as she surreptitiously watched Mr Ransleigh manoeuvre the pony trap.

Goodness, what was wrong with her? First her runaway tongue, and now this firestorm of sensual awareness!

Granted, she'd never been shy about expressing her opinions, but what had possessed her to be so free with her advice—to a man she'd scarcely met, and one with whom she needed to establish good relations, if she hoped to settle her orphans at this location? If that almost instantaneous sense of rapport she'd felt with him was an illusion, she might have doomed her mission before it even began.

And yet, she was convinced Mr Ransleigh, too, felt the connection between them.

After an initial surprise and dismay upon discovering her potential landlord to be the one-armed man she'd been so rude to in the lane, she'd been immediately drawn to this ex-soldier, who matched her apology with a generous one of his own. Then, to confirm that his life had, like hers, been upended in the aftermath of Waterloo and to learn they shared the same army experiences...

Having made her awkward way these last few months through an unfamiliar civilian society in an unfamiliar land, to stumble upon someone who'd been part of the world she'd lost was like coming home. Within a few moments, she'd been more comfortable in his company than she'd felt since leaving the regiment in Belgium.

Yet at the same time, upon meeting the man again, properly garbed and in his own element, she'd been struck by the potent masculinity he radiated, in spite of his injuries. The fever-induced thinness of his frame only served to emphasise his impressive height and the broadness of his shoulders. Caught up in gazing at the strong chin, sensual lips and brilliant blue eye, she'd several times, like a moment ago, lost track of where she was in the conversation.

A fact as sobering and even more dismaying than learning the identity of her new landlord.

Just sitting beside him in the pony trap, close enough that the next bump in the road might bounce her into contact with his body, kept her heartbeat skipping at an accelerated pace. The air between them seemed to simmer with a palpable tension.

As an unmarried woman, society might expect her to be an innocent, but she was no stranger to passion. In the arms of the man who'd intended to make her his wife, she'd revelled in kissing and touching, eager to explore Marshall's body, wanting him to explore hers. Though she'd lived mostly in the company of men for the years since his death, not until today had she felt again that unbidden, instinctive, intensely physical connection.

She knew exactly how powerful it could be—and how dangerous.

Oh, this would not do at all!

She should have insisted on delaying this visit until Ransleigh's estate agent could accompany her.

Instead, disbelieving, intrigued—and tempted—she'd permitted his company, compelled to discover if that incompatible pairing of feelings—welcome ease, and dangerous attraction—would dissipate upon further acquaintance.

Well, it hadn't. Despite the distractions of the drive and the delight of the bluebell wood, the ease had only increased, and so too the attraction. As evidenced a moment ago by her losing track of every thought save the impulse to run her finger over his lips and watch that undamaged eye drift closed as she tangled her fingers in the shaggy mane of blond hair and pulled his mouth to hers.

Just recalling that desire sent another flush of heat through her.

But there was no time now for her to figure out what she was going to do about this unwelcome complication, with Mr Ransleigh pulling up the pony trap in front of the stone building. Forcing her thoughts away from that dilemma, she made herself calm.

The spark that singed her fingers as he helped her down momentarily distracted her. But Theo would never have survived the last four years had she not been able to summon the will to focus only on the problem at hand.

Putting a deliberate distance between them, Theo followed Mr Ransleigh as he led her on an inspection of the stone building.

The fact that the structure appeared nearly perfect for her purposes helped her concentrate. Originally designed as a barn, the building had a main floor of smooth paving stones; the stalls had been removed, leaving an open, rectangular space that would do well as a schoolroom. The hayloft above, its partially floored area finished out and with railed wooden stairs constructed to reach it, would serve splendidly as a dormitory.

'This will be excellent!' Theo declared as, having made use of the railing rather than her escort's arm to steady her, she returned from the upper floor to the main room. 'It will require very few alterations: partitions upstairs, to divide the boys' area from the girls', and cordoning off a small section on this floor to install a kitchen, where meals can be prepared and girls can be schooled in cooking and household management.'

'Are you sure?' Mr Ransleigh said dubiously. 'It looks like a cobweb-infested wreck to me.'

'Compared to some of the structures I had to make habitable on the Peninsula, it's a virtual palace! I dare say the roof will not leak, half-drowning some hapless orphan in the middle of the night, nor a wall give way, letting in cows to munch next morning's bread, nor do I see any ancient piles of rotted straw that might house a host of vermin.'

'Sounds like you were billeted in the same places I was,' Ransleigh said.

'Doubtless,' she agreed, dragging her mind back before it could jump to contemplating the idea of being billeted... or bedded down...with her compelling landlord. 'A good scrubbing and a competent carpenter, and I believe I can turn this into just the school I envisioned. If you're agreed, I'll consult the solicitor at once to find the necessary workmen, so they may begin as soon as the lease is signed.'

'You might consult Bildenstone's steward, Winniston. He seems to have kept the manor house in reasonable repair, despite the family not having resided there for years. And he would know where to find the craftsmen you'll need.'

'That would be most helpful, if it won't be too much bother.' Laughing ruefully, she shook her head. 'Here I've been assuring you I wouldn't intrude on your peace! I've already dragged you from your house and am now thinking of imposing upon your estate manager.'

Mr Ransleigh shrugged. 'He hasn't been imposed upon for years. Every soldier needs a little prodding to keep him marching in the right direction.'

'Very well, I shall ask. Now, I should allow you to get

back to Bildenstone and whatever business I interrupted when you felt obliged to accompany me here.'

Theo worked to keep the wistfulness from her voice. Unwise as it was, she was enjoying this outing more than she could remember enjoying anything in a long time. The easy camaraderie and sense of shared experience made her forget for a while that she was now alone in an unfamiliar world. And his tantalising presence revived dim memories of what an energising delight it was to bandy words with a handsome man, a titillating buzz of attraction humming between them.

Settling the details of the lease was a matter for solicitors; once they completed their tour today, there would be no need for her to consult again with the property's owner. She would go back to her children and their needs, and firmly shut behind her the door into this glimpse of what life spent with a congenial, beguiling man might have been like.

Since that life was lost to her for ever, the sooner she did so, the better.

Setting her shoulders, she walked back to the pony trap and hauled herself to the bench before her escort could offer a hand.

Which didn't mean she was any less cognizant of the simmering heat of him, once he climbed up beside her, she thought with a sigh.

'That was exceedingly dusty,' Mr Ransleigh said as he set the vehicle in motion. 'Can I offer you tea when we get back?'

Theo steeled herself against the temptation to accept. 'That's very kind, but I shouldn't.' A more disturbing thought occurred and she frowned. 'Indeed, now that I think of it, with you being a bachelor and having no lady mother in residence, I seem to recall that it would be considered improper of me to take tea at your house—or indeed, even to call upon you.'

She sighed with exasperation. 'English mores! Dashed inconvenient, with you being our landlord, but there it is. I only hope I haven't blotted my copybook already! It wouldn't help the children's reception—already dubious, according to what you've told me—if your servants carry tales hinting that I'm a lightskirt.'

Her companion choked back a laugh. 'You really are plain-spoken, aren't you?'

'I'm completely devoid of maidenly sensibilities,' Theo admitted. 'Perhaps I should try to acquire some, if it will make the idea of the school more acceptable to the neighbourhood.'

'Though you may be right, I'd hate to see it. I find your candour refreshing.'

'So is a dunk in the Channel, but most people would rather avoid it,' Theo said wryly. 'I'll have to learn to curb my tongue—and think more carefully about my actions.' She made a mental note to ask Aunt Amelia, before she returned to London, to review with her the most important rules of propriety.

'You're probably right about tea,' Ransleigh allowed. 'Talking over experiences on the Peninsula, it's too easy to fall back into army ways and forget the rigid notions of conduct that apply here. Since I've been back in England less than a month, after years away, my memory of those rules is probably as rusty as yours. But let me assure you, no tales of our lapses today will be heard beyond the walls of Bildenstone—or the offenders will answer to me.'

Surprised, she looked up at him. Though linked by their memories of campaign, he was still little more than a stranger. No connection between them required him to watch over her reputation, and she was impressed that he intended to do so.

He truly was an officer and a gentleman.

'I wouldn't expect you to go to such trouble, but I do appreciate it.'

'Don't want you to run afoul of the Lady Wentworths of the county before you've even got your building renovated,' he said, turning his attention back to his driving.

All too soon, they arrived back at Bildenstone Hall. Once again resisting the temptation to continue their conversation, Theo refused his offer to proceed to the drawing room while a groom fetched her horse.

'There's no need for you to tarry here, truly!' she said when he gallantly insisted on waiting outside with her. 'I shall be off as soon as Firefly is brought up. The children will be missing me, and there's still so much to do, getting the house up to snuff and filling in until I can secure a teacher.'

He raised an eyebrow. 'You don't intend to teach the children yourself?'

'No. While we were with the army, I helped Jemmie with his letters and sums, but we hadn't the materials, nor I the training or inclination, to give him a proper schooling. Not that the children should study languages and philosophy—just gain a thorough grounding in reading and arithmetic. While they learn, we shall ascertain what most interests them, then train them to that trade, for which I'll need to hire instructors as well. I doubt I could sit still long enough to manage a classroom. I have to be out and about, moving around, accomplishing things.'

'I can appreciate that. After months of being cooped up, mostly bedridden, I can't tell you how much I've enjoyed this drive in the fresh air.'

'Then you must drive about often—as long as you don't tire yourself. You're not fully healed yet, remember.'

'Don't worry. My arm and shoulder will remind me, should I be tempted to forget.'

From the stable lane, a groom paced up, leading her mare. 'Here's Firefly,' she said, turning back to him, 'so I will take my leave.'

After giving the mare a quick inspection, Mr Ransleigh nodded his approval. 'Good, deep heart, nice level croup, and well muscled—she must be a fine goer.' Reaching out to stroke the horse's neck, he crooned, 'What a lovely lady you are! Such a graceful neck, pretty eyes and small, perfect ears!'

As the mare nickered and leaned into Ransleigh's massaging fingers, Theo chuckled. 'I believe she's preening for you. Which is quite a compliment! Firefly doesn't take to just anyone. You must have a way with horses.'

'I've always loved them. Spent most of the last fifteen years when not in the army breeding and training them. Hunters and steeplechasers who—' Abruptly he went silent, leaving the sentence unfinished.

Even if I just had my limitations forcefully demonstrated, his cryptic comment came back to her as she recalled the fractious stallion who'd almost trampled her. *But oh, he can fly like the wind and jump anything in his path.*

'You trained that black beast from yesterday,' she said, putting it all together.

'And many more like him,' Ransleigh said tightly. 'For all the good it does me now.'

All horses he could no longer ride. Theo felt an ache in her chest. One more loss, one more joy stolen from him. How terribly cruel life could be!

'It must have taken remarkable skill, just to get him to accept a rider,' she said, wanting to ease the tension in that clenched jaw. 'He looked like he would have enjoyed running us down.'

He rewarded her with a slight smile. 'He would have, the evil-tempered devil.'

The urge to linger and question him further teased at her. Clenching her teeth against it, she told herself she should bid him farewell before this intriguing man charmed her any further.

'Well, I must be off. You're welcome to call any time at Thornfield Place and meet the children. Or not, as you choose,' she added, unhappily aware he was unlikely to take her up on that offer.

Before the groom could assist her, Ransleigh offered his hand. 'You were right,' he said as he lifted her into the saddle. 'I can do it, if I want to.'

Our last contact, she thought with a little sigh as he released her boot. 'I am sure you will soon be able to do whatever you wish, Mr Ransleigh. Thank you again for giving my orphans a chance.'

With a wave of her riding crop and a foolish sense of regret, she turned Firefly and set off towards Thornfield.

She felt the warmth of his gaze on her back, all the way to the turn in the drive.

By the time she'd ridden most of the way home, Theo had convinced herself she'd not really responded as strongly to Mr Ransleigh as she'd first imagined. After all, it was only natural that she would feel comfortable around a man who'd spent nearly as many years with Wellington's army as she had, especially after more than a month of dealing with civilians.

Nor did she deny he attracted her. The scarred face and eye patch did nothing to detract from his commanding profile, nor the missing arm from the vitality that emanated from him, despite the fact that he was not fully recovered from his injuries. Indeed, in her eyes, the marks of the suffering he'd endured in defending his country enhanced his already arresting physical attributes.

But that attraction, like the welcome relief of finding herself once again in a soldier's company, had doubtless been heightened by not having experienced the feeling in so long.

She could only imagine how much more potent his appeal would be when he was fully healed. A heated flutter stirred in her stomach.

Fortunately, she was too old and wise now to be caught again in passion's snare. Or she certainly should be—she need only remember the agony she'd suffered over Marshall.

Still, she was a woman, and vain though it might be, she was glad she'd worn the most attractive of her gowns for the call. She'd couldn't help being pleased that, if her instincts were correct, that compelling man had found her attractive as well.

A flush of embarrassment heated her face as she suddenly recalled she'd actually told this wealthy, well-connected bachelor how handsome she thought him.

Drat candour! Hopefully, he would only think the comment shameless—and not suppose her to have marital designs upon him. The very idea that he might interpret her comment in that manner made her a little sick.

Nothing she could do now to correct that impression, if he had so interpreted her remark. With any luck, there'd be no further need to contact him, so any awkwardness on that score could be avoided.

Then perspective returned, and she had to laugh at herself. How foolish of her to think this commanding man, whose wealth and pedigree doubtless focused upon him the attention of every woman in the vicinity, would think twice about any supposed lures cast his way by a plain, outspoken spinster—with a crowd of orphans in tow!

The only lasting result of her visit today was her landlord's agreement to lease her the property. Once she was immersed in overseeing its renovation, adding that task to those of getting Thornfield running properly and finding the necessary teachers, today's interlude would fade to a pleasant but vague memory.

Ignoring the eddies in her stomach that warned otherwise, Theo fixed that conclusion firmly in mind and turned Firefly down the drive to Thornfield's stables.

Chapter Six

Dom awoke the next morning with a sense of anticipation, the first he could recall since his injuries. Questioning the source of that unexpected sensation, he remembered meeting his unusual new neighbour the previous day, and smiled.

The drive to the stone barn had been energising. As he recalled, there was a tilbury in the carriage house and a high-stepper with a bit more fire to pull it. After his successful driving of the pony cart, he was reasonably sure he wouldn't end up flat on his back in the mud again if he tried taking it out.

This morning, he decided as he rang for Henries, he would.

After consuming breakfast with a keener appetite than he'd possessed in some time, Dom walked down to the stables to collect horse, carriage and a stable boy to watch them, should he need to stop and inspect a field or cottage. It required but a moment's thought to decide where he meant to drive first.

Miss Branwell had invited him to call at Thornfield Place, and so he would.

Setting the carriage in motion, he wondered at himself. After all his firm intentions to avoid contact with the neighbours, here he was, the day after meeting Miss Branwell, ready to encounter her again. If he felt like visiting, he ought to first return the Squire's call.

He pictured his bluff neighbour and frowned. Stopping there didn't appeal in the least.

Seeing Miss Branwell again did.

Perhaps it was because she didn't expect anything of him but to be her landlord. Unlike every other resident in the county, she didn't know his reputation, had no connections to hunting or its enthusiasts—she didn't even recognise the name of the great Meynell! And, praise heaven, she wasn't evaluating his worth on the Marriage Mart.

Indeed, Miss Branwell, self-confessedly ignorant of English customs, might not even be aware that, with his wealth and connections, he was still a prime matrimonial prospect.

No, all she had seen was a dishevelled one-armed soldier walking down a lane—and decided to offer him employment. He laughed out loud.

Direct, plain-spoken and completely focused on her objectives, she worked and thought like a soldier. Only she was much better to look at.

Picturing her immediately revived the strong attraction she'd inspired yesterday. His mind explored the idea of dalliance and liked it, his body adding its enthusiastic approval. However, Miss Branwell was still a *miss*, a gently born virgin. As strongly as he was attracted to her character and her person, he'd never debauched an innocent, and he wasn't about to start.

With a disappointed sigh, he allowed himself to regret she wasn't the widowed *Mrs* Branwell. They couldn't, alas, be lovers. But perhaps they could be friends. A friend who knew him only as the man he was now.

There was freedom in that: no preconceived notions to

meet, no pressure to perform up to the standard of what he'd once been.

Besides, he had to admit he was curious to see this assortment of orphans she'd collected. He tried, and failed, to imagine the problems one must overcome in order to follow the army with a troop of children in tow, then to transport them to England.

He shook his head and laughed again. What a remarkable girl!

Without doubt, calling on her would be much more interesting and enjoyable than perusing the London papers to determine the current value of hunters.

An hour later, at Thornfield Place, Theo was sipping a second cup of coffee while her aunt finished breakfast when Franklin informed them that Mr Ransleigh had called.

Surprise—and a delight far greater than it should have been—sent a thrill through her. After instructing the butler to inform the visitor that the ladies would receive him directly, she turned to her aunt.

'Thank goodness I had Mrs Reeves straighten the parlour first thing this morning,' she said, trying to pass off her enthusiasm as approval of prudent housekeeping. 'It appears my new landlord is paying us a visit.'

Her aunt opened her lips to reply, then froze, her eyes opening wide. 'Did Franklin say a Mr *Ransleigh* had called?' she asked at last.

'Yes. Mr Dominic Ransleigh. The building I want to turn into the children's school sits on his land. I told you I planned to call on the landlord yesterday, remember?'

'Of course I remember. But why didn't you tell me your landlord was a Ransleigh?'

'The owner of that much land would doubtless be a

member of a prominent family. I didn't think it mattered which one.'

'Not matter? Good heavens, child, don't be ridiculous! One must always be aware of the social position of the individuals with whom one associates—as you army folk want to know the rank of a military acquaintance.'

'I suppose you're right,' Theo conceded. 'Enlighten me, then.'

'Do you know anything of his background?'

'Only that he was in the army for the duration of the war.'

'So he was—he and his three cousins. The 'Ransleigh Rogues,' the boys have been called since their Eton days. They grew up inseparable, and when Alastair Ransleigh ran off to the army after being jilted by his fiancée—quite a scandal that was!—the other three joined up to watch over him. The eldest, Max—younger son of the Earl of Swynford, who practically runs the House of Lords!—was involved in a scandal of his own, something about an affair with a Frenchwoman at the Congress of Vienna and an assassination attempt on Wellington. The youngest, Will, the illegitimate son of the Earl's brother, spent his first decade on the streets of St Giles before being recovered by the family.'

'My, that is an assortment!' Theo said with a laugh.

'Your landlord, Dominic, was known as "Dandy Dom", the handsomest man in the regiment, able to ride anything with four legs and drive anything with four wheels.' I don't know about the former, but I've seen him in Hyde Park, impeccably dressed, navigating a coach and four through the crowd as easily as if it were a pony cart on an empty country lane. He is—was—absolutely fearless on the hunting field, I'm told. His late father moved the family to Quorn country so long ago, I'd forgotten their primary estate was in Suffolk.'

The details about his family drifted into the background of her mind like dust settling on a window-sill. All that struck Theo was the image of a runaway horse and a one-armed man shuffling down the lane, his garments spattered with mud and leaves, his face strained and angry. *Able to ride anything with four legs...*

Her heart contracted with a sympathetic pain. How much more bitter it must be to bear his injuries, knowing he'd been renowned throughout the polite world for those skills!

'Does he seem...recovered?' her aunt asked, pulling her from her thoughts. At Theo's questioning look, she continued. 'I only wonder because he was engaged to a duke's daughter, and broke with her as soon as he returned from Belgium. It was quite the *on dit* before I left London, the young lady making it known that it was Mr Ransleigh who wished to cry off, not her.'

'I had no idea,' Theo said. She ran through her observations of his behaviour before continuing, 'He didn't seem to be brooding over a lost love, but then a man would hardly wear his heart on his sleeve, especially before a stranger. Certainly he's not yet fully recovered physically.'

'Retired to the country to finish healing,' her aunt said, nodding. 'Here, rather than in Leicestershire, where the memories of his hunting days would be sure to torment him.' Lady Amelia shook her head wonderingly. 'Dominic Ransleigh, living practically at your doorstep! Thank heaven you wore something at least moderately attractive when you called on him yesterday!'

Then she realised what she'd just said, and gasped. 'Oh, Theo, you called on *him*? You took Constancia with you, I hope?'

'I'm afraid not. Really, Aunt, I had no idea my landlord was a bachelor. I was expecting a doddering old man with an ear trumpet, rather than a most attractive young man.'

'He is—still attractive? I'd heard he was grievously wounded.'

'He lost an arm and an eye, and his face is scarred. But he's still a very handsome man.' A heated awareness shivered through her as she remembered just how arresting he was. 'Perhaps even more compelling now, given the grace with which he bears his injuries.'

Her aunt's expression brightened. 'And he's once again unattached!'

'Don't look at me with that light in your eye!' Theo warned. 'For one, if Mr Ransleigh has just broken an engagement, he's unlikely to start angling after some other female. Nor, having rejected a duke's daughter, is he apt to consider anyone less lofty. I expect he came to the country to find space and time…especially if his circumstances have changed so drastically. So promise me, no hints from you about how superior my lineage and prospects are, despite my current situation.'

The very idea that Ransleigh might suspect she was trying to attach him made Theo feel ill. Patting her hand, Lady Amelia said, 'Don't upset yourself, my dear! I would never do anything to embarrass you.'

Theo relaxed a little—until her aunt gave her a smile Theo didn't entirely trust before saying, 'In any event, we've kept him waiting long enough. Shall we go in?'

A few moments later, Theo and Aunt Amelia entered the parlour. The warmth of Ransleigh's smile as he rose to acknowledge them sent an immediate surge of response through her. Trying to curb it—and her dismay at how strong and involuntary a reaction it was—Theo made the necessary introductions.

'Delighted to meet you, Lady Coghlane,' Ransleigh said.

'As I am to meet you, Mr Ransleigh. And may I add my thanks for your gallant service with the Dragoons? I can't tell you how much better we all sleep, knowing that Napoleon is vanquished for good!'

Ransleigh inclined his head. 'Doing my duty, as so many others did. My condolences on the loss of your brother, by the way. Too many good men fell at Waterloo.'

Her aunt's eyes misted over. 'Richard's life was the army, but it's been…difficult. Enough of that, now. By the way, I knew your late mother well—we came out together. A lovely, sweet girl, who became an elegant and much-admired lady. The carriage accident which claimed your parents' lives was a sad day for all of us. Though it's been years, you have my deepest sympathy. It's not a loss from which one recovers easily.'

Ransleigh nodded. 'I was fortunate to have my cousins and their families to help me bear it. So my mother was said to be elegant?' He laughed and shook his head. 'I remember her in a worn riding habit, mud on her boots and her windblown hair escaping from her bonnet. She was as hunting-mad as my father, at a time when ladies weren't supposed to hunt.'

'I seldom leave London, so I didn't see her often after the family relocated to Upton Park. Which happened so long ago, as I told Theo, I'd forgotten Bildenstone was your primary estate. How are you finding it?'

'After being away with the army for so many years, I'm just reacquainting myself with it. My grandfather did accumulate a superb library, which I'm enjoying.'

'I understand my niece wishes to rent one of your buildings for her project. Though I applaud the tender feelings which inspire her, I have to admit, I have tried to talk her out of it. Such a weighty responsibility for someone so young, do you not agree?'

Theo threw her aunt an indignant look, to which that lady returned a bland smile. 'Really, Aunt Amelia, delighted as I am that you journeyed here to welcome me back to England, I'll not be so happy if you induce Mr Ransleigh to have second thoughts about allowing me to use his building!'

'I, too, think establishing the school a laudable aim— if a bit unusual an undertaking for a gently born lady,' Ransleigh said. 'However, from my brief acquaintance with your niece, Lady Coghlane, I don't think she's likely to be dissuaded.'

Her aunt sighed. 'She takes after her father in that— once she's fixed a project in her head, there's no dislodging it.'

'Will you be staying to help her begin the school?'

'Heavens, no! I have neither training nor inclination. As Theo said, I came only to welcome her to England. I'm too fond of London's comforts to tarry long in the country. I have been trying to persuade her to visit me, perhaps for the rest of the Season.' She gave Theo an arch look. 'There are, after all, other laudable goals for a young lady to accomplish.'

'If you're hinting at marriage, Aunt, I've no intention of accomplishing that goal, as you well know,' Theo said, irritated. 'I'm happy in the country, and I fully expect the children to occupy all my time. That is—' she looked over at Ransleigh as the dismaying thought suddenly occurred '—assuming you didn't come here to tell me you intend to withdraw your permission to rent your building.'

'No, I have not,' Ransleigh replied. 'Although I hope that won't put me in your black books, Lady Coghlane.'

'For the fondness I bore your mother, I shall try to forgive you,' she said with a twinkle.

'I am relieved! I should hate to offend my mother's good friend. As for why I appeared on your doorstep, it's such a fine morning for a drive, I decided to take your good advice, Miss Branwell, and get some fresh air. While pondering where I might drive, I recalled your invitation and thought perhaps I might meet the orphans whose school building I've agreed to lease to you.'

Surprised—and impressed, for how many young men would trouble to acquaint themselves with a group of children—and orphaned commoners at that?—Theo said, 'I'm sure they would be delighted to meet you. Especially Jemmie, the oldest, who will have to be restrained from monopolising you, once he discovers you're a soldier. I've already ordered a farm wagon brought up so I might drive them over to the building this morning. They've walked so often in the van of the supply wagons; the opportunity to *ride* in one is quite a treat. If you don't mind including in your drive a stop at the stone barn, may I wait to introduce them until after we arrive? They will be much more attentive once the ride takes the edge off their exuberance.'

'Of course. I brought my tilbury, Lady Coghlane. May I offer you a ride?'

'That's kind, Mr Ransleigh, but I will not be going. The prospect of a gaggle of children running about, shrieking at each other at the top of their lungs, does not appeal. As for the barn, Theo tells me it is presently unoccupied, needing a good deal of work before it will be fit for her purposes.' Lady Coghlane shuddered. 'Not a task I'd willingly undertake! I prefer my rooms already cleaned, polished, heated and well furnished before I enter them—preferably to find a comfortable couch upon which to sit, and a butler at the ready to bring refreshments.'

Theo laughed. 'It's good that Papa didn't ask his sister to follow the drum, then. Shall you feel neglected if I leave you for a time?'

'Certainly not, my dear. I have letters to write.'

'I'll bid you goodbye, then,' Ransleigh said, making her a bow. 'Once again, it was a pleasure to meet such a charming lady, and doubly so to meet a friend of my mother's.'

'Goodbye, Mr Ransleigh. Do call if you find yourself

in town. I would be pleased to receive you in that comfortable parlour and offer some excellent refreshments!'

Ransleigh laughed. 'I will certainly avail myself of your hospitality when I'm next in London.' Turning to Theo, he said, 'Shall I meet you and your charges at the barn, Miss Branwell?'

'Yes. I'll go collect them at once. Until later, Aunt Amelia. Let me escort you out, Mr Ransleigh.'

While they walked towards the entry door, Theo said, 'As she told you, my aunt has been trying to dissuade me from establishing the school. Failing that, I suppose she hopes I'll set it up and then turn it over to some good vicar to run, resuming my place as a proper English maiden.'

Her attraction to him, doubtless evident to a man of Ransleigh's experience, made it even more important to her that Ransleigh understand her views on marriage. So, despite the embarrassment of discussing such a topic with an eligible bachelor, she forced herself to say, 'Having no daughter of her own, Aunt Amelia always hoped Papa would ship me back to England so she might launch me into society and find me a husband. Neither Papa nor I were ever interested in accepting her kind offer, and with the school to establish, I certainly am not now.'

'Are you so uninterested in marriage?' Ransleigh asked, his tone curious.

'Papa left me very well settled. Unlike most of my sex, I don't have to marry for security or to have a place in the world.'

'What of…companionship?' he asked, his expression turning warmer.

Ah, *companionship*… With him standing at her shoulder, his gaze locked on her face, the physical pull between them intensified. Resisting the desire to step close enough to feel the heat of him up and down her sensitised body, she said, 'I was once engaged, I believe I told you. Having already found—and lost—the love of my life, I don't expect to find another. Nor would I even wish to. Losing Marshall w-was...' Her voice breaking, she swallowed hard, unable to find words to express the shock, horror and desolation of learning that he'd been killed in battle.

They'd reached the stairs, giving her an excuse to wrest her gaze away from his. She took a deep breath to slow the pounding of her heart. 'I'll leave you here, and see you at the barn in half an hour?'

Tacitly accepting her retreat, he nodded. 'Half an hour it is.'

Theo watched him walk away, then headed up the stairs to the nursery.

She hoped her avowals of uninterest in marriage had negated any little hints Aunt Amelia, drat her, had made about London and a maiden's duty. She also hoped Ransleigh didn't feel as strongly as she had the tingling connection that seemed to hum between them from the moment he'd entered the parlour. That had intensified as she walked beside him down the hallway, a tantalising hand's breadth apart.

Only recalling the agony of losing the man she loved had broken its bewitching hold over her.

Alas, the immediate attraction she'd felt at their first encounter at Bildenstone, that she'd tried while riding home to convince herself had been a trick of the moment—an amalgam forged of an unexpected meeting with a like-minded soldier who also happened to be a handsome man—had resurfaced in full force upon their second meeting. Every instinct, reinforced by the innuendo in his tone when he mentioned *companionship*, told her he found her alluring, too.

She wrestled with that fact, finding it at once deliciously appealing and alarming.

Focus on the 'alarming' part, her sensible nature urged. If only she could, without having to arm herself against him by calling up painful memories she would rather keep buried. And she absolutely must submerge again the dangerous passion he seemed to call forth so readily from where she'd banished it after Marshall's death.

Like putting the genie back in the bottle, the task was proving much harder than she'd anticipated.

She'd probably not see Ransleigh again after today. Surely she could restrain her inclinations for one more outing—with a bevy of children as chaperones!

Chapter Seven

As she'd expected, the children chorused their excited approval of a drive. Exuberant, Charles jumped up and down, clapping his hands in glee before delighting her with a kiss on her cheek. She gathered him close, drinking in the cherished feel of his small body nestled against her.

The ever-silent Maria merely nodded, but even the new children, Anna and Georgie, left off their guarded looks to smile at her.

She shepherded them downstairs to where a groom had pulled up the wagon. After helping Constancia settle the little ones in the back, Jemmie climbed up beside her, begging to handle the ribbons. Promising she would offer driving lessons on another occasion, when they did not have someone waiting on them, she took the reins and set the horses off.

A short while later, she pulled up the wagon in front of the stone building. Mr Ransleigh, already arrived in his tilbury, awaited them before the entrance. Just seeing him standing there sent an anticipatory shiver through her.

She tried to quell it while she helped the children down from the wagon—though, alas, she did not need to be looking at the man to be fully aware of his presence. Once they were safely disembarked, she said, 'Mr Ransleigh, may I present Jemmie, Charles, Maria, Anna and Georgie. And this is Constancia Bracamonte, their nurse and my assistant.'

'Pleased to meet you, children, Miss Bracamonte,' Ransleigh said, inclining his head.

'Mr Ransleigh owns this building, which as I told you, children, we plan to make into a home and school for you.'

Five young heads turned as one to look at it. 'Seems sturdy enough,' Jemmie said after a swift inspection.

'Very sturdy—made of good stone. Why don't you all go inside and have a peek?'

Charles, who'd been impatiently shifting from foot to foot after the introductions, needed no further invitation. 'C'mon, Georgie, I'll race you!' Shaking his head, Jemmie loped off after them.

Anna looked at Theo, who nodded. 'It's quite safe. Maria, would you take Anna's hand? Constancia will accompany you, too, so you will be all right.'

'Come, *meninas,* I will see you take no harm.' Beckoning the girls to follow, the maid walked them after the boys.

Theo turned back to Ransleigh. 'Your colour is better this morning! I believe driving agrees with you.'

'You may have the satisfaction of knowing you were right; I do feel better, getting out into the fresh air. Shall we walk towards the pasture while the young ones explore?' He offered his arm.

She hesitated. Given his effect on her, it would be wiser not to accept—but it would seem rude to refuse. At the questioning lift of his brow, she capitulated, laying her fingers on his arm. Despite the layers of broadcloth and kidskin, she felt a connection sizzle between them.

She suppressed a sigh, torn between annoyance and letting herself, for the few more moments she'd have to spend with him, simply enjoy the delicious disturbance he created whenever he was near her.

'So, tell me about your little group,' he was saying. 'Where did you find them?'

Glad that he'd invoked the children—the surest way to ground her—she said, 'Jemmie, the oldest, is the son of Father's sergeant-major, who was already with the regiment when we joined it in India. His mother died in childbirth—all too common an occurrence for English women in Calcutta, I'm afraid. The sergeant-major was killed by a sniper while directing the rear guard during the retreat to Corunna. Jemmie's about twelve, we think, and more than ready to begin training for an occupation.'

'Maria, the older girl with the sweet smile, is about seven. We found her at a convent after the Siege of Bajados, brought there with her dying mother, who'd been… abused by French soldiers. The sisters suspected Maria had witnessed the attack, for she's never spoken, and is very shy around men—quite a disadvantage for a female travelling with an army! She grew to be easy with my father, and accepts Jemmie and Charles, but she prefers to stay close to me or Constancia.'

'Anna and Georgie are the newest, just arrived from Belgium. I understand Anna's mother died in Brussels right before Waterloo, and her father was killed in the battle, leaving the five-year-old orphaned. Georgie we found at the docks in Calais, as he was about to be turned over to a gendarme for filching a meat pie from one of the army provisioners. He's about seven as well.'

Jemmie had approached them as Theo finished that last, and shook his head. 'Still not sure it was such a good idea, taking in a thief, Miss Theo! The Colonel always said them that thieves small will thieve big, sooner or later.'

'Which may be true for soldiers, but I don't know that the rule applies to a starving child, Jemmie,' Theo said.

Jemmie shrugged. 'S'pose we'll see. Right clever she was about nabbing him, though,' he said, turning to address Ransleigh. 'Fat pieman about had his thumbs around ol' Georgie, hollering as how he'd stolen a pie and he was goin' to turn him over to the provost. Miss Theo nips over, cool as you please, and spins him this faraddidle about how she'd sent Georgie to get pies for us, and how Georgie was naughty to make the man chase after him, rather than just buyin' the pies from his stand.' Jemmie chuckled. 'The man just stood there, gogglin' at her, cause he weren't born yestiddy and knew as how she was bammin' him, only when Miss Theo gets her "colonel's daughter" agoin', who's to gainsay her?'

He turned back to face Ransleigh. 'So you see, sir, Miss Theo kin look after herself, what with me to help out. And Miss Theo, though that building is sturdy enough to make a fine shelter if we wanted a billet, I don't see why we need a school. I'm too old for one, Maria never lets out a peep, and Master Charles will be getting a tutor anyway, won't he?'

'That's as may be, but remember, there will be more children coming to join us. All of you will need to learn your letters and a trade.'

The boy's frown deepened. 'Sure you got enough blunt to keep more army brats, after paying to rent that fancy manor house?'

'You watch my money closer than I do,' Theo said with a chuckle.

'Don't want you to run short,' the boy said seriously. 'Not afore I'm old enough to join the army, so's I can earn enough coin to support us. I promised the Colonel before he died that I'd take care of you, and I mean to.'

'I know you will,' Theo replied, an ache in her throat as she looked at his earnest young face. There would be time later to argue over his desire for an army career—

and its potential financial returns. 'But to earn enough to take care of a family, one has to have schooling. You'll like it, Jemmie.'

'Mebbe,' the boy conceded. 'I'd rather watch out for the horses, like I did for the Colonel. I will be able to tend horses here, won't I?'

'We'll see,' Theo replied diplomatically. 'You'll need to do lessons as well, though. Now, will you round up the others for me? It's time we went back.'

Jemmie nodded. 'Whatever you say, Miss Theo.' Turning to Ransleigh, he said, 'Nice to meet you, sir. I expect we can manage on our own now.'

After giving Ransleigh a bow, he trotted back towards the barn.

'I think I've just been warned off,' Ransleigh said, watching the boy walk away.

Theo shook her head ruefully. 'He's grown quite protective since Papa died. Though he's a boy still, he's at that awkward age, not yet a man, but thinking to take on a man's responsibilities.' She laughed. 'Which I guess explains why he tried so hard to demonstrate how clever I am and how well we are able to hold our own in the world, without anyone else's help.'

'You *are* clever. Nor do I think I'd want to cross swords with you when you've got your "colonel's daughter" goin'.'

'You already know I'm managing. I suppose it doesn't take much of a stretch to think of me as manipulating as well.'

He raised his eyebrows. 'I seem to remember a caller waiting on a wall in the rain until the reluctant host felt obliged to receive her.'

She laughed again. 'I object, sir! That was tactics, not manipulation.'

'And quite effective,' he admitted. 'You've told me about the others, but what about the one he called "Master Charles"'? Who's not to attend the school, but to have a tutor?'

'Ah, Charles.' She gathered herself to give him the story she always told of how the boy had become like her own. 'He is an orphan, but not the offspring of a common soldier. His late father, Lord Everly, was the youngest son of the Marquess of Wareton. Before joining his regiment on the Peninsula, Everly persuaded the daughter of a curate to run away with him. They were both of age, and wed by an army chaplain after their arrival, but the marquess, who was furious at his son's union with a girl whose father was barely a gentleman, never recognised the marriage.'

'Everly,' Ransleigh said, frowning. 'I knew him slightly. He was at Cambridge when I entered Oxford. Didn't last long, as I recall; sent down before the first term ended. Wild to a fault. Poor girl.'

'Poor girl, indeed. He got her with child almost immediately, and a very difficult time she was having of it. I persuaded her to accompany me back to London to my aunt's house for the birth, but before we reached Lisbon, we received word that Lord Everly had been killed. Distraught and hysterical, she was unable to travel further. We ended up staying at a convent until the child was born, and sadly, she did not long survive his birth. I brought Charles back with me, only to learn upon my return that Lord Everly's father had no intention of acknowledging the woman or a brat from a marriage he refused to recognise. So Papa and I kept Charles. Indeed, I look upon him as my own son now, and shall do my upmost to see that he receives an upbringing and education suitable to his birth—whether or not he is ever received by his grandfather.'

'Raise a child on your own? Once again, a commendable aim, but isn't that an even weightier responsibility for a young lady?'

'With Papa gone now, too weighty, my aunt would say.

But why should an innocent child suffer for the folly of his parents, the hard-heartedness of a grandfather and the death of a male sponsor? Especially as dear and clever a boy as Charles. Which is, of course, another reason a Season in London would only disappoint my aunt. I don't imagine many gentlemen would be eager to court a lady who comes with a child attached, one whose blood family refuses to receive him. And I will never give him up.'

Before Ransleigh could attempt a reply—fortunately, for Theo wasn't sure what a gentleman could safely respond to such a startling revelation—Constancia trotted up with the children in tow.

The full truth of her circumstances should effectively snuff out whatever attraction he might have felt for her, she thought, both relieved that the temptation he represented would soon be removed—and a little sad to lose it. Like the last vestiges of her youth, disappearing for good.

Immured in the country, he might find flirting with a safe but willing female mildly attractive. Even flirting with one who had a troop of orphans to supervise might not be too daunting. But trying to flirt with a woman surrounded by a gaggle of orphans who also had a child clinging to her skirts would doubtless not seem worth the effort.

'The children are all here, Senhorita Theo, except for Jemmie,' Constancia said.

Pulling herself back to the present, Theo said, 'I thought he was doing the gathering. Where could he have got to?'

She was about to call him when her attention was drawn to a flicker of movement glimpsed from the corner of her eye. Turning, she saw in the adjoining pasture the boy approach a tall, prancing stallion.

Jemmie—drawing near the black beast who had nearly trampled her.

At Theo's gasp, Ransleigh saw them, too. 'Great Lucifer, is the boy mad?'

'Too late to warn him! What should we do?'

'Stay here, and don't call out to Jemmie!' he said, restraining her when she would have run towards the fence. 'Any loud noise or sudden movement could set the horse off and he'll kick out, or run the boy down. Don't come any closer, and for heaven's sake, keep the rest of the children away!'

But as he set off at a measured pace for the pasture, Maria gave a guttural cry and leapt forward. Before she could take a second step, Ransleigh grabbed her, murmuring soothingly to the child as he turned slowly, calmly towards Theo, who stepped forward to take the girl in her arms.

'Keep her safe,' he said softly, and set out again towards the pasture.

Much as it chafed Theo to stand still and do nothing more useful than murmur reassurances to the trembling Maria, she knew Ransleigh, from his long association with the horse, would be more likely to safely rescue Jemmie.

As she watched anxiously, Ransleigh approached the fence. Meanwhile, rather than retreating from the agitated stallion, Jemmie—whose neck she was going to wring once Ransleigh extracted him from the pasture—had moved slowly closer. As she held her breath, he leaned towards the huge beast, his lips moving, doubtless talking in the soothing tones he used with the army horses.

The stallion stopped pawing the ground and watched the boy. Cautiously he extended his head, his nostrils quivering. A moment later, his body and muzzle relaxing, he let Jemmie stroke his neck.

Slowly and silently Ransleigh scaled the fence, his gaze never leaving the boy and horse. As the stallion's aggressive posture changed to curiosity and then acceptance, he walked slowly over to the pair and put a hand on Jemmie's shoulder.

'That's enough of a visit for now,' he said, giving Jemmie's shoulder a tug.

'Is he yours?' the boy asked, awe in his tones. 'What a prime goer he must be!'

'He is, but with a disposition to match his name—Diablo,' Ransleigh said, a touch of acid in his tone. 'Let's leave while he's still feeling amiable.' Keeping his body between the horse and the boy, he walked Jemmie back and over the fence.

Theo rushed over to greet them. 'Jemmie, what were you thinking? You shouldn't just go right up to a horse you don't know!'

Jemmie looked at her, puzzled. 'But I done that all the time, Miss Theo. The cavalry boys always wanted me to tend their horses.'

'Yes, but we're not with the army now, and Diablo isn't a cavalry mount, he's much less steady! Besides, one shouldn't approach a horse in a private pasture without getting the owner's permission first.'

'Which would not have been granted, not for that horse!' Ransleigh said. 'You might have been bitten, at the least, kicked in the head at worst. I've seen Diablo scatter a stall full of grooms on a whim.'

'He'd never hurt me, sir,' Jemmie said. 'I could see he were a bit riled up at first, but once I started talkin' to him, he calmed down right quick. They generally do, once they know you understand them and don't mean them no harm.'

Ransleigh shook his head and looked at Theo.

'He does have a way with horses,' she explained.

'That may be. But, young man, you are not to approach Diablo again. He was moved to be amenable today, but he can change in an instant. Promise me you won't go near him.'

'You don't need to worry he'd be harmin' me,' Jemmie

repeated confidently. 'But it's your horse, so I guess I have to promise. Will you let me visit him again?'

'We'll see about that later,' Theo said. 'Now, please help Constancia load the children back into the wagon.'

'Yes, Miss Theo. Thank you again, sir, for lettin' me talk to your horse.'

'As if I'd given him permission,' Ransleigh muttered to Theo as Jemmie ushered the children away. 'He does have the touch, though. I've seen grooms with years of experience afraid to go near that horse.'

'Perhaps Diablo allowed it because he sensed that Jemmie was not afraid. I, however, was terrified! Thank you so much for seeing him safely out!'

Ransleigh made a gesture of dismissal. 'It seems he would have been fine on his own. But I couldn't risk that.'

Theo felt a swell of gratitude, which only redoubled her admiration for him. 'I do think Jemmie would make a fine trainer—which would be a better use of his skills than sending him to the army.'

Ransleigh nodded agreement. 'A skilled trainer can forge a fine career working for a large stable, like the Duke of Rutland's racing stud. If he can quiet Diablo, Jemmie should be able to work wonders with more even-tempered beasts.'

'From what you've told me of your work with horses, you should know.' A sudden thought occurred, and Theo's eyes lit. 'Might you work with Jemmie? If you were able to train Diablo, there must be so much you could teach him!'

As soon as the words left her lips, she caught herself. 'No, don't answer that,' she said before he could speak. 'Forgive me again! I get so caught up envisioning their futures, I blunder on as if everyone takes a similar interest. But I would ask one other, more acceptable favour.'

He shook his head at her. 'Poor Lady Coghlane. I sincerely doubt she's going to be able to tempt you away to London. Now, what would that favour be?'

'In your years of working with horses, you must have met any number of trainers. I do think it would be a perfect occupation for Jemmie. If you can think of a good one who might consider working at the school, I would very much appreciate the recommendation. I'd like to see Jemmie—all of them—become useful members of the society their fathers gave so much to protect.'

'You may have trouble convincing the Lady Wentworths of the neighbourhood, but I wholeheartedly agree.' He shook his head. 'Despite the fright Jemmie gave me over Diablo, I'll even see if I can think of a trainer you might use.'

Nothing could incite her gratitude more than his engaging himself to help her orphans. 'Thank you for understanding,' she said fervently. 'And for your compassion.'

Impulsively she grasped his hand, intending to shake it. But the moment she touched him, a palpable current flashed between them, so strong she nearly gasped at its force.

He must have felt it, too, for his pulse leapt under her fingers. But rather than pulling his hand away, he tightened his grip.

Her breathing stopped, her vision narrowed until only he filled it—the handsome face with the slash of the scar running down from the eye patch, his vivid blue gaze watching her so intently. Her hand throbbed beneath his touch, the vibrations radiating from her fingers up her arm to the whole of her body.

He murmured something, her name maybe, and bent his head. Her eyes fluttered shut, her lips tingling in anticipation of his touch.

A sharp tug at her gown snapped her eyes back open.

Dazed, she looked down to find Charles beside her. Her face flaming, she yanked her fingers from Ransleigh's.

'Can we go back now, Miss Theo! I'm awfully hungry.'

Shaken by what had passed between her and Ransleigh, she seized the boy and lifted him into her arms, hugging him against her, a reassuring reminder of where she belonged.

Heavens, Theo, pull yourself together!

'I'm ready to get in the wagon now,' Charles said, squirming in her grasp.

She set the boy down and gave Ransleigh a curtsy, her breathing still unsteady. 'Thank you again for lending us your barn, Mr Ransleigh,' she said, relieved that the words emerged in a natural tone, rather than a gasp. 'Perhaps you will honour us with another visit after the school has begun, if your engagements permit.'

'I expect they might. Good day to you, Miss Branwell,' he said with a bow.

She felt his gaze on her as she walked away, her body still humming and fizzing like a Congreve rocket about to erupt. Which she might have done, had Charles not interrupted them. Or would Ransleigh have come to his senses first?

She'd need to regather her wits in order to drive the children home without running them into a tree, she thought as she hoisted Charles into the wagon and took her seat. And leave until later, when her brain was functioning again, the problem of figuring out how to halt the madness that seemed to overcome her every time she came near Dominic Ransleigh.

Chapter Eight

After watching Miss Branwell drive off with her orphans, Dom reclaimed his vehicle and set the tilbury in motion. What was it about the lady that affected him so strongly? Though she looked no more like a siren than a sparrow resembles a peacock, something about her seemed to light him off faster than a fuse touched to powder.

She felt it too, he was certain, just as unbidden and just as strongly. And seemed to have no more idea where it came from or how to counter it than he had.

It certainly wasn't her beauty, nor a sophisticated wit that played seduction's game. To be sure, she had a natural grace and a keen, if often biting, intellect. But far from trying to entice him, she proclaimed she had no interest in men or marriage. He had to believe her; the surprise and confusion with which she reacted, each time attraction flared between, was too convincing to be a sham. Besides, if she were trying to lure him on while playing the innocent, she'd surely allow a touch or a kiss, just to inflame him further.

Even if she weren't too straightforward to make those claims to try to cozen an eligible bachelor, the fact that she had taken in a child she intended to raise underlined the truth of her uninterest.

A child she meant to keep even without her father to help smooth his way, she'd said, raising her little chin as if she meant to defy everyone and the world who might try to take him from her.

Which should provide protection enough from seduction and wedlock. As she'd noted, few men would want to begin married life with someone else's cuckoo in their nest, a boy his own blood family refused to recognise.

Nor could he blame his reaction to her on the fact that he'd been too long without a woman—though it had been too long. Just two days ago, he'd kissed the hand of delectable blonde, blue-eyed Miss Wentworth, whom any sane man would consider far more beautiful than Theodora Branwell. And felt…nothing.

Was it the passion so evident in her eloquent defence of her orphans and her brisk, restless movements that called to him? A strain of barely controlled wildness he sensed thrumming beneath her skin, which drove him on some instinctive level to try to free it?

Whatever fomented it, the urge was strong. If that urchin hadn't distracted her, he would have kissed her in full view of the whole group of orphans and their nurse. For no more reason than something primal in her called urgently to something in him.

Just thinking about taking her mouth, pulling that lithe, slim body against him, made his pulses race and his body harden further. He sighed and blew out a breath.

Pay attention, Dominic Ransleigh, he told himself sternly. Had that long fever addled his brain? Nothing about Miss Branwell's circumstances had changed since the last time he'd speculated about his attraction to her. She was still a gently born virgin, therefore not a female available for seduction.

Unless he was thinking of marriage.

Ah, there was a brake to halt this runaway carriage!

Attracted he might be, but having just extricated himself from one attachment for the express purpose of discovering what he meant to do with his life before committing himself to anyone, he had no business letting his senses lead him into another entanglement. Miss Branwell was not some experienced widow or bored society matron, whom he could dally and then part with amicably, both satisfied with the arrangement and no one the wiser. Keep less than a stranglehold over his passions, and he might compromise her, forcing him to do the honourable thing and compelling into wedlock a girl who'd expressed even less desire to marry than he had.

To save himself frustration—and temptation—he probably ought to avoid her.

Except…he'd just more or less promised her he'd look into the matter of a trainer.

Though he might know nothing about children, he did remember being a boy mad about horses, an enthusiasm he saw mirrored in Jemmie. He shuddered as he recalled the boy in the pasture with Diablo. A lad who could get near that beast without injury already possessed instincts that could not be taught, that needed only refining to turn him into a superb trainer.

Maybe he should help, sharing his love of and skill with horses. Guiding the sergeant-major's orphan into a secure future would be a worthy task.

Then he had to laugh. Was that his destiny—becoming an orphanage instructor? He could just imagine the shock, disbelief, and derision among the toffs of the *ton*, were they to learn Dandy Dom had turned his hand to bear-leading youths.

But then, who cared what the toffs of the *ton*—or Lady Elizabeth's ducal father, or the earl his uncle, the 'King of the Lords', thought of what he did? It was his life—his to remake.

He'd felt for so long like the old brown leaves scattered beside the lane he drove down, crumbling into nothingness as the new grass of spring grew through them. But maybe he was more like a skittering seed pod blown on the wind, just needing to reach fertile ground to take root.

Still, he'd be prudent not to make a premature offer he might later decide was unwise.

Besides, training the orphan would mean spending way too much time around Miss Theo.

Recalling her allure heated his simmering senses anew.

He could seduce her—he was sure of it. Contemplating the passion promised in that lush mouth, those vibrant eyes sent an anticipatory thrill through him.

Wise or not, he couldn't seem to bury that fact that he wanted her. More intensely than he'd wanted a woman in a very long while.

If he couldn't subdue the craving, maybe he should try to assuage it in a more acceptable way. He'd had mistresses before his engagement to Lady Elizabeth. If it would distract him from this frustrating desire for Miss Branwell, maybe he should consider setting up another.

He conjured up the image of a lush female in a diaphanous gown, her mouth in a seductive pout, her bosom covered with jewels and little else. Somehow, beside Theo Branwell's fresh, straightforward appeal, such a woman seemed...overblown.

He uttered a curse, startling the horse he'd just turned down the drive to Bildenstone.

He had too much free time on his hands—that was part of the problem.

Now that he could manage more than sleeping half the day and lifting his head to sip some gruel, he needed something more challenging to occupy him.

He'd been with the army so long, he had trouble recalling the rhythm of his days before he'd become a soldier.

Blocking out the hunting and steeplechasing activities still too bitter to contemplate, he tried to remember. In the country, he'd been up early, he mused, consulting with his grooms, training horses, or travelling to fairs or farms to evaluate others he might wish to purchase. Studying bloodlines in the evening if alone, or socialising with like-minded friends. In town, he'd stop by Tattersall's to check out the horses for sale, visit the tailor and bootmaker and haberdasher, pay calls by day and spend his evenings at dinners, balls or entertainments, charming the ladies.

Contemplating returning to most of these activities still evoked distaste. The only endeavour that called to him was working with horses.

Putting that thought away to consider later, he returned the tilbury to the stable and walked to the house.

Wilton met him at the entrance. 'Some refreshment in the library, sir?'

'Thank you, some ham and ale would be good,' he said, pleased to find, after months of no appetite, that a morning of driving and walking about had left him both hungry and not too fatigued to eat.

He'd found his place again in Herodotus by the time Wilton knocked at the library door. Miss Branwell's advice came back to him as he watched the man carry the tray to the table. To his chagrin, it did seem the elderly butler struggled to manage the heavy item, his thin frame bent back under its weight as he balanced it.

Deciding on the instant, he said, 'Wilton, a word, if you please.'

'Of course, Mr Ransleigh.'

'I've been intending to ask you to convey my appreciation to the staff for the excellent work they did, preparing Bildenstone Hall for my arrival. I know it took a great deal of effort, after the house had been closed up for so long.'

Expressions of surprise, then gratification, illumined the butler's face. 'I'm pleased you found everything satisfactory, Mr Ransleigh, and I'll certainly pass your approval on to the others.'

'With the increased workload of having a family member in residence, we should hire some additional employees. I'm thinking we will need an under-butler, an assistant for Cook, plus a couple of maids and perhaps another footman, as a start.'

The butler's eyes lit with enthusiasm. 'That would indeed be helpful, sir. We had nearly twice the staff when the late Mr and Mrs Ransleigh resided here. Though as a bachelor, of course, you won't do as much entertaining.'

'Consult with Mrs Greenlow and hire as many as you think necessary. '

The butler nodded. 'Very good, sir. I shall be honoured to assist you in reviving Bildenstone Hall.'

'Thank you, Wilton.'

The butler bowed himself out. Dom sat for a moment with a bemused smile. *Well, Miss Branwell, I've taken care of the house,* he thought, satisfaction warming him. Perhaps it was time to arrange a tour with his estate agent and check on the tenants. If the lord of the manor was going to reside here—and it appeared he was—he ought to become better acquainted with his land and the people who farmed it.

That should keep him occupied, away from the school— and the tantalising Miss Branwell.

Though even as he resolved it, he doubted he'd stay away long.

Chapter Nine

Two days later, the afternoon turning fair, Dom toted the volume of Herodotus to the bench in his mother's rose garden. An agreeable hour of reading later, a footman trotted up to inform him Miss Branwell had called.

Surprise, pleasure—and a bit of alarm—filled him. He thought at their last encounter they'd settled, regrettably, the fact that propriety forestalled her from calling on him again.

It might be wiser to send her away unseen, but it took him only an instant to conclude he'd not be able to force himself to do that. Curiosity alone demanded he discover what was so urgent that she felt moved to disregard the irksome rules of proper conduct and come to Bildenstone.

While he debated whether it would be better to receive her inside, in the parlour, where there would be fewer prying eyes to observe them, or out in the garden, in the open, where the many household staff could witness nothing improper was transpiring, the lady herself walked over.

'Good day, Mr Ransleigh,' she said with a smile.

It was certainly not prudent, but Dom couldn't help himself—he *had* to walk forward and take her hand, just to see if the tingling connection fired between them again.

He felt it immediately as he touched her—shock, then a force surging through him, flooding his senses. Without further thought, instead of shaking her hand as he had before, he turned the hand palm up and kissed it, fiercely resenting the buttons that prevented him from moving his lips to taste the bare skin at her wrist.

After a moment of savouring her warmth and an intoxicating violet scent that made his senses swim like strong brandy, he made himself release her. Straightening, he saw her gazing down at her still-extended hand, eyes wide, lips parted, her breathing quick and shallow.

Ah, she'd felt the connection just as strongly! he thought, triumphant. Desire ignited, sending awareness and need flaming through him. Had she leaned even infinitesimally closer, he could not have stopped himself from kissing her. Fortunately, more discreet than he, she took a wobbly step backward. He had a moment of furious regret before reason returned to make him glad she'd halted the encounter before it flared ever further out of control.

It took him a moment to reassemble his scorched wits.

'Good day to you, Miss Branwell,' he managed to say at last. 'I'm very happy to see you—though I am surprised you called, given the conclusion of our last conversation on the matter. Nothing alarming has happened, I trust?'

She gave a shaky laugh, further defusing the sensual tension. 'No, nothing alarming. Encouraging developments, actually. Not only am I emboldened to call on you, I believe you can offer me tea with impunity. Which, in fact, I should very much like. The day seems to have become suddenly over-warm.'

He could sympathise; his cravat—not to mention his breeches—now seemed over-tight. 'Let's walk back to the house, then. I'll order tea, and you can explain.'

He offered his good arm, and to his delight, she took it. Though as a result, he scarcely heard what she was saying, too distracted by her body so near his and that elusive violet scent, which seemed to emanate from her glossy brown hair—or perhaps from behind her ear. His mouth watered as he envisioned tasting her there, before his gaze drifted down to focus on the glimpse of tongue behind soft lips as she spoke. Wind-loosened wisps escaped from the braided tangle beneath her hat, and he itched to pull the hair fully free of its pins.

In short, he wanted her more than ever. It took all his will-power to force back that need and focus on her words.

'…probably not wise to visit too often,' she was saying as he guided her to the large receiving room, 'but I did need to call just this once, to warn you. I'm afraid you may be angry when I confess the rather presumptuous statements I made to Lady Wentworth, whom I called on this morning.'

'Presumptuous?' he echoed, amused. With so outspoken a girl, he couldn't imagine what outrageousness she'd uttered—and to Lady Wentworth! 'So you bearded the lioness in her den? I'm impressed by your courage,' he said as he waved her to a chair and sent a footman off for tea.

'Papa always said it's best to take initiative and confront your adversary on ground of your choice, rather than wait and wonder when and where you're going to be attacked. If Lady Wentworth intended to be an impediment to my establishing the school, I needed to know sooner rather than later.'

'Will she be an impediment?'

Her grin looked almost—smug. 'I think I've defused the problem, for the present, at least.'

'Have you, now?' he said, dubious. 'She seemed rather strongly opposed to it when she and the Squire called on me, and she didn't strike me as a person who is easily persuaded to change her opinions.'

'Quite true. But Papa also said one must learn everything one can about one's adversary before facing him, so I preceded my visit with a call on the local solicitor, Mr Scarsdale. I wanted to thank him anyway for his efforts in helping me staff Thornfield Place and discover from him which were the most influential members of the community, whose approval I must obtain if the school is to succeed. '

'Your father is right—that was good tactics,' he said approvingly. 'I'm sure Mr Scarsdale was gratified to be consulted.'

'I believe he was. Solicitors seem to me akin to sergeants in the army, performing many useful functions, knowing everything about everyone in their community, yet too often undervalued by those outranking them.'

Struck by the comparison, Dom nodded. 'I expect you are right. So, what did you discover?'

'After describing the most important families in the area—Squire Marlowe, Baron Southwick, and the Ransleighs—' She halted as Dom groaned.

'I hope he didn't recount too many adventures of my misspent youth.'

She shook her head, regarding him seriously. 'You must know how very highly you are regarded here, both your reputation before you entered the army, and for your valour in serving. He merely repeated what you yourself already told me—your ability with horses, your family's growing interest in breeding foxhounds and hunters, which led to their removal from Suffolk, to the great disappointment of all in the county. But he also provided the information I needed about Lady Wentworth.'

'Such as?'

'An only daughter doted upon by her father, she was the most beautiful and the most richly dowered maiden in the county in her début Season. Which makes it more understandable that she is accustomed to pronouncing judgements that permit no opposition, expressing desires that must be swiftly accommodated, and having others defer to her. I discovered the local charitable organisation of which she is now the head was established by her father, which she carries on in his honour. So naturally, in our conversation, I emphasised how the greatest wish of my late father, one of the heroes of Waterloo, was to establish a home and school for orphans of the soldiers he'd led into battle. That after his death, I felt it my solemn duty to carry out his wishes.'

Dom lifted an eyebrow. 'Was it his greatest wish?'

'Well, he never said it *wasn't*,' Miss Branwell said, with a twinkle in her eyes that made him laugh. 'To be fair, he had a war to win before he figured out what was to be done with the orphans we'd begun to accumulate. It's quite possible he would have decided to establish a home for them.'

'I begin to believe you incorrigible, Miss Branwell,' he said severely, his amused expression belaying the censorious comment.

'Determined, certainly,' she allowed, seeming not at all apologetic about manipulating her adversary.

After a break while Wilton brought in the tea tray, she continued. 'Mr Scarsdale said her father was a man of strict morals. So I emphasised that children brought up around an army are instilled with discipline from their earliest years, which makes them more amenable to following directions in moral training and improvement—moral improvement being something else her late father felt quite important.'

'I never noticed that strict discipline had any morally improving effect on soldiers.'

'As adults they have grown too set in their ways,' she countered. 'In any event, I ended by begging that she avail me of the experience she's garnered in running her own establishment. Which is quite true—I *would* appreciate her recommendations in staffing the school, and I certainly can't obtain the calibre of employee I want or find positions for the students later, if she sets the neighbourhood against me.'

'Very true. Well done, Miss Branwell!'

She nodded, her cheeks pinking at his praise. After draining her cup, she set it down and lifted her chin. Taking a deep breath and looking for the first time a bit uncomfortable, she said, 'I'm afraid I haven't yet confessed the truly incorrigible bit.'

Intrigued, and bracing himself for something outlandish, Dom said, 'Better do so straight away.'

'Well, if you're angry, there's nothing for it, but under the circumstances, I felt the…evasion justified. You see, before I left, Lady Wentworth took me to task about the nature of my relationship with you.'

Irritation washed through him. He'd never before resented quite so fiercely that birth and position would make everything about him of great interest to his neighbours for ever. 'Interfering creature,' he muttered. 'However, with the servants at Bildenstone all interrelated to families in the county, the fact that we've met several times was bound to get out.'

'Yes, and this is the…presumptuous part. I felt I'd mostly won her over, but with an unmarried daughter who might need to look closer to home for suitors if her Season isn't a success, and with her initial opposition to the orphans still making her approval uncertain, I knew she'd seize upon any reason to discredit me—and any stain upon my honour would give her exactly the excuse she needed! So I'm afraid I inferred that our acquaintance was of long standing, that you were a sort of protégé of my father's whom I looked upon as a sibling, and had been pleased to meet again as a fellow campaigner.'

Dom paused a moment to absorb the implications. 'You told that plumper without a blink? You *are* shameless!' he cried, torn between annoyance and admiration.

'Oh, no, I didn't lie!' she protested. 'I simply mentioned that Papa had mentored a number of young officers, of whom I grew quite fond and looked upon as brothers. As my comment followed her enquiry about our relationship, she *assumed* that you were one of the young men I was describing. Though I did not, I confess, contradict that erroneous assumption. In any event, I felt you should know about it, so you may decide how you wish to respond if anyone dares to question you about it.'

'So I can be prepared to insert a suitable evasion, which infers a relationship that never existed without precisely lying about it?'

She grinned. 'If your conscience will allow, I would much appreciate it.'

'Miss Branwell, I begin to have serious doubts about your character.'

She lifted an eyebrow and shrugged. 'Subterfuge and misdirection, when necessary, are legitimate tactics.'

'Perhaps you should abandon the idea of caring for orphans and take a post in strategy at Horse Guards.'

'With Boney on St Helena, they don't need me any more,' she said, then burst into laughter. 'Very well, I admit, I enjoyed leading her on. Someone so obviously full of herself, with a heart hard enough to consign innocent children she's never met to poverty without a blink, deserves to be hoodwinked from time to time.'

He shook his head, wondering at what a marvel she was. 'I only wish I'd been there to witness the performance. It must have been masterful!'

'Adequate, at any rate. With effects lasting long enough,

I hope, that I can launch the school and staff it before she has second thoughts about my respectability. Though it would still be wise not to invite those second thoughts by visiting here too often. So I'd best take advantage of this opportunity and ask you now if you've come up with any trainers whom you think I could approach about teaching at the school.'

'I did make a list. But I fear all those with the qualifications and experience you'd prefer are presently employed training horses for very wealthy men. It would probably be beyond your budget to hire any of them.'

She gave a negative shake of her head. 'If adequate salary is all that prevents them from accepting a position, that won't be a problem.'

'I should think, for one who's always managed on an army officer's pay, finances would be a pressing concern. Unless you have tucked away somewhere an India nabob or a rich brewer for a grandfather?'

'Actually, as you may have discerned with Lady Amelia being my aunt, my grandfather was an earl. My father, his youngest son, bedazzled my mother, a marquess's daughter with an enormous dowry that made her the prize of her début Season. I've inherited wealth from them both.'

Unconventional, outspoken, independent—and an heiress. Dom whistled. 'Miss Branwell, you amaze me!'

She looked down, her cheeks pinking again. 'I know, I hardly look the part,' she said, totally misunderstanding his compliment. 'Another reason I've resisted my aunt's urging that I come to London for the Season.'

Before he could come up with a tactful way to reassure her, the thought struck him of how Lady Wentworth would react to the news, and he had to laugh again. 'Wait until the officious Lady Wentworth discovers you outrank her—with a lineage that makes you far outshine the attractions of her daughter!'

'Not in that young lady's estimation,' Miss Bran-well said, and chuckled. 'I met her during my call on her mother. One look at me and my less-than-stylish raiment, and Miss Wentworth accorded me half a curtsy and a mur-mured greeting before relegating me to the background, as being of no more interest than the sofa.'

Having often observed the treatment acclaimed beau-ties meted out to those they considered of lesser stature, Dom wasn't surprised by the girl's discourtesy. He *was* surprised to find how strongly he resented the treatment on Miss Branwell's behalf.

'Sad to discover her breeding doesn't equal her beauty.'

'No harm done; I found it amusing. In fact, her dis-dain turned out to be useful. Deciding it might be help-ful in securing Lady Wentworth's approval, I let slip my aunt's name. Upon realising her daughter had just been rude to the niece of one of society's leaders, she couldn't have turned more agreeable. So agreeable, she offered to scotch any rumours that might be generated by my calling on you—allowing my visit today. So I can only be thank-ful for the beauty's self-absorption. Though,' she added, her smile faded, 'it would be less amusing, were I forced to put up with such treatment through the whole of the Season Aunt Amelia would drag me to.'

'Your aunt would guarantee you were too fashionably gowned and too surrounded by persons of superior in-tellect and breeding to receive snubs from ill-mannered country nobodies.'

'I'm not so sure. Nor could I imagine enduring the rounds of visiting and shopping my aunt described as nec-essary for acquiring a suitable wardrobe. And the cost! I may have inherited wealth, but I find it almost scandalous that society ladies fill wardrobes with gowns intended to be worn only once or twice.'

'What sacrilege!' he said, even more amused. 'Quite

true; with opinions like that, you'd not only *not* become fashionable, you'd be lucky if society's female population did not hire a sharpshooter to silence you before their men-folk could be exposed to so treacherous a notion.'

'No danger of my becoming fashionable, Aunt Amelia's protests notwithstanding. New gowns wouldn't change who I am—and what I am not. You can put a wagon mule into shiny harness, but that won't make him a cavalry horse.'

'That's a bit harsh,' Dom protested. Giving her shabby habit a glance, he said, 'You may not follow the latest fashion, but you have many admirable qualities.'

She raised an eyebrow. 'Such as?'

'Honesty, courage, ingenuity, perseverance, and a keen wit,' he shot back, naming off what had so quickly impressed him.

Obviously taken aback, her eyes widened. 'Thank you for that,' she said after a moment. 'But surely you can't claim those to be qualities highly prized by society gentlemen on the lookout for suitable wives!'

Before he could find a way around that irrefutable statement, she said, 'Not that it matters a particle. Only desperation would ever drive me to the Marriage Mart, and with Papa's inheritance and Mama's portion, I don't see that happening. As I mentioned before, unlike most of my sex, I'll never need to marry to avoid ending up with no roof over my head, or be reduced to begging a post as a companion or governess. Which is fortunate,' she added with a grin. 'Since I've never learned to keep my opinions to myself, I probably wouldn't last long as anyone's employee.'

Dom couldn't imagine her in that role, either. Though he did find it somehow sad that she seemed to think it her destiny to remain alone in the world. Such a unique, engaging personality deserved nurturing and appreciation—just as the sensual side to her called out for a lover's fulfilment.

His breath quickened and his body hardened at the thought; ah, how he'd like to guide her along that path, explore their explosive connection to the inevitable, exquisite conclusion!

While he once again struggled to rein in that fruitless desire, she rose and shook out her skirts. 'Thank you for the tea. With my news now delivered, I should get back to Thornfield Place.'

An immediate reluctance to let her go had him scrambling to his feet. Seizing on the first excuse that came to mind, he said, 'Before you leave, let me show you my grandfather's library. Anyone who could spend hours sitting on a wall, reading in the rain, must appreciate books, and Grandfather amassed quite a collection.'

Her face brightened. 'You mentioned to my aunt how extensive it is. I would love to see it! We could carry so few books with us on campaign. What I missed most about not having a settled home was the lack of a library.'

'So did I,' he said, struck by how she'd echoed his own feelings on the matter, and delighted to be able to share his grandfather's treasure with someone who would appreciate it as much as he did. Like braiding another thread into a strand of rope, that common interest further reinforced the bond that pulled them together.

Offering her his arm, Dom led her from the parlour to the library.

Three steps into the room, she came to a dead halt, her eyes wide with wonder as she looked up and down the shelves that covered every wall, from the floor up to the high vaulted ceiling.

'It's magnificent!' she breathed. 'May I?' She gestured towards the shelves.

'Of course,' Dom replied, her response all he had hoped. 'I must warn you, though, Grandfather's passion was collecting, not archiving, so I'm afraid the books are not shelved in any particular order.'

As Dom watched, she practically ran to the nearest bookcase. Something tightened in his chest as he watched her avidly scanning the shelves, sometimes running her fingers reverently over the spine of a particular volume, occasionally removing one to browse a page or two before carefully replacing it.

A lady who disdained new gowns, but went into raptures over a well-stocked library, was a unique creature indeed. The avid delight with which she examined the books, completely absorbed in discovering the treasures surrounding her, reinforced his instinctive sense of the deep passion that animated her, simmering beneath her matter-of-fact façade—and calling to him to fully reveal it.

After ten minutes, she shook her head and looked back at him.

'You warned me it was extensive, but this is overwhelming! How wonderful that your grandfather had a passion for collecting books, instead of rocks or jewellery or snuff boxes! I haven't enough time now to explore as I'd like. Might I come back later?'

'Whenever you wish. It's a pleasure to make it available to someone who truly appreciates it. Should I chance to be away when you call, Wilton can show you in.'

She turned towards the exit, then halted and looked back at the shelves, as if the volumes had an almost physical hold she was reluctant or unable to break. Then, with a sigh, she crossed the room to his side and looked up, her expression rapturous.

She stood so near, he burned to touch her, the delight still animating her face intensifying that desire. Struggling to restrain himself, Dom could barely breathe. When she placed her hand on his arm, his body tensed as he fought the need to pull her into his arms.

'I know life treated you cruelly, but you still have such blessings. A beautiful home, loyal servants, this magnificent library—and a bluebell wood!'

'And an enchanting new neighbour who appreciates books as much as I do,' he murmured.

'It is enchantment,' she whispered, and raised her chin.

Mesmerised, he cupped her face in his hands. As he lowered his mouth, her eyes drifted shut, one hand coming up to clasp the back of his head, the other trailing beside her, over a stack of books on a side table.

Which tumbled over the edge and hit the floor with a tremendous clatter.

At the sound, Miss Branwell gasped and jerked away from him. Bereft, shocked, Dom let her go.

For a long moment, they stared at each other, panting. Miss Branwell, her eyes wide and unfocused, brought a hand to her trembling lips, as if unable to sort out what had just happened.

A knock at the door, followed by Wilton bowing himself in, broke what remained of the spell holding them motionless. 'Should you like me to bring refreshments here, Mr Ransleigh?' the butler asked.

'N-no,' Miss Branwell answered for him. 'Thank you, Wilton, but I'm already overdue to return to Thornfield.'

'Very good,' the butler said, bowed himself back out.

Miss Branwell turned back to Dom, high colour still in her cheeks. 'I suppose I should be grateful for disorganised stacks of books. Otherwise, my actions might have been… embarrassing, to say nothing of scandalous.'

'I'm the one who should apologise, Miss Branwell,' Dom said, making the obligatory statement, though he was not sorry at all. Or, with his needy body still clamouring for the kiss denied it, only sorry they'd been interrupted.

'I should not have taken such advantage of you, a guest in my house.'

'You hardly "took advantage",' Miss Branwell admitted frankly. 'It goes without saying that the lapse mustn't be repeated, but in honesty, it was as much my fault as yours. And quite unsisterly! That's what I get for browsing through Ovid.'

Before his shocked mind could come up with a reply, she went on, 'I should like to browse through the library again, but next time I'll bring my maid as chaperone. And oh, how I would like to borrow some of the books for the school!'

As soon as the words left her lips, she shook her head. 'Forgive me! Presumptuous again! You would certainly not wish to risk loaning valuable books to children who would not appreciate how costly and delicate they are. But if you would permit it, might I myself borrow some books? I could copy out passages for the students.'

'Of course you may. Though you are correct; it would not be wise to put them into the hands of grubby schoolchildren.'

'I shall ensure they are not.' Not meeting his eyes, she bent to gather up the scattered books and stacked them back on the table. 'I should leave before I wreak any more havoc. Thank you again, for your hospitality—and your understanding.' She turned to go, halted a moment to press his hand, then hurried out.

Fingers tingling, Dom watched her walk away, then took himself to the sofa. His unsatisfied body still raging, he tried to settle a mind in turmoil and make sense of what had just happened.

Only one thing was clear: Miss Theo Branwell, unlikely siren, just made him forget a host's duty to protect his female guests, a precept that had been drilled into him since childhood. He'd better stay away from her until he figured out what he was going to do about it.

Shaken, Theo gripped Firefly's reins with trembling hands as she directed the mare down the lane back towards Thornfield Place, alarm over the episode in the library extinguishing her satisfaction in having outmanoeuvred Lady Wentworth. Whatever had come over her?

Her ladyship's chagrin over her daughter's discourtesy might have initially put to rest the worry that Theo's association with Dominic Ransleigh might harm her orphans' cause. But had the butler entered the library a few moments earlier, with her practically embracing his employer, even Aunt Amelia's influence as a society hostess wouldn't have been enough to salvage her reputation. Loyal retainer Wilton might be, but such gossip would be too delicious to repress—and impossible for Ransleigh to halt or punish.

Hadn't she learned that lesson well enough, having to endure Audley Tremaine's sly innuendoes after Marshall's death? She'd paid dearly for her indiscretion in slipping away into the sunset-washed Portuguese hills to spend one halcyon evening alone with the man she loved. She should know better than to act so impulsively.

Besides, her imprudence now would injure not just her, but the innocent children she'd pledged to nurture and protect.

A part of her protested the clear conclusion that, having shown herself so susceptible to Ransleigh's appeal, she should avoid him entirely. True, in his company she was able to recapture the ease and comfort of her years in the army with Papa, and she'd been completely delighted by the treasures of his library. But Ransleigh's ability to slip through her guard and fire a passion she'd thought long extinguished was a danger against which she needed to remain much more vigilant.

Work was the answer, she told herself, shutting out the pleading voice that urged her not to end her association with her intriguing neighbour. Set up the school, care for the children, and fill her days loving the little boy who meant more to her than any transient passion.

No matter how much, at this moment, she might regret letting it go.

Chapter Ten

A week later, Herodotus finished, additional staff hired, and restless, Dom wandered around a rose garden freshly weeded by the new assistant gardener. Though he was pleased at returning Bildenstone to the elegance and comfort he remembered from his childhood, he hadn't yet managed to force himself to proceed to disposing of his now superfluous horses and carriages, nor had he ventured out to inspect the estate.

Having only recently been able to manage more than eating, sleeping, and reading, Dom told himself that taking on restoring the house was task enough for the moment. As he regained strength and immersed himself in the rhythm of country life, he'd feel more like he belonged here, begin figuring out what he was meant to do next—and find it easier to part with the relics of the past.

At least, he hoped so.

With a sigh, he halted his aimless ramble and turned back towards the house. He'd check on the progress the carpenter from the village had made on the repairs to the kitchen roof, then find another book to replace Herodotus.

Pacing into the kitchen, he found a neat pile of supplies, but no carpenter. The assistant cook looked up from peeling vegetables to bob a quick curtsy.

'Can I help you, sir?'

'Is Young Joe around?'

'He left after setting the new beams in the corner,' the cook replied. 'He said while he was waiting for the plaster to dry, he'd be down at the stone barn, building some partitions for Miss Branwell.'

'Did he say how much longer it would take him to finish the work here?'

'No, sir. Shall I send one of the boys down to the barn to ask him?'

Dom hesitated. He should tell her to dispatch someone, or wait until the carpenter returned on his own. But if work were being done on the school building, Miss Branwell was undoubtedly present.

After the incident in the library proved beyond doubt how strong his attraction to her was and how difficult to resist, he'd told himself to put her out of mind. Had Wilton or any of the other servants come in while he was practically devouring her, the vicar would even now be calling the banns. Since compromising her meant marriage, something neither of them wanted, the best remedy to buttress a suddenly deficient will-power was to avoid her.

But damn, he missed her. That keen wit, the winsome smile, the sparkling laugh, how she could shock and amuse him with her honest, unexpected and sometimes outrageous observations. She'd brought back to him the pleasures of driving and pointed him towards increasing the staff, which had led him to the admittedly limited activities that now occupied his days.

And that dangerous, irresistible, visceral attraction that sparked between them had made him feel more virile, more alive, and more happy to be alive, than he'd felt since before his wounding.

Why not go to the barn himself? In addition to consulting Joe about the progress on Bildenstone's kitchen, as the owner of the barn, he probably ought to inspect what alterations were being made.

Once admitting the possibility of seeing her again, the need to do so rose to swamp him.

And why shouldn't he? A man who'd faced down a company of Napoleon's fiercest cuirassiers needn't fear handling one tall, brown-haired girl. If he felt his willpower slipping, there would be workmen and children about, chaperones aplenty to restrain him from making any untoward moves. Besides, as eager as Miss Branwell was to avoid being compromised, she'd undoubtedly be on her guard as well.

He could indulge in the pleasure of her delightfully unconventional conversation for a few moments, with little risk. Before returning to his lonely existence at Bildenstone.

There was no need to be so blue-devilled. If he were beginning to regret burying himself alone in the country, there were any number of friends and at least two of his cousins he could invite to divert him.

But after running through a list of possibilities, he didn't hit upon a single one whose company tempted him to alter his solitary state.

No one but Miss Branwell.

The implication of that truth was so unsettling, Dom shied away from considering it.

Hell and damnation, enough introspection! He wanted some intelligent conversation, and he wanted it with Miss Branwell. Surrounded by workmen and urchins, he could indulge in half-an-hour's chat without requiring a priest and a wedding band at the end of it.

Suddenly aware the cook was still staring at him, awaiting an answer, Dom shook his head. 'No, you needn't send someone. I'll speak with Joe later.'

About thirty minutes later. Nodding as the woman

bobbed him another curtsy, Dom paced out the kitchen door and headed to the stables to order the tilbury.

Scarf around her hair to keep off the dust, an apron over her oldest gown, Theo was directing Jemmie and Maria to carry in water to wash down the grimy stone walls when she heard the rattle of a carriage and the clop of hoofbeats. Looking up, she saw a familiar tilbury approaching, and a shock of anticipation raced through her.

Her landlord, coming to inspect the alterations to his property, that was all, she rebuked herself, trying to settle her fluttering pulse. After her shameless behaviour in his library—her cheeks burned hot as she recalled how, but for some carelessly positioned books, she would have made a complete fool of herself—he'd not wish to be near *her* unless a number of chaperones provided protection.

She would concentrate on behaving like a proper lady and give neither of them any further occasion for embarrassment.

But she couldn't seem to stop the thrill that ran through her as he pulled up the vehicle and she watched his lithe, broad-shouldered form climb down. A technique, she noted, he'd now mastered, swinging down on his single arm with none of the awkwardness he'd displayed on their first drive ten days ago.

Nor could she slow her accelerating heartbeat when a shock of energy flashed between them as their gazes met.

Not daring to permit his touch, she tucked her hands behind her and made a quick curtsy. 'Good day, Mr Ransleigh.' *It is, now that I've seen you.* 'Have you come to check our progress, or to reclaim the carpenter I stole from you? Young Joe told me he's doing some work in Bildenstone's kitchen.'

'I need to talk with him, yes. But I also wanted to see the changes you're making.'

His tone seemed normal, friendly, with no edge of the disapproval she might have expected after he'd had time to consider her forwardness in the library—and no embarrassment, either.

Reassured, she said, 'Young Joe has most of the partitions constructed in the sleeping loft, and is now framing out the part of the downstairs that will become kitchen and dining areas. Should you like to see them?'

'I would, if I'll not be taking you from your work.'

'I'd enjoy a break from scrubbing and sweeping, and I'm sure the children will, too. Jemmie, Maria, there's a basket in the wagon with water, cheese, and some of the apple tarts Cook made for dinner last night. Have a bite while I show Mr Ransleigh around the building.'

To her surprise, Jemmie, who normally would have set off at a run to claim apple tarts, merely stood, eyeing Ransleigh. 'I can show him around, while you rest yourself with Maria.'

The bitterness of loss echoed within her. She appreciated Jemmie's protectiveness—the need he apparently felt to take over from Papa. Then a less sanguine thought occurred: did Jemmie, a young male of the species, sense something between her and Ransleigh?

Devoutly hoping he could not, Theo said, 'No, go enjoy your treat. The inspection tour will not take long.'

'I don't think Jemmie trusts me,' Ransleigh murmured. 'Perhaps you'd better assure him I won't ravish you in the sleeping loft.'

'I might rather assure him *I* won't ravish *you*,' Theo muttered, feeling herself flush. 'Once again, I do apologise—'

'Please, don't!' he interrupted, his teasing tone turned serious. 'First, I assure you that, if circumstances permitted, I would welcome being ravished by you, and second, the…mistake in the library was mutual. An episode that, much as I regret the fact, cannot safely be repeated, so I suppose we shall both have to be on our best behaviour. See, I have not even attempted to take your hand.'

Grateful there was nothing further she was required to say, she murmured, 'Thank you. That forbearance will lend me the courage to escort you up to the sleeping area. Though as a mercy, there aren't yet any beds.'

His quick chuckle made her smile, too, and relax—at least, as much as she could, with every hair on her arms and neck quivering at his nearness. Forcing herself to concentrate on the building, she showed him the girls' and boys' sleeping areas, the sections partitioned off for washing up and for storage. Descending the stairs again, over the racket of Young Joe's saws and hammers, she described the planned addition of two fireplaces, finishing up with the news that the stove and kitchen equipment, desks for the schoolroom, tables for the dining room, and beds for the dormitory were expected from various providers within a fortnight.

'So, what do you think?' she asked, dropping her voice back to normal tones after leading him back outside. 'You approve of the alterations, I hope.'

'I think you've done a wonderful job, though I would hate to estimate the cost.'

'That's of little consequence, as long as it turns the building into a home and school the children find welcoming. By the way,' she recalled, thinking it might amuse him, 'I've just received the first fruits—or perhaps the second, if I count my permission to call on you—of my interview with Lady Wentworth. We now have a teacher!'

'Indeed? Who did Lady Wentworth deign to recommend?'

'One of the charges from her institution, Helen Andrews, the orphaned niece of a retired governess who passed away, leaving the girl with no resources. Her aunt had completed her education, but being so young and without references, she'd been unable to secure a post. Lady Wentworth sent her to Thornfield; she's quite eager to take the job. Jemmie approves, and he's very cautious about accepting strangers.'

'So I noticed.'

Flashing him a look, she continued. 'Maria liked her, too. Not that she actually spoke with her, of course, but she consented to sit beside her when Helen came up to meet the children. I think she'll do very well.'

'When will classes start?'

'Probably next week.' After which time, she should be busy enough that squelching her stubborn attraction to a certain dashing neighbour should become easier. 'As soon as the schoolroom is finished and the desks arrive. The dormitory and kitchen will not be fully functional for several weeks yet, so we'll be bringing the children back and forth from Thornfield, but I'm anxious to have Helen begin the lessons. Travelling in the van of an army makes for a haphazard education, and I'm eager for the children to catch up.'

Since she could think of nothing further to discuss about the school, she ought to say goodbye and send Mr Ransleigh on his way. Still, protected by the presence of so many chaperones and knowing, once classes began, there would probably be few occasions to indulge in the delicious thrill of his nearness, she found herself hunting for conversational excuses to make him linger.

'Young Joe tells me you are doing a good deal of work at Bildenstone,' she ventured.

'Yes, I took your advice and hired more staff—doing my bit to contribute to employment in the county. Then, since I needed to give them something to do, it seemed a good idea to begin restoring the old place to its former glory.'

'It must be satisfying to watch it become the showpiece you remember.'

'It's a long way from that yet. With dusting and polish, the rooms are looking better—and the kitchen roof no longer leaks! But my favourite place is still the library. For several reasons.'

Those words drew her eyes to his face as steel to a magnet, to find him regarding her with an intensity that brought back all the mesmerising passion of that interlude. Her body heating, she gave him a little nod, silently acknowledging she remembered the episode as vividly as he did.

His molten gaze and her subtle response suddenly recalled the looks she'd exchanged with Marshall after their engagement, when they were in camp, surrounded by soldiers…smouldering, secret glances that reminded her of intimacies exchanged, promised intimacies to come.

Flustered, she shook her head. How ridiculous a comparison! In this case, there would be no intimacies to come. The fact that she could even erroneously connect the experiences, however, did warn her to be mindful of the strength of her attraction to Ransleigh, a passionate connection the like of which she'd not experienced since she had fallen in love with her fiancé.

This time, she'd not be able to indulge her passion.

She should only need to recall the spectacular heartbreak in which that passion ended to be thankful there would be no repetition.

Annoyed at herself for the turmoil Ransleigh seemed to provoke in her, she steered him towards his tilbury, which the stable boy was walking on the verge by a fence that divided the roadway from a field of newly sprouted wheat, the tiny plants swaying in the light spring breeze.

The younger children not being of practical use in cleaning the building, she'd had Constancia take them for a walk. The maid, Charles, Georgie and Anna approached from down the lane as she and Ransleigh reached his vehicle.

Anna ran up and held out a bouquet of wildflowers. 'They are pretty, just like you, Miss Theo!'

'How sweet of you, Anna,' Theo said, accepting the gift.

Warmth filling her as it always did when she saw Charles again after an absence, no matter how brief, she drew the boy to her for a hug—which he tolerated for a moment before wriggling free.

Growing up already, she thought, releasing him with regret.

Meanwhile, Georgie had wandered to the fence. Leaning over it, he took a deep breath. 'The dirt smells good. Not like in the cities.'

'It's rich, fresh earth, newly turned over so the crop could be planted,' Ransleigh said. Gesturing towards the young plants, he added, 'That's wheat growing in the field. When it gets tall, it makes kernels that are ground into flour. The kind that is made into bread, not the sort Anna just picked.'

Georgie looked up at him. 'Those little plants turn into bread?'

'It's a bit more complicated than that, but, yes.'

As Georgie surveyed the field, rows of plants rolling into the distance, his eyes widened. 'There's so much of it! We never had enough bread on the march. That there's probly enough so's we'd none of us ever be hungry again. Wish I had a field I could grow bread in,' he said, his voice wistful.

'Would you like to learn how to plough the land and grow wheat?' Theo asked.

Georgie wrested his gaze from the field to look up at her. 'Could I really, Miss Theo?'

Theo turned to Dom, who held up a restraining hand. 'I

know, I know. Let me check with the estate manager and see if any of the tenants would take on a young farmhand.'

Georgie looked from Theo to Ransleigh and back. 'Do that mean I'll get to grow the bread plants?'

'Wheat,' she corrected. 'We'll see. You'll still need to go to school, though. Now, you must all be thirsty from your walk! There's water and apple tarts in the wagon; Jemmie will help you get some.'

'Apple tarts!' Charles said, clapping his hands. 'C'mon, Georgie, let's go fast before Jemmie eats them all!' The two boys pelted off, Anna and the maid following.

'Do you really think you could arrange for one of your tenants to take Georgie under his wing?' Theo asked. 'I would so appreciate it.'

'When you look at me with that appeal in your eyes, how can I refuse?' he murmured. 'As long as you don't expect me to find positions for all your urchins.'

'Of course not. But I cannot tell you how much I appreciate your kindness in looking out for them—Jemmie, and now Georgie.' Holding up Anna's bouquet, she laughed. 'I suppose I should thank *you* for the flowers, too, since they were filched from your lane. They are beautiful.'

'Spring is such a lovely time of year here—I've been away so long, I'd almost forgotten. With your school about to start, I expect you'll soon be too busy to notice, and it would be a shame not to enjoy it. If you can spare a few hours, why don't I drive you around the estate tomorrow? So you can say you didn't miss the beauties of your first Suffolk springtime.'

Shirk her responsibilities for a morning, and explore the verdant paths, mossy woods and brilliant fields of wildflowers of this homeland she was just discovering? Guided through the lanes and fields by a man whose similar interests and experiences made her feel as much at ease as she'd been since losing Papa?

Theo wanted very much to accept the offer, but…being seated beside him as he drove her down deserted lanes and paused to explore bluebell woods and newly planted fields would be dangerous. As much as she felt secure with him, she'd also proven on several occasions how very strong the attraction between them was—far stronger than the rules of propriety, strong enough to lead them into disaster, if her vigilance in resisting him lapsed for even a short time.

If the treasures of an exceptional library hadn't been enough to restrain desire, she doubted the English countryside, no matter how delightful, would succeed in distracting her from its insidious call.

She'd reluctantly decided prudence demanded she refuse the offer when an alternate solution occurred—and she pounced on it.

'I should love to have a tour—but I'd much rather ride. Firefly could use the exercise, and surely you have something in your stable less temperamental than Diablo.'

He started to speak, then halted, looking troubled.

'You've not attempted to ride any other mount, have you?' she guessed. When, with a wry grimace, he nodded, she said, 'Your balance is still excellent. There's no reason you shouldn't be able to ride—as long as you don't choose a bully who'd rather bite, buck and unseat you than follow your commands.'

'I've always rather enjoyed mastering those bullies who'd rather bite, buck and try to unseat me.'

'Why not try a more amenable mount, and see if you can enjoy that, as well?' If she could only persuade him, she'd win herself an extended ride through the countryside—a pleasure she'd not realised how much she'd missed until Ransleigh proposed this expedition. It would enable her to spend a few more precious hours in his company, stashed in a saddle a safe distance from him, the need to pay attention to her mount distracting her from the constant temptation of his nearness.

She was reasonably sure she could manage it—as long as she stayed in the saddle.

Finally, he shrugged. 'I suppose I must try riding some time, though the prospect of mounting a slowtop doesn't appeal.'

'There are alternatives between a beast and a slug,' she pointed out.

His unexpected smile was like the sudden appearance of a winter sun on snow, dazzling in its brilliance. *Gracious, but he was appealing,* she thought dazedly, curling her fingers into fists to keep herself from reaching out to touch him.

'You're right, and I should stop being churlish. Very well, I'll give it a try. I warn you though, if I can't abide it, I reserve the right to return to Bildenstone and fetch the tilbury.'

'Agreed,' she said, delighted she would have her treat. 'But I'll wager you won't need to.'

'Shall I call for you at Thornfield—about nine?'

'Nine would be quite convenient.'

'Until tomorrow, then, Miss Branwell.'

'I shall look forward to it.' *More than you can imagine,* she added silently.

Prudently he refrained from taking her hand, and prudently she didn't offer it. But she felt the lack of his touch almost like a physical ache as he turned to climb up into the tilbury. She waved as he flicked the whip and the equipage set off down the lane.

After it disappeared from sight, she turned back to her buckets and brooms, savouring the knowledge that before the responsibilities of managing the school and caring for the orphans relegated her permanently into matronhood, she could look forward one last time to spending a few hours in the company of that attractive, witty and intriguing man.

And it had better be the last time, she warned herself. Before her growing yearning for her dazzling neighbour destroyed any chance that she could satisfy herself with a lifetime of mere contentment.

Chapter Eleven

Just before nine the next morning, Dominic Ransleigh trotted a seasoned gelding down the lane towards Thornfield Place. He'd trained this horse, too, rejecting him as a mount since the animal lacked the fiery temperament he always sought in a hunter. He would have sold him off, but the animal had a soothing effect on Diablo and the speed and endurance, if not the spirit, to match the stallion. Still, though responsive to command, he wasn't so docile Dom felt he was riding a hobbyhorse.

A little more spirit wouldn't have been amiss, though. Any challenge that forced him to direct his attention away from the beguiling lady he was about to meet would be helpful.

He really did want to introduce Miss Branwell to the beauty of an English spring, but she had been wise to suggest they do so on horseback, not seated in the far too intimate confines of a carriage. Somewhere along the way to recovering his strength and vitality, he seemed to have misplaced most of his good judgement and all of his powers of resistance.

At least when it came to the appeal of the unconventional Miss Branwell.

Still, he was glad she'd overcome caution and agreed

to accompany him. Were she any other maiden, she'd be bringing along a maid or a groom, but Dom bet the notion of a chaperone would never occur to her. Riding alone wouldn't be as proper, but if she met him unescorted, he certainly wasn't going to suggest adding one to the party.

For this excursion, he wanted her all to himself. He had a strong feeling she meant to severely limit their interactions in future—and an even stronger feeling he was going to miss them acutely.

A rising excitement gripped him as he approached Thornfield Place. To his relief, Miss Branwell, sans groom, stood near the entrance, her mare on a lead. As he rode up, she climbed on to a mounting block and tossed herself into the saddle.

She wore the same old riding dress—Dom thought again how he'd enjoy introducing her to more fashionable styles and colours that would bring out the chestnut in her hair and the velvety brown of her eyes. He recalled the disdain she'd expressed for shopping and laughed. How 'Dandy Dom' would love teasing and bedevilling her through a succession of modistes and dressmakers!

How much more he'd love easing her out of the old habit, using lips and hands to show his appreciation for her unclothed form, before fitting the new garments over her naked skin…

To his frustration and regret, there'd be no chance of that, so he'd best enjoy the innocent delights of conversation and companionship. They made excellent friends, after all. In fact, she was the cleverest, most entertaining and engaging individual he knew, excepting his Ransleigh Rogue cousins.

She rode up to meet him. 'Good morning, and what a glorious one it is! As if England herself ordered up a perfect day to show me her wonders.'

'What, you're not going to credit me with arranging it?' he teased.

She chuckled. 'Very well, Mr Ransleigh. I'm sure there is nothing you could not arrange! So, which way first—to the bluebell wood?'

'No, it's been a fortnight, and their display will have faded. Along the lane leading north, there's a stand of jonquils that should be coming into bloom, as well as meadow buttercup and red clover. The land rises as we go; from the highest point, we'll get a good view over the estate.'

'Lead on!'

They set off at a trot. Dom didn't attempt conversation, content to watch Theo ride. As he'd expect for one who'd followed the army, she sat the horse effortlessly, moving as one with her mount, fluid, graceful, and lovely to observe.

They exited the Home Woods into an area where fields bordered both sides of the road. And just as he remembered, up ahead was a glorious stand of jonquils.

With an exclamation of delight, she spurred her mount. He followed, smiling at her excitement as she gazed at the tall yellow flowers nodding in the wind.

'Papa told me about England's daffodil meadows—but this is more beautiful than I imagined. And the scent! Sweet as vanilla.'

'Heavenly, isn't it?' he agreed. 'Shall we ride on? I seem to recall a patch of wood violets along the banks of the brook just ahead.'

For the next hour, they rode slowly from wildflower display to wildflower display, past a handful of farms. But as the ride continued, Dom's initial enthusiasm began to dim.

The first farm they'd passed had seemed somewhat run-down, the roof thatch of the farmhouse old and dark, some of the surrounding field still fallow, with an old wooden-bladed plough left in the soil, as if the farmer had been unable to force it to finish its task. He'd noted it with some concern, wondering whether the tenant was old and in need of assistance.

But by the time they'd passed four such farms, each seeming more dilapidated than the last, he knew it couldn't be a question of aged tenants.

Angry and troubled, he pulled up near a patch of red clover.

Looking at him soberly, Miss Branwell said, "I'm no agriculturalist, but it seems something is wrong. I thought your estate was profitable?'

'It has been. It is. I'm no agriculturalist either, but the places we've just passed remind me more of the abandoned farms we saw in Spain after the French had plundered them, than a prosperous estate in the heart of England. I cannot imagine how they have deteriorated to this point, but I certainly intend to find out.'

She nodded. 'Of course you must. These are your people, dependent on your leadership as surely as the men who served under you in the army. They need you to watch out and care for them.'

She hadn't meant the words as a reproof, but they stung anyway. 'These *are* my lands and my people, and their welfare *should* be my concern. I'd thought about riding the fields ever since I arrived—but there's no excuse for my not having done so sooner. I find it strange, though, if the farms are in such dire straits, that I've not heard a word of complaint or dissension from anyone on the household staff.'

'You said you'd been absent for seven years, and your family hadn't resided here for much longer. It's probably been like this for some time.'

Dom nodded grimly. 'It might well have been. My father had little interest in agriculture. He prized Bildenstone only for the income it provided him to spend on his hounds and horses. Winniston, the agent, has been here for years, and his father before him. Trusting them to manage things, Papa came only to collect the rents. If the amounts were sufficient, he probably didn't even check the account book.'

'He must not have ridden the estate, either.'

'Probably not. I know he was never gone long from Upton Park.'

'Well, someone needs to fix this.' She waved her hand towards another pasture half-grown up in weeds, with a dilapidated farmhouse in the distance. 'Do you think you could take up the tasks of an agriculturalist? I shouldn't think it would be so different than evaluating and cultivating horses—though less exciting than a gallop across the countryside.'

Memory returned in a vivid flash: mounting a horse so fresh he fought the bit, coaxing him to accept Dom's weight, moving him forward. And then the sheer soul-filling wonder of leaning low over the beast's head while the countryside flashed by him, the exhilaration as the horse gathered himself and threw heart and body over fence or pond or fallen log, the possibility of a rough landing or a fall ever present, adding a spice of danger.

Wonder, exhilaration, and excitement he'd never experience again.

'I don't know,' he answered frankly. 'By the time I went up to Oxford, I knew I wanted to spend my life breeding and training horses that were the strongest, fastest, most fearless jumpers in England, both to follow the hounds and to race cross-country.'

'Like Diablo.'

'Like Diablo,' he said. 'Horses which, as you know, I can no longer ride. With the endeavour that was the focus of my life since I outgrew short coats no longer feasible, I've come back full circle, to Bildenstone, looking for something to replace it. Thus far, singularly bereft of inspiration, I've been drifting along, unable to force myself to sever those ties with the past, unable to see a future I want to pursue.'

She nodded, offering him no empty platitudes, for which he was grateful. But as she sat regarding him thoughtfully, Dom wondered what had possessed him to confess his failings to her. Just because they'd shared the same experiences and challenges in the army—just because a potent sensuality pulled them together—didn't mean she was interested in his inability to redefine his life. A difficulty, incidentally, about which he'd said nothing to Max or Alastair, and admitted only to Will, who'd tended him with a mother's care after his injuries.

'So many never made it off the killing fields of Waterloo,' she said softly, startling him out of his reverie. 'For you to be so severely wounded and survive, yet be ill equipped to continue your previous pursuits, it seems to me that you must have been spared for a purpose. To become a new man, meant to pursue something that lies in an altogether different direction. Your challenge is to resist looking back, regretting what you've lost, and discover instead what is meant for you now.'

'As you have?' he asked, well aware that his wasn't the only life whose course had been shattered by the case shot of Waterloo.

She gave him a brave smile. 'Easy for me to offer advice. I already know what I'm to do.'

'Taking care of soldier's orphans. Are you so sure that's your destiny?' he asked, wishing he could find such a clear sense of his own.

'Despite Aunt Amelia trying to dissuade me, I believe it is.'

A new man with a new purpose. Maybe that's why it seemed so easy to confide in her, he thought. Because, rightly or wrongly, he felt Max and Alastair and even

Will would always be comparing him to what he'd been, whereas she knew only who he was now.

She saw him and his future as a blank slate, and she expected him to pick up the chalk.

Right before him loomed at least one worthwhile endeavour. And she was right; it was past time for him to start moving forward.

'Is that why you broke your engagement—because you felt your future would be completely different from your past, and you didn't think the lady would want to go there with you?'

The question startled him, but by now he should expect Theo Branwell to boldly ask what no one else would dare enquire about. 'Yes. I didn't feel it was fair to hold her to her promise when I was no longer the sportsman whose suit she'd accepted. When I no longer could, nor wanted, to move in the same circles, doing the things I'd done before.'

'So she didn't pass the test.'

He frowned, not sure what she meant. 'Test?'

She nodded. 'If she'd really loved you, she wouldn't have let you walk away.'

'That's a little unfair!' he protested. 'I didn't give her a choice.'

'That may be, but if Marshall had been wounded and sent me away, I wouldn't have gone. I've have stayed and tended him, and if he wouldn't permit that, I'd have sat at his doorstep until he relented.'

'Like you sat on my wall?' he said, bemused.

'Yes. And if he had me evicted, I would have written him every day, telling him how much I loved him and wanted to be with him. I would never have given up.'

Dom sat silently, pondering. Had he, on some level, meant his insistence on breaking the engagement as a test—for them both?

If so, he had to admit, he had failed it, too. Since coming to Bildenstone, he'd hardly thought of Elizabeth.

'Well, in any event, look at me! I'm not the gallant cavalier who had the gall to persuade a duke's daughter to marry him.'

She stared at him, her eyes narrowed. 'Maybe that was part of it—the audacity of carrying off the prize on your part, the thrill of flouting convention on hers. Of course, it's not my place to speculate.'

He chuckled. 'But you did anyway.'

'What *I* see when I look at you is a man as audacious as he ever was. Brave, powerful, immensely attractive, and full of potential. He may be a bit nicked up on the exterior—' she motioned to his eye patch and missing arm '—but the outside isn't important. It's the essence of the man within that matters.'

'I'm not sure what my essence is,' he admitted. 'I suppose, before this, I could always rely on what was outside, so I never had to look. I'm looking now, and I'm not sure I like what I'm seeing.'

'What did you do before?'

'Oh, followed the seasons as a sportsman. Buying, training and hunting horses in the autumn and winter; balls, entertainments, cards at my club, visits to the tailor in London during the Season, house parties and more horse training in the summer…'

His voice trailed off at the look of incredulity on her face. 'Pretty useless stuff, actually,' he allowed, 'when compared to fighting Boney—or caring for orphans.'

'Maybe what happened, happened, so you'd have to confront your life and choose to do something different. Something more…important.'

'Had this not happened, I probably never would have examined it,' he said, realising that fact for the first time.

'Nor am I sure what that "something more important" should be.'

'While you ponder it, do something for the tenants here.'

'Like hiring an estate manager who knows what he's doing,' he said acerbically.

'Yes. And hopefully,' she added with a grin, 'one willing to take on some junior apprentices.'

'Ever watching out for your orphans! Maybe I *should* become an estate manager. Fattening up little boys like Georgie would be an aim worth striving for. My cousin Alastair is master of his own profitable estate—I'll write and seek his advice. I also remember him nattering on about the spring shearing at Holkham Hall in Norfolk; where a group of agriculturalists gather to discuss new techniques. Maybe that will ensure I no longer let my tenants down,' he added, his ire resurfacing.

'You didn't know they'd been let down. What matters now is what you do to correct the deficiencies.'

They set off again, Dom still angry and unsettled. How he wished he had Alastair's expertise, so he would know immediately how to rectify all the problems he'd seen!

As they reached the next farm, Dom noted a man in the field, ploughing behind a heavy-set draught horse. Pulling up his mount, he said, 'If you don't mind, Miss Branwell, I'd like to speak with that farmer. I can at least assure him that I intend to begin at once to correct some of the problems he will doubtless want to point out.'

'Please, go speak with him as long as you like. I even promise not to gift you with my opinions on his suggestions.'

He smiled slightly, appreciative of her efforts to make him feel better. Though nothing but a transformation of the cottages and fields he'd just seen would do that.

'I won't be long.' At that, he slid from the saddle and set off, leaving his mount to graze at the roadside.

Seeing him approach, the man pulled up his horse, watching him warily.

'I'm Ransleigh,' Dom said as he approached. 'And you are…?'

A flash of emotion—resentment, probably—briefly coloured the man's expression before he nodded a greeting. 'Willie Jeffers. Heard you'd come back to Bildenstone, Mr Ransleigh.'

'Pleased to meet you, Mr Jeffers. That's a fine horse and plough you have. Unfortunately, I haven't seen others like it on my inspection today.'

'I reckon not,' Jeffers said with a short laugh.

'Your fields look to be in prime shape as well. As you know, I've not been to Bildenstone for years, and am shocked by the condition of the farms. Can you tell me what has happened here? Please, speak frankly. Anything you say will be held in confidence. I give you my word.'

After studying Dom for a moment, the farmer said, 'Folks say you were a brave soldier and a man that keeps his word. So, you want the truth about the farms?'

'I do,' Dom replied, meeting the man's steady gaze.

'The truth is that Winniston's always been more concerned with collecting rents than using any of the blunt to improve things—even make necessary repairs. Don't think he holds back extra for himself. Just doesn't seem to understand he'll get more profit from the land if he ploughs some back into it, instead of wringing out of it every farthing he can get.'

'You seem to have held on to enough to improve yours.'

'Aye,' Jeffers acknowledged. 'My family has farmed these acres for generations, and I'm always looking for ways to do it better. I've a brother up near Holkham Hall, and he passes along to me the things they've tried up there.'

'To very good effect, judging by what I've seen. First, let me assure you that Winniston will not be supervising

Bildenstone's farms much longer. I *am* interested in improving things, and want to do so as soon as possible. But as you noted, my experience is with the army, not the land. I'd appreciate any suggestions on techniques you've found useful in your fields.'

The wariness in the farmer's expression turned to the enthusiasm of a master describing his craft. 'Iron-tipped ploughs help, especially when the ground's mostly clay. And having the right draught horse. At the last county fair, I talked with a farmer from around Needham Market way. He'd heard of breeding a Suffolk sorrel with a Norfolk trotter, to give the offspring more flesh and stamina. Gentle, tractable, strong, and love to work, those sorrels! If we could breed more stamina in them—now that would be a combination! I already have a trotter—can't ride around all these acres on some weak-kneed thing that would give out under my weight in an hour. One of the farmers the other side of Hadwell has a sorrel out of Crisp's stallion. But when it came right down to it, neither he nor I knew enough about breeding to give it a try.'

The idea immediately piqued Dom's interest. 'I might. Not by borrowing your stallion—you need him to ride your fields. But I must return to Newmarket soon to complete the sale of some stock, and will see about purchasing a good trotter stallion and several sorrel mares.'

'A lot of your tenants would like a horse that could hold the plough longer over heavy ground,' Jeffers said. 'Especially further east, where the land's low and marshy.'

'Thank you very much, Mr Jeffers. I shall certainly look into it.'

'Right happy to have you back in residence, sir,' Jeffers said, before turning back to his plough.

I hope you will be, Dom thought, energised by the conversation. He'd never considered breeding anything other than steeplechase animals, but creating a crossbreed that

could allow farmers to plough their fields faster and perhaps grow crops in land previously thought too heavy to
cultivate would be an admirable goal.

Was this to be the worthy endeavour he was meant to
pursue? A rising sense of anticipation dispelled the last
vestiges of his anger and frustration.

'Looks like it was a profitable conversation,' Miss Branwell observed as he walked back to her.

'It was. I may have found something useful to do after
all.'

'Excellent! That calls for a celebration. How about a
good gallop? Let's find an unploughed field just begging
to be ridden.'

The disaster with Diablo had so shaken his confidence,
Dom wasn't sure he could manage more than a canter.
Well, why not? he thought, buoyed by a newfound enthusiasm. If he could discover a new vocation, maybe he could
find a way to keep his seat at a gallop.

'I'll see if my mount and I can oblige.'

As if sensing his hesitation, Miss Branwell said, 'You
need only pretend you're mounted on your cavalry horse,
sabre in hand, leading the charge.'

If he were going to land on his rump, better to find out
now. He couldn't envision another person whose witness-
ing of that failure would bother him less than the compassionate Miss Branwell.

Not only would she neither laugh nor carry tales, she'd
probably make judicious notes about the cause of the fall
and advise him how to correct his position.

Smiling at that notion, he rode with her past the rest of
Jeffers's acreage, down a hill and around a bend, where
they found an invitingly fallow meadow.

'Ready?' she asked.

'Ready.' *As I'll ever be,* he added silently. Dom set his
mount off slowly, signalling the gelding through his paces.

He found him responsive to his touch, not fighting him for control, as Diablo always had. He'd about convinced himself he was ready to try a full-out gallop when Miss Branwell, in the lead, looked back over her shoulder and shouted, 'Race you to the stone wall!'

No Ransleigh had ever refused a challenge. As her mare took off in a burst of speed, Dom spurred his gelding to follow.

As the horse moved faster and faster, he found his body adjusting instinctively into the rise and fall of the horse's stride. His hips and legs easy, the shift of his weight automatic, within minutes, he was able to transfer energy from worrying about balance to urging on his mount.

The gelding accelerated, stretched himself out to a ground-eating pace. Wind whipped at his hat, air rushed through his lungs, his heartbeat accelerated...and joy began to bubble up from deep within, the pure joy he always felt when he became one with his mount in a full-out gallop.

Miss Branwell looked back once, a brilliant grin on her face as she saw him closing behind her. Taking that as a tossed gauntlet, Dom pushed the horse harder. Just before they reached the stone fence at the far end of the pasture, he edged her mare out by a nose.

Miss Branwell pulled her horse up and sprang down from the saddle. Energised, exuberant, he slid down beside her.

'Not very chivalrous to beat you at the end, I'm afraid.'

'Oh, but what a run! How I've missed the good gallops I used to have with Papa, out on the plains of Spain and Portugal. And you—you were magnificent! Not many could beat Firefly when she's got a lead, but you managed it. I knew you could do it!'

With a joyous laugh, she threw her arms around him and tilted her head up.

Despite a whisper of conscience that warned it was dishonourable to take advantage of her impulsive act, a company of French cuirassiers at the gallop couldn't have kept him from claiming the lips so temptingly close.

The kiss began slow and sweet, a soft brush of his mouth against hers. But then she made a small sound deep in her throat and parted her lips.

A surge of heat and desire swamping him, he swept his tongue to claim hers. To his elation, she met his and fenced with it, laving him with slow, lush strokes that fired passion to a searing heat.

With his one good arm, he pulled her against him and deepened the kiss while she wrapped her arms around his neck. He slid his hand down to cup her bottom, bringing her closer still, and she rubbed herself against his aching groin.

White-hot lust obliterated everything but his need for her. One tiny, still functioning part of his brain applied itself to considering whether there was any usable surface where he could lay her down, raise her skirts and lose himself in her.

The sound of a horse's whinny finally penetrated the fog of lust. Shocked that he'd almost tried to ravish her at the edge of a field, where some farmer might at any moment have come by and discovered them, he released her and staggered a step away.

Her eyes dreamy and unfocused, she stared up at him, her moist, kiss-rosy lips so appealing it was all he could do not to step closer and kiss her again.

'If you apologise for that, I'm going to punch you,' she murmured.

Trust his Theo to say the unexpected, he thought, her unconventionality a joy. 'If I did,' he replied, smiling, 'it would only be for form's sake. I've wanted to kiss you practically from the moment I met you.'

'As I've wanted to kiss you. Shocking, I know, and unmaidenly, but there you have it. So I am very, very glad I got to kiss you—and it was everything I'd dreamed it would be. But it must stop here. I wish…' she sighed before continuing '…but wishing changes nothing. Episodes like this, if discovered, would ruin my reputation, and I cannot risk that, when any disgrace of mine would harm the future of my orphans. And you—well, you need to find that new direction for your life before you involve yourself with anyone.'

Dom knew what she intended. Everything within him wanted to resist the conclusion, but she was right—which didn't mean he had to like it. 'Time to part?' he said.

'Time to part,' she agreed. 'Thank you, Dominic Ransleigh, for making my return to England easier and more joyful than I could ever have hoped, so soon after losing Papa. Thank you for all you've done, and continue to do, for my orphans. I wish you the best as you work towards your future—and you *will* find what you're meant to do, I'm sure of it. I would ask only one more thing.'

'Only one?' he asked, amusement at that unlikely possibility breaking through his dismay over the note of finality in her speech.

'Well, I can't promise never to ask anything in future for the children, but I do promise never to ask anything else for me. Nothing but this. May I kiss you goodbye?'

After a moment of shock at the unexpected request, he answered by pulling her into his embrace. She slid her fingers into his hair, sending shivers down his body as she tilted her head up and opened her mouth to him.

Twining her tongue with his and moulding herself against his body, she kissed him with everything in her— lips, tongue, fingers stroking his head, legs and torso rubbing against him, even her booted foot wrapped around his ankle. She kissed him as if the world were about to end, as if there would never be anything of fire and passion and intimacy again.

He took everything she offered, and returned it.

When at last she released her hold on him, he was breathless and so dizzy he nearly fell over. For a few moments, there was nothing but their panting breaths and the almost tangible connection sparking in the air between them.

'I would really rather consider that hello,' he muttered when he'd assembled wits enough for speech.

She gave him a little smile, so sad he felt an immediate need to assuage whatever hurt had caused it. His confusion and concern mounted as tears sheened her eyes.

While he stood frozen, unsure what to do, she opened her lips as if to speak, closed them and shook her head, as if the situation were hopeless. 'Goodbye…my very dear Mr Ransleigh,' she whispered and turned away.

Before his muzzy brain decoded her intent, she'd led her grazing mount to the rock ledge, scrambled up and launched herself into the saddle. Without another word, she kicked the mare to a gallop.

Dom stood watching her ride away, his body still afire with unsatisfied desire, his thoughts in turmoil, while within the raging cauldron of chaotic emotion something shouted that letting her go was *wrong*.

After a few more dazed moments, he shook himself free and went to claim his own horse. Leading it to the ledge, he remounted and nudged the gelding towards Bildenstone Hall.

Hello, not goodbye, kept echoing in his brain.

Chapter Twelve

Two weeks later, Dom was looking through records in the estate office, trying to make sense of harvest quantities, when Wilton came in, out of breath. 'Sorry to disturb you, Mr Ransleigh. We've just had a soldier stop by, asking for directions to the stone barn. He said he meant to call on Miss Branwell.'

An immediate stab of jealousy struck him, so surprising he didn't quite hear Wilton's next words.

'...so you might ride over and check on her,' the butler was saying.

'Ride over and check on her?' he repeated.

'She may be there by herself, with just that young female teacher and the little ones, and no man to protect her.'

'Did this soldier look like someone she might need protecting from?'

'I can't rightly say, sir. But he was young, and...vigorous.'

While that observation didn't make Dom's struggle to suppress the unaccountable jealousy any easier, he did wonder about Wilton's unusual level of concern for a girl he'd met only a handful of times. Had Miss Branwell confided to the butler that increasing the staff at Bildenstone—and thus easing his burdens—had been her idea? Somehow, that didn't sound like her.

'You seem rather worried.'

'All the neighbourhood thinks highly of her, sir. Giving a place to Miss Andrews, when other families in the area that could have didn't lift a finger. Employed many others, too, and Young Joe told me that she paid all the workers she hired twice the going rate, since she wanted the building completed as soon as possible. And made sure there was ham, cheese and ale available for all, so they didn't have to bring their own. Mrs Greenlow was just telling Cook what a shame it was she lost her man in the war and fair broke her heart, her being so young to be alone, no matter but it's noble for her to dedicate herself to those poor unfortunates. Anyways, no one would want to see any harm come to her.'

Good thing she's not hunting a new butler, Dom thought, awed at that paean of praise from the normally laconic Wilton. Still, he felt a swell of pride in her; some Christian folk gave lip service to the need to do good in the community, but the concern Theo Branwell showed for her orphans, the care she urged him to show for his employees, she showed to everyone.

A pang of longing echoed through him. While he was dampening down that equally unsought-for emotion, Wilton said, 'You will ride over and make sure everything is all right, won't you, sir?'

A rush of excitement stirred his senses. Though he felt somewhat guilty at taking advantage of this situation to break their self-imposed separation, he wouldn't be staying long, and there would be a school full of witnesses to make sure he didn't indulge any carnal longings. And though he was reasonably certain the redoubtable Miss Branwell, who'd followed the army from India to Portugal to Brussels, would have no trouble taking care of herself if some soldier turned importunate, she might still be alone and unprotected out there.

Maybe it would be wise to check on her, he thought, a niggle of unease stirring.

'Better send to the stables for my gelding.'

'Thank you, Mr Ransleigh,' Wilton said, obviously relieved.

'I shall do my best,' Dom assured the butler before trotting up the stairs to change into his riding gear.

Ten minutes later, spurring his mount down the lane, Dom let his thoughts stray to the object he'd been trying so hard *not* to think of since the incident by the wild-flower meadow.

That kiss—heaven and stars, what a kiss! It's a wonder he hadn't turned molten on the spot. If she kissed like that, he couldn't imagine what ecstasy a full loving could promise.

But what pulled him to Theo Branwell was more than just a promise of sensual heaven. The fact that she'd shared and understood the demands, the sacrifices and the un-equalled camaraderie of the army had drawn him to her from the first. He'd been gratified and delighted to find they shared a love of books and horses. She stimulated his mind as much as she stirred his body, challenging easy assumptions, jolting him to think in different directions, startling him with her unusual perspectives and her clear, bright honesty. She made him think more, dared him to do more, to *be* more.

How much brighter his days had become since he stumbled into her in that lane! She'd pushed him into trying to drive and ride again, restoring those pleasures to him much sooner than he probably would have discovered them on his own.

He admitted to himself that he'd been jealous when she'd talked about her lost fiancé. From what he'd seen of Theo Branwell, the man she loved would have been wrapped in a devotion so complete, so intense, nothing would ever have been able to penetrate it. Her fierce declaration of unlimited loyalty only underscored how easily he'd been able to part from Elizabeth, and how easily she'd let him go.

In fact, thinking back on that kiss—a pleasure he'd sternly denied himself—he was convinced that, though Miss Branwell might be still unmarried, she was not completely inexperienced. She *had* been engaged to a man she loved completely; it wasn't beyond possibility that they'd anticipated their vows.

His body rejoiced at the idea of Theo Branwell coming to his bed, prompting his mind to consider possibilities for making that happen.

Only a moment's contemplation reminded him there were none. Experienced or not, he concluded with a sigh, she was still technically a maid. And she was quite right that an affair discovered would tarnish her reputation and make the lives of her orphans that much more difficult.

Unless…unless he decided to court her with honourable intent?

Shockingly, the voice of self-interest and prudence didn't immediately reject the notion. Though, as they'd discussed, he didn't yet have a clear idea of his future, and thus had no business asking anyone to share it, he could at this juncture not imagine finding a lady more delightful, challenging, and sensual than Theo Branwell.

Fortunately, there was no need to make an immediate decision. He could let the tantalising notion rattle around in his brain and see where it ended up. Miss Branwell and her orphans were only just getting established in their new homes, and neither he nor she were going anywhere else any time soon.

Pleased and intrigued by the possibility of being able to

pursue an association with Theo Branwell after all, Dom kicked his mount to a canter and guided him down the lane to the stone barn.

Meanwhile, Theo stood in the kitchen area at the school, supervising the installation of the new cooking stove. In the open space beyond, students at their desks recited a lesson, after which Miss Andrews had asked Theo to read them a story copied out of Bildenstone library's volume of *Arabian Nights*.

She needed to make one more trip to Thornfield, to fetch the rest of the linens for the beds and the kitchen. Within a few days, her vision would be fully realised as the students began using the building as both home and school.

She'd not seen Dominic Ransleigh when she ventured back to Bildenstone's library, a bored Constancia at her side. She hadn't really expected to, but she'd been shaken anew by the strength of her disappointment and regret at missing him.

The hard truth was she'd already grown too attached to him, and not just by the physical magnetism that drew her to him whenever he was near. She had come to crave his company and look forward to discussing all manner of topics with a mind as active and even more far-ranging than Papa's. She loved listening to him talk about horses, discuss farm management and reminisce about his army days. She would love to scour the shelves in the Bildenstone library while they compared their favourite books.

She recalled their wildflower ride, the disarming humility with which Ransleigh confessed he was still floundering to find his place, the deepening intimacy of friendship that had surrounded them as they talked so frankly, a bond as close and powerful as the more physical connection they'd shared after.

Even now, she felt the urge to throw herself and all her energies into helping him identify the life's work that would replace the calling he'd lost, sure whatever endeavour he settled upon, he would pursue it with vigour and competence.

It would take but very little more involvement to find herself falling in love with him. Which would be a disaster on so many counts.

First and foremost, she had only to remember the catastrophe of losing Marshall. She'd fallen for her fiancé quickly and completely, investing every particle of her mind and heart. Imbued with the confidence of youth, she'd expected him to go through all the campaigns unscathed, as Papa always had. The loss of Lord Everly and his bereaved wife's pain had scarcely shaken her confidence in the future she and Marshall would share.

When, on the road to Lisbon, she'd received the terrible news of Marshall's death in battle, she'd been at first incredulous and denying. Once the messenger her father dispatched was able to convince her of its truth, she'd fallen to her knees, struck down by a physical pain as great as if her chest had been cleft in two.

She'd told everyone their long sojourn at the convent was because of Alicia's ill heath, but in truth, her companion could probably have made it to Lisbon. It was Theo who, after reaching the nunnery where they'd arranged to spend the night, had collapsed, inconsolable. Paralysed by grief and despair, she lay for days unmoving, pushing away the meals the nuns brought her, scarcely able to dress or groom herself.

If it hadn't been for the need to care for the infant Charles, she wasn't sure she would ever have emerged from that spiral of misery.

Now, when she looked up at Ransleigh's face, caught in that mesmerising blue gaze, wrapping herself up in his brilliant smile, her mind captivated by his wit and beguiled by his charm, she thought how easy it would be to fall again just as completely for Dominic Ransleigh.

Her illusions of safety destroyed by the deaths of Marshall and her father, she wasn't sure she could survive losing anyone else.

And if she couldn't risk falling in love with him, no more could she risk *making* love to him. She no longer had any doubt about the strength of the physical pull between them; if she kept seeing him, sooner or later the siren song of passion would drown out the voice of prudence and caution—she'd been reckless enough already, kissing him with total abandon in that farmer's field. The results of discovery, for herself and her orphans, would have been too dire to contemplate.

But even if she did become so lost to reason and prudence as to take those risks, an involvement between them wouldn't be fair to Ransleigh. He'd shown disarming candour in confessing that he was still at his life's crossroads. It would be wrong to try to attach him now. Sooner or later, he would find the occupation he sought, and land on his feet again. Once launched upon the new endeavour—and some interaction with society would inevitably be part of it—he deserved far better than an old maid past her last prayers with a troop of children in tow, a woman whose position in society would do him not a particle of good in advancing along whatever path he chose to pursue.

The keenness with which she missed him, and strength of temptation to seek him out, only reinforced her conviction that parting from him was necessary.

It was also miserable. Well, she'd endured 'miserable' before; she must simply grit her teeth, keep moving forward, and wait until the need for him faded.

As it must, eventually. Mustn't it?

A touch at her arm shocked her out of her melancholy

reverie. Beside her stood one of the footmen who'd accompanied her from Thornfield to transport the heavy items. 'Miss Branwell, there's a soldier outside asking to see you.'

Curiosity replaced introspection. She didn't recall that any of Papa's troopers hailed from Suffolk. 'Did he give you his name?'

'Lieutenant Audley Tremaine. He said he'd worked with your father.'

Distaste soured her stomach and she frowned. What could Audley Tremaine want with her? She wished she'd been able to repeat to her father some of the crude insinuations he'd made after her return from the convent; Papa would have used him for target practice, and she'd not have to deal with him now.

Though she had no wish to see him, neither would she give him the satisfaction of thinking he intimidated her. Still, not wanting to have the children witness the unpleasantness that would probably arise at their exchange, she decided to meet him outside.

'I don't want the students disturbed. Tell the lieutenant I'll join him by the pasture fence.'

After giving the footman time to deliver her message, she took a deep breath and girded herself for what was probably to come. *You will be cool, distant—and will not let him make you lose your temper,* she instructed as she exited the building.

She saw him immediately, lounging by the fence, his black gelding tied to a nearby tree. Before she'd met Marshall, she'd found the attentions of the tall, handsome, arrogantly charming Lieutenant Tremaine flattering and exciting. Until acquaintance with a man far his superior made his attractions look as insignificant as a copper farthing beside a gold sovereign.

He straightened when she reached him and made a

mocking bow. 'Well, well, Theo Branwell, imagine finding you in the wilds of Suffolk!'

'Indeed,' she said, not offering her hand. 'Whatever brings you to the wilds of Suffolk?'

'The desire to renew your charming acquaintance?'

'Since we didn't part on friendly terms, I doubt that.'

'We could have been friendly. We could still be very… friendly.'

Trying not to grit her teeth, she said, 'Weren't you selling out? So you could resume attending house parties where there are bored matrons to seduce?'

The smile on his handsome face faded. 'Not kind to remind me that my ancient name came unaccompanied by the funds to maintain it. Yes, I've sold out, but ladies find a man in uniform so appealing! I'm sure you noticed the effect.'

'I'd say it depended on the man.'

Ignoring that jibe, he continued. 'My business elsewhere didn't preclude my stopping by to see you. Quite a fuss you've created in the neighbourhood, I understand! Over a pint at the King's Arms in Hadwell, I heard all about your pious zeal for the poor orphans. How are the little tykes?'

'Please don't pretend now you have any interest in them. I remember too well your disdain for father's sergeant-major's son.'

'Hanging on to them after the old man's death to remember him by? How pious and proper. Ha!' He laughed. 'If the townspeople here only knew.'

'Now that you've offered the usual insults, isn't it time to leave?'

'I might have offered you marriage instead, once upon a time. Though after Marshall arrived with his handsome face, large fortune, and future title, I knew I didn't have a chance. Now that he's met his sad end, however, there might be…other opportunities. Not marriage any longer, of course.'

'Not now that I'm "damaged goods", you mean?'

Tremaine laughed. 'I always admired your spirit. I knew a lass with your energy and enthusiasm would have to be passionate—and we both know how right I was, eh? I figure by now, you've had time to finish grieving and become…lonely.'

'I will never be *that* lonely. But don't despair; at this house party or the next, you may find an heiress with less-than-vigilant relations you may cozen into marrying you before she realises what you are. Not everyone can be as fortunate as I was.'

He merely smiled. 'You always had a sharp tongue on you. I've always hungered to taste it…and more.'

At that moment, Charles ran over to tug at her sleeve. 'Miss Theo! Teacher says she needs you to come tell our story now.'

'Very well,' she said, patting the boy on the shoulder. 'Tell Miss Andrews I'll be with you in a moment.'

Turning back to her tormenter, who stood regarding her with a smirk she longed to slap off his face, she said, 'I'm afraid I can't stay and trade insults any longer.'

'Cute little urchin, and too well spoken to be an enlisted man's leavings,' Tremaine said, watching Charles skip back towards the building. 'Was that Everly's brat? Funny, with him and his doxy so dark, to have the boy turn out so fair. He's almost as blond as…'

Tremaine's words trailed off and amazed recognition lit his eyes. Consternation filled Theo as the lieutenant turned back to scrutinise the child until he was lost to sight inside the building.

'Well, now, what an interesting development,' he murmured, looking back at Theo. 'Ah, the stories I could tell! Maybe you'd like to reconsider my offer?'

Desperately Theo schooled her face to indifference, hoping Tremaine hadn't seen the flash of fear in her eyes.

'Why ever would I wish to do that?' she asked in a bored tone. While her mind raced, trying to decide whether it would be more effective to add another dismissive disclaimer, or say nothing further, she suddenly noted the sound of approaching hoofbeats. Relief filled her when she turned to see that Dominic was nearly upon them.

'You'll have to excuse me. Here's my landlord, coming to consult about the property.'

Tremaine looked over her shoulder. 'Dominic Ransleigh! Might not have recognised him, but for the missing arm. I'd forgotten his family had an estate in Suffolk. "Consulting about property", eh? Darling, if you're still giving it away for free, why waste your charms on a cripple? A real man could make it so much better for you.'

At that insult to Ransleigh, her control, already pushed to the edge by Tremaine's insinuations and her own panic, finally snapped. Stepping forward, Theo slapped his face with all the force she could muster.

Chapter Thirteen

Trembling with rage and dismay, Theo jumped when Ransleigh suddenly materialised right behind her.

'Is something amiss?'

Theo forced her voice to calm. 'Nothing I can't handle. Lieutenant Tremaine was just leaving.'

'Am I? With all the stories I have to tell?' Tremaine said, a challenge on his face as he rubbed at the scarlet mark of her palm on his cheek.

With a great show of indifference, she shrugged. 'Tell whatever tales you like. No one of discernment gives any credence to what you say anyway. Now, you really should be leaving.'

'Perhaps you need further encouragement?' Ransleigh said, his voice a snarl and his one hand curling into a fist.

Tremaine looked from Theo to Ransleigh and back. 'Not this time. Wouldn't want to distress the urchins. But you may be hearing from me again, Theo.'

Motioning Ransleigh, who looked ready to have a go anyway, to stay where he was, Theo said, 'I devoutly hope not. Have a pleasant life, Lieutenant Tremaine.'

He stared at her, but she faced him down, unsmiling, until finally he broke eye contact. 'Sure you won't reconsider?'

At her curt negative shake of the head, he said, 'Your choice. Don't blame me if you—and your little urchins—have cause later to regret it.'

At that, with a negligent nod to Ransleigh, Tremaine strode to his mount, threw himself in the saddle, and rode off.

As Theo took a shuddering breath, trying to slow the racing of her heart, Ransleigh said, 'Why did you stop me? If that varlet said something meriting a slap, I would have enjoyed planting my fist in his face. Although, accustomed as I am to your plain speaking, telling him no one believes anything he says was a bit harsh.'

'It wasn't kind, perhaps, but I hope to prevent him carrying tales. My reputation is…already sullied, but I would like to prevent him tarnishing yours.'

'Sullied?' Ransleigh said, an odd note in his voice. 'Forgive me, I overhead some of your conversation as I approached. Surely he didn't say you were "giving it away for free"? How could you keep me from punishing him for uttering something so scurrilous?'

Theo sighed. 'Will you walk with me? I don't want the children to overhear, and after what you saw—and heard—you'll want an explanation.'

'I wouldn't wish to pry into the private details of your life.'

She laughed without humour. 'Unlike me, who had no hesitation about prying in yours. But there has always been honesty between us, and you ought to know the truth about your tenant—unless you'd rather not hear it.'

After a short pause, he said, 'If it concerns you, I'd like to hear it.'

'Very well. Let me tell Miss Andrews I'll be another few minutes.'

After informing the teacher she'd be delayed, Theo rejoined Mr Ransleigh. She hoped he'd have enough compassion for the children not to reveal to anyone what she was about to confess. Even though, she knew with a sick certainty that made her stomach churn, she would surely forfeit his respect once she'd told him.

No point delaying the unpleasantness any further.

Waving him to follow, she set off walking. Once they were out of sight and hearing of the school, she said, 'Let me come straight to the point. While Tremaine's wording was crude, it's still…true. I suppose, after that kiss in the wildflower meadow, you suspected that I'm not an innocent. I've told you how much I loved Marshall. We were to be married as soon as I returned from escorting Lord Everly's wife back to England.'

She fell silent a moment, lost in the memories. Probably shocked speechless to find that a woman he'd thought virtuous, wasn't, he didn't prompt her to continue.

'How many times I've regretted not insisting we find the nearest chaplain to marry us before I left!' she said at last. 'But Marshall wanted me to have a proper wedding when the army went into winter quarters in Lisbon, with a reception for all our friends and Papa giving me away in a smart new gown. So we waited—for the wedding. But I didn't want to wait to belong to him completely…and he didn't deny me that.'

'Unfortunately, the night we slipped away, Tremaine followed us. And watched, apparently. When I returned from the convent with Charles, he started shadowing me, making suggestive overtures whenever he caught me alone. He seemed to think that if I'd allowed Marshall to touch me, I was fair game for any man.'

'And you never told your father of this?' Ransleigh interrupted. 'I can't imagine he would have tolerated it!'

'No, Papa would probably have shot him, or at least run him out of camp. But Tremaine was very careful not to make his insinuations where others could overhear him.

It would have been difficult to accuse him to Papa without having to confess the whole and I…I dreaded forfeiting Papa's good opinion. As, I fear, I've now lost yours.'

He frowned. 'Do you know me so little as to think I would disdain you for giving yourself to the man you meant to marry, when men take women lightly all the time without reproof? If I did not know you must be upset by Tremaine's visit, I'd be insulted.'

Her throat felt tight, and tears threatened. 'Most men have different standards for themselves and for women. When a maid gives herself to a man, and does not end up marrying him, she is scorned.'

'Miss Branwell, I have never known a woman more principled and honourable than you! And before you insult me again by asking, I have no intention of betraying your confidence to anyone.'

Knowing what she'd *not* told him, his unqualified support was almost worse than disdain. She considered confessing the whole…but gentleman though he was, the risk was still too great.

Swallowing hard, digging her nails into her palms to keep the tears at bay, she whispered, 'You are too kind.'

'Not at all,' he retorted, 'though I was too courteous. For his insults and for upsetting you, I should have pummelled Tremaine anyway, despite the possibility of the children overhearing us.'

'I'm glad you did not. I have a singular dislike of a man being punished for telling the truth. Besides, he was the best pugilist in the regiment.'

'All the better to prove what I can still do with one hand. But can he make trouble for you?'

'If he were to cast aspersions on my character, Lady Wentworth—and others—would likely withdraw their support. But with the school already staffed, and with agreements in place for the local masters to apprentice willing students, the effect wouldn't be as devastating as it would have been earlier. I'd have to press Aunt Amelia to find places for the girls.'

'I couldn't do much for the girls, but I'd certainly be willing to help find positions for the boys.'

'I don't think it will come to that—but now you've made the offer, I will hold you to it!' she warned. 'Tremaine probably only discovered I was here by chance, when he broke his journey at the public house in Hadwell. A younger son with expensive tastes and no means, before the war he cultivated those who could entertain him in the style he prefers, drifting from country estate to hunting box to the London town houses of wealthier friends. Technically now out of the army despite the uniform, he's taken up that pastime again.'

'I am glad that his call provided me opportunity to see you.'

She looked up at him, surprised. 'You knew about it?'

'Tremaine stopped at Bildenstone for directions to the school. Wilton—and the rest of the staff, apparently—were concerned about the safety of you and the children out here, alone and unprotected.'

Embarrassment—and gratitude—warmed her face. 'That was kind of them.'

'You shouldn't find it surprising. The Lady Wentworths of the county may look down their noses at your efforts, but your concern for the welfare of the lowliest in the parish has won you the admiration of everyone else.'

'Take care of your soldiers and your sergeants, and the men will take care of you, Papa always said,' she murmured, feeling again that ache at his loss.

'True, and some commanders do so out of self-interest. But the men recognise those who treat them well out of respect and concern, and they don't forget it.'

'Much as I appreciate your reinforcements, I hope you

didn't feel compelled to interrupt your work to come rescue me. As you saw, I was able to handle it myself.'

'I was glad to come. I know we agreed—or rather, you dictated—that we should avoid one another, but I owe you thanks for your advice. After the horrors you observed when we rode about the estate, I thought you might like to know how things are progressing.'

Despite knowing how important it was to start distancing herself from him, she couldn't help feeling a flush of pleasure. 'I would indeed.'

'The first project was riding the rest of Bildenstone's acreage, followed by an inspection of the estate ledgers. Unsurprisingly, I concluded that Winniston was at best incompetent and worst, skimming more off the top than he was entitled to. After Father's death, he had no oversight; all the estate income was kept by him or deposited in the accounts, with nothing reinvested in the land or the tenants.'

She nodded, thinking of the old equipment and rundown dwellings they'd passed. 'That was rather evident.'

'I've removed him, with a pension only because of his family's generations of service at Bildenstone. As soon as I complete the rest of the ledgers, I'm going to Newmarket to consult with the stable manager about selling my hunters. I may stop afterward at Holkham Hall to see Thomas Coke and consult with him about the latest in agricultural techniques. Perhaps get a recommendation for a new estate manager.'

Theo searched his expression—which looked resigned, but with none of the despair she'd seen in it before when he talked of selling off his hunters. He seemed...at peace with the decision, and ready to move beyond his loss.

'I'm glad. Letting go isn't easy, but acceptance is the first step in forging ahead.' Then she had to laugh. 'Listen to me, pontificating, when I've never been any good at it myself.'

'Some things, you never want to let go,' he said quietly.

Something in the timbre of his voice pulled her gaze back to his. A shimmering cloud of sensation enveloped them, breathtaking as a thousand dust motes gilded by the sun. But there was sweetness too, empathy, and a deep connection that curled around her heart like a pair of loving hands and made her bones ache with longing.

Ah, Dominic Ransleigh, you are so dangerous to my peace of mind, she thought, struggling to keep from reaching for him. *Good thing you're going away, before I blurt out how much I want you to stay.*

Finally, losing the battle, she let herself take his hand, almost sighing at the jolt that tingled through her. 'Best of luck.'

He held her fingers a few moments longer than was strictly necessary. 'I won't be ready to leave for a week or so. If you'll permit, I'll check with you when I return and let you know how it went.'

'I'd like that,' she said, even as the protective voice within protested she mustn't see him again. 'I shall be interested in your plans for the improvement of the estate,' she answered it back.

Liar, it whispered.

Ignoring it, she said, 'I must get back. I owe the children a story and Miss Andrews a break.'

'What are you offering them? Not Bowdlerised Shakespeare, I hope.'

'Never!' she said with a laugh. 'I was delighted to find in your library an edition of Galland's *Les Milles et Une Nuit.* I'd seen the English *Arabian Nights* translation, but the original French is so much better. What child could resist stories of sorcerers and jins?'

'So you will be their Scheherazade. They will love it.'

'I expect they will clamour for more. Good thing there were one thousand and one nights.' And could there be anything in those Far Eastern stories more outlandish or shocking than the tale she didn't finish telling Ransleigh?

By her omission, she'd managed to retain his good opinion. Keeping it gave her an even more compelling reason to hold him at arm's length.

Two weeks later, Theo sat at the desk in her study at Thornfield Place, looking over the replies to her advertisement for a tutor for Charles. Though he'd continued accompanying her to the school and shared in the lessons, she brought him back to Thornfield Place every night, despite his protests that he'd rather sleep in the dormitory with Georgie and Jemmie. Soon he must start preparing for the more rigorous academics required of the gentlemen who sojourned at Oxford or Cambridge before taking up the management of their acreage. Though, she thought, envious of the men who could pursue study forbidden to women, most of the scions of the aristocracy devoted more of their time at university to entertainment and developing friendships among their peers than pursuing scholarship.

Once the time came, she'd not renew the leases and instead turn several of the properties she'd inherited over to Charles. She was idly wondering how soon they ought to visit the estates to decide which were the most promising, when a knock sounded at the door.

'Miss Branwell, there's a lady to see you,' Franklin said.

'Did she not give her name?' Theo asked, curious. She'd been graciously introduced to several local ladies by Lady Wentworth, but having assured them she was seldom at Thornfield during calling hours, none had ventured out.

'She said you'd not recognise her name, but that she had heard much of you and was very interested to meet you.'

Which told her exactly nothing, Theo thought, a little

uneasily. Had Tremaine managed to drop a few words in some interested ears before he'd taken himself out of Suffolk?

If so, there'd be nothing for it but to face down the rumours. Fortunately, her dress and manner were so far from brazen or seductive, she had a good chance of successfully refuting whatever he'd insinuated.

'I put her in the Green Room, miss,' Franklin recalled her.

Conveying the visitor to the most formal receiving room, with its Wedgwood plasterwork and Adamesque ceiling, told Theo that the butler considered the caller a lady of rank and position. Not that the fact helped her narrow down the identity of her unexpected guest.

Glad she owned no gowns that weren't modest in the extreme, and already thinking about tactics to counter any initial hostility and engage the woman's sympathy, Theo girded herself for the fray and headed for the Green Room.

Normally, she paid little attention to the rituals of greeting, but if this were to be a subtle dance of step and counterstep, she meant to begin with every advantage. 'You'd better announce me,' she told Franklin, to his surprise.

Start from strength, Papa always said. So she'd play Lady of the Manor.

Walking in as the butler intoned, 'Miss Branwell', she sank into a curtsy. Her visitor, a woman some years her senior whose fashionable, obviously expensive gown and dashing bonnet justified the butler's estimation of her status, rose to return it.

'Miss Branwell, I am so delighted to meet you at last.'

Puzzled, Theo gazed down into earnest green eyes that looked vaguely familiar. The visitor was not any of the ladies she'd met after church, nor could she recall Mr Scarsdale informing her about any other family in the county with the wealth and status to dress its matriarch in such prime fashion.

'As am I, I'm sure,' she murmured. 'Although you must excuse my ignorance. My butler did not give me your name.'

'My subterfuge, I'm afraid. Shall we sit? It's a bit of a strain on my neck, looking up.' The woman smiled. 'Marshall wrote me about how tall you were.'

Recognition knifed through her in a stab of horror. Those green eyes—that soft blonde hair waving out from under the stylish bonnet. No wonder they looked so familiar.

This woman had to be Lady Hazlett. Her dead fiancé's mother.

For a moment, Theo thought she might faint, before the primal instinct for self-preservation kicked in and rushed her brain back into action.

Too late to worry about what the woman had gleaned from her initial response. Lady Hazlett might not know anything at all. Her unexpected visit could be just a pleasant coincidence.

Theo could still pull this off, if she went about it cleverly.

Belatedly putting a smile on her face while touching a hand to her heart, Theo said, 'You're Lady Hazlett, of course! I'm sorry, it was such a shock. I'd always hoped to meet you some day…under much happier circumstances.' Trying to make her motions smooth instead of jerky with panic, Theo motioned her guest to a chair and took one herself.

'By the way,' she added belatedly, 'I'm so sorry for your loss. I intended to send you and Lord Hazlett a note. But I was…ill for some time afterwards, and putting anything in writing would make it too…final. It took me a very long time to face the fact that Marshall was gone for ever.'

Grief shadowed Lady Hazlett's face. 'I miss him dreadfully still. Yet, I know that your loss was greater.'

Marshall's mother's words ripped open the lid on the box in which she tried to keep all the anguished memories contained. Hammered by a blow of desolation, Theo couldn't get any words to form, all her energy concentrated on holding back the sobs.

Lady Hazlett poured a cup of tea and handed it to her. Grateful, Theo gulped down a sip, the scalding liquid shocking her back to the present.

'Thank you,' she said after a moment. 'Goodness, where are my manners? *I* should have served *you*. Are you staying long in the area? Not that I'm not delighted to meet you at last, but how did you know I was at Thornfield Place?'

Annihilating Theo's last hope of brazening through, Lady Hazlett said quietly, 'I think you know why I'm here.'

After a moment of agonised silence, Theo said dully, 'Audley Tremaine visited you.'

'Yes. And now, may I see my grandson?'

Chapter Fourteen

Through the roaring in her ears, Theo dimly heard the clatter of her teacup as it dropped back into the saucer. She found herself on her feet, chest so tight she could scarcely breathe, desperately trying to decide what to do next.

She could laugh, look puzzled, tell Lady Hazlett she had no idea what she meant—though her obvious distress would make such a denial rather unbelievable.

She could walk out, order her butler to show Lady Hazlett the door, and hope that was an end to it.

Lady Hazlett had risen, too, and looked up at Theo, an anguished appeal on her face. 'Marshall was my only remaining child, you know. I lost two little boys as infants and one dear daughter, and then, two years ago, our eldest and heir, Edward, died after a hunting fall. When Tremaine told me Marshall had a son, I had to come. Your precious child is all I have left. Surely, you won't be so cruel as to keep him from me!'

'I never set out to hide him,' Theo said softly. 'I didn't know if you and Lord Hazlett would want to acknowledge him, since Marshall and I never married, but I *had* planned to contact you. But then, when I arrived back at the army with him, and everyone assumed he was Alicia and Everly's child whom Everly's family refused to acknowledge, I saw a way of keeping him that would avoid shaming my father. That would avoid having Charles branded a bastard.'

'Good heavens, girl, what were you going to do if the Marquess of Wareton changed his mind and wanted the boy back?'

'I would have told him then about Charles's true parentage. It's all recorded in the register at the convent, so there would be proof. But unless and until that happened, Charles could remain legitimate in the eyes of the world, and free from the true scandal of his birth.'

'As could you,' Lady Hazlett said tartly.

'As could I. For what it's worth, I cared very little what happened to me. I couldn't imagine ever loving anyone again as I had Marshall, so being ruined and unable to marry didn't matter to me. I would have grieved at the loss of my father's respect, but protecting my father from embarrassment and Charles from the stigma of bastardy were my primary motivations. Which you can believe, or not.'

'Oh, child, I didn't come here to harangue you! Only to reclaim a part of myself I thought lost for ever. Blood of my blood, flesh of my flesh.'

Furious determination boiled up from the depths of her soul. 'You can't have him. He's all *I* have left of Marshall, too! I've cherished him and nurtured him since the sisters placed him in my arms after he drew his first breath. Besides, how could you claim him, without the facts of his birth coming out?'

Lady Hazlett shrugged. 'Why could we not continue the fiction you've already promulgated? All my friends know how devastated I was by Marshall's death. We can put it about that, after your return to England, I called on my son's former fiancé, to meet her and commiserate over our common loss. While there, I met this noble orphan whose family didn't wish to claim him. Delighted by the child, I took him up in place of the boy I'd lost. It would make as much sense as the version you've told thus far.'

'He'd be much more visible then. Much more likely that the Marquess would hear about him, and perhaps change his mind about acknowledging him.'

Lady Hazlett laughed. 'That old miser? I've known Wareton since my come-out, and a more selfish, clutch-fisted man would be impossible to find. If he didn't want the boy years ago, he'll not claim him now. If he thought at all about my taking Charles on, he'd look upon it as a fine joke that someone else was paying the bills for one of his son's by-blows. As for the girl's family, I understand they are of slender means, and would doubtless be happy to have the boy recognised by someone of more wealth and influence.'

'Which,' she continued, rounding on Theo, 'is why you should give him up, if it's truly his welfare that concerns you. What can you do for him, compared to what Lord Hazlett and I can offer? Yes, I know you are well funded, but you can't claim to have the influence in society of a vis-count, nor can you promote Charles's career through a long association with other landed gentlemen in their colleges, clubs, and Parliament. Would you deny Marshall's son all those advantages? Besides, I understand you've started a school for soldier's orphans. I can't imagine how you can run that and give proper attention to Charles's upbring-ing, nor is it right that he grow up associating solely with orphans much below his station. How is he to learn to be-come a gentleman in an orphanage for paupers?'

It didn't help the panic roiling through her that Lady Hazlett was echoing all the arguments Aunt Amelia had always given her about securing Charles's future. And then it came to her.

A battle never went as you'd envisioned, Papa always said, the attack often coming from an unexpected foe or an unforeseen direction. One must fall back into a more defensible position.

And there was only one defensible position in this battle. If she wanted to keep Charles, she would have to find a stepfather for him who could offer the same advantages as his grandfather.

'I can't refute those arguments. I've agonised over them myself from time to time, but never could bring myself to consider marriage. Threatened with Charles's loss, though, I'm prepared to act. So I propose a bargain.'

'A bargain?' Lady Hazlett echoed. 'I don't understand.'

'We're agreed that we both love Charles and want what is best for him. I believe that remaining with me, who has cared for him since birth, is better for him than being sent away with strangers. But I also understand your desire to claim a child who, but for unfortunate circumstances, would have been a grandson you could have loved and acknowledged openly. I propose to marry a gentleman of standing and substance, who can be the mentor, teacher and example your husband would be, while allowing Charles to remain here, with those he knows and loves. But we will also adopt your story of visiting me, being charmed by the orphan, and wanting to take him under your wing. I'll accompany him on visits to you and Lord Hazlett several times a year, and when he's older and knows you better, will let him come alone. It was never my aim to deny him the love of his grandparents.'

Lady Hazlett sat thoughtfully silent. 'Who do you propose to marry?'

'I don't know yet,' Theo said frankly. 'I'll have to consult with my aunt, Lady Coghlane, and see what's possible. I do promise that whoever I agree to wed would be of sufficient stature and wealth to secure Charles's future. In the meantime, you will keep our secret.'

'Will your…potential husband know?'

'I would never deceive a gentleman about something so important. Of course, I would not reveal his true parentage until I was certain of a suitor's esteem, superior character, and willingness to act as Charles's mentor.'

'Finding such a paragon may be difficult,' Lady Hazlett said sceptically. 'And if I do not agree to your terms?'

'I understand there is much fine property available in Belgium, now that the war that killed so many of its owners is finally over. And I have a good deal of ready income.'

The two women faced each other for a long moment.

'I didn't come here to be your enemy,' Lady Hazlett said at last. 'For all I knew, you'd be happy to give up the boy. But I understand only too well what it is like to lose a beloved child; I wouldn't be the means of parting a son from his mother. *If* he can be raised, not in an orphanage, but with a mentor who can offer him all the advantages due his station, and *if* we have assurance Hazlett and I can make him a part of our lives.'

'Then we are agreed?'

Lady Hazlett reached out her hand and Theo shook it.

'Now that that unpleasantness is settled, may I see my grandson?'

'Why don't you follow me up to the nursery?'

A little lightheaded, her hands still trembling in the wake of the confrontation, Theo led Lady Hazlett from the Green Parlour up the stairs. As they got closer to the nursery, she could hear Charles singing a Portuguese folk song with Constancia, his piping voice slightly off-key.

Nausea crawled up her throat and a wave of panic crashed over her. Should she have sent Lady Hazlett away and barred the door? If she mustered her forces poorly, would she lose the person who meant most to her in the world?

Don't concede the field after the first skirmish, she steadied herself. Lady Hazlett wanted what would make

Charles happy, and he wouldn't be happy parted from his friends and the woman who had cared for him his entire life. She needn't figure out every bit of strategy this very moment; she would have time to plan.

Plan to marry.

She swallowed another wave of nausea.

Then Charles heard her footsteps, and rushed to the nursery door. 'Miss Theo!' he cried, popping out. 'Did you hear us? Constancia taught me a new song! Shall I teach it to you?'

'In a minute, Charles. Right now, there's a lady I'd like you to meet. She was a…a good friend of your papa's.'

She led Lady Hazlett into the nursery, where Constancia curtsied and Charles made a fine proper bow. As he looked up, his bright green eyes fixing on a lady whose similar green eyes stared back at him, Lady Hazlett gasped.

'He's so like Marshall at that age,' she whispered. 'May I?' At Theo's nod, she reached out to brush a lock of golden hair off his brow.

Theo felt her heart constrict. How could she deny Marshall's mother the chance to know and love his son?

She couldn't. But that didn't mean she wouldn't fight sword, pistol and whip, take him abroad if necessary, to have him remain with her. He was *her* son, too.

'Why don't you show Lady Hazlett your soldiers before we have some nuncheon?'

'Then can we go to the school?'

'Then we can go to the school.'

'Why can't I stay at the school with my friends? Why do I have to have a—a too door?'

With an anxious glance at Lady Hazlett, Theo said, 'Because you're going to grow up to be a great gentleman, like my father the colonel, and your papa. And to do that, you must go to university. The tutor will help you get ready.'

'I'd rather get ready to teach horses with Jemmie, or plant fields, like Georgie.'

'That's only because you don't know yet how much fun it will be to learn many things and go to university. And afterward, you'll have lots of horses to train and fields to tend.'

'Should you like to have a horse of your own?' Lady Hazlett asked.

Charles's gaze hopped back to his grandmother. 'Oh, I would! Miss Theo said after the school got ready, she would get me a pony.'

'Your papa loved ponies. I think you should have one straight away.'

While Theo absorbed that challenge, Charles subjected Lady Hazlett to a frank stare. 'I like you. Would you like to see my soldiers now?'

'Will you show me?' she asked.

'Of course. I better help you, though. It's awful narrow in the corner for a lady.' He offered his arm.

Theo watched, anguish throbbing in her chest, as the son she could never acknowledge assisted his grandmother to the low eaves in the corner where his lead soldiers were displayed. How she wished Marshall had lived to see this!

But he hadn't, which left her with quite a dilemma.

Now she, who had never wished to marry, needed to find a husband. A *suitable* husband.

And quickly.

A week later, Dom sat in a parlour of the Palladian masterpiece that was Holkham Hall, agricultural tracts spread out on the desk before him. He was immersed in the merits of the Norfolk Four-Crop Rotation system when a footman in gilded livery bowed himself in. 'Mr Ransleigh, there is a…young person to see you.'

'Young person?' he echoed blankly.

'When he arrived first thing this morning, the butler sent him away, thinking it most unlikely a rough sort like that would have any acquaintance with a gentleman. But he stationed himself in the kitchen courtyard, claiming that you do know him and that he will not leave until he's spoken with you.'

The memory of another person a butler had been unable to shoo away popped into his mind—but the footman said this was a 'he,' not a young lady. Besides, he thought with a smile, if contested, Theo would doubtless put her 'colonel's daughter' on and not be put off by a mere butler.

The smile faded as he considered the only other 'young person' he knew whom a butler would not consider receiving—and who had the gumption to refuse to be dislodged from his intent: a boy who'd grown up emulating his sergeant-major father. And Jemmie would never have come looking for him, unaccompanied by Theo, unless something was drastically wrong.

Having gone within an instant from amusement to alarm, Dom said, 'Where is he? I will see him at once!'

The footman shifted uncomfortably. 'I don't think the butler would approve my showing him in here, sir. Perhaps…perhaps I could convey him into the servants' hall?'

'Nonsense!' Dom snapped, agitation lending an edge to his voice. 'I don't intend to conduct my business in front of the servants—or in the kitchen yard. Bring him here at once!'

'Very well, sir,' the footman said, still looking dubious.

Wondering what could have happened at Thornfield or the school that would have prompted Theo to send Jemmie, Dom jumped up to pace the room. He was about to set off and fetch the boy himself when the door opened and an exasperated Jemmie trotted in.

'Think I was tryin' to break a prisoner out of stocks,'

he muttered. 'I was about ready to find an open window and comb the place for ya meself.'

'I'm sorry, Jemmie. I only just learned you were here. But why have you come—and how did you find me? Has something happened to Miss Branwell?'

'Aye, something's happened. Nay, she's not hurt or nothin',' he added quickly at the concern he must have seen in Dom's face. 'Though I can't make any sense of her takin' such a crack-brained notion of a sudden.'

'You'd better tell me the whole.' Dom motioned to a chair, on which, after giving the gold-corded brocade upholstery a dubious glance, Jemmie perched. Seating himself at the sofa, he said, 'Now, what has happened?'

'Everything seemed just fine until about a week ago, when she come to school like she always does, but leaving Master Charles back at Thornfield. And she's all agitated and fidgety-like. I asked her what was wrong—thought mebbe the boy'd taken sick or something, cause she sets great store by the little nipper. She said he was fine, but a lady who knew Charlie's da had come to visit. Then she goes in and has a long talk with Miss Andrews, and after that she talks with Mr and Mrs Blake—that's the cook and her man, what lives with us at the school. And off she goes again, without a word to any of us.'

Jemmie frowned. 'I knew somethin' bad was happenin', cause Miss Theo never left any place, ever, without tellin' me first where she was goin'. She didn't come to the school at all the next day. Then the next day, she comes ridin' up in the carriage with Master Charles and tells us she's goin' off to London, to see her aunt, and mebbe she'd be gone a good while. Then she said goodbye.'

The boy twisted his hands, distress on his face. 'I knew there was somethin' powerful wrong; she ain't looked so broken up since they brought the colonel back after Waterloo, just afore he died.'

'Didn't she explain why she needed to go?' Dom asked, his concern beginning to mirror Jemmie's.

'Nay. I follered her out, cause I weren't goin' to let her go off to London all alone, not til I knew why. She hugged me, and there was tears in her eyes. And she told me she was goin' to London to find a husband! That her aunt would help her, and she might not come back till after she was married. She said she was sorry, and she loved me like her own son, and then she got back into the carriage and drove away.'

Jemmie stared into the distance. 'We been through a lot together, Mr Ransleigh, Miss Theo and me. And it sounded like she was tellin' me goodbye for g-good.'

Tears glittered in Jemmie's eyes before he rubbed them away with a grubby fist. 'Why would she want to get married now, when she's told me for years, after she lost her lieutenant, she'd never marry nobody? And when she knows I'll soon be growed and kin take care of her like her pa did, so she won't never be alone no more?'

Only desperation would ever drive me to the Marriage Mart, he recalled her saying. 'I can't imagine.'

'We need to know what's wrong so we kin do somethin' to help her. She tells me lots, but she prob'ly won't talk to me about marryin'. That's why I lit out to find you straight away. Folks up at Bildenstone told me you was goin' to Newmarket and then here, so's when I didn't find you there, I come to Holkham. But we got to hurry. She'll be in London, with her aunt by now.'

Dom looked at him, astonished at his journey. 'How did you manage to travel all—?' He broke off abruptly. A child who'd scrambled along in the wake of an army probably knew things about transporting and feeding himself Dom would rather not enquire about too closely. 'Never mind. You think Miss Branwell is in London, then?'

'By now, sure as sure. You got to make her tell you

what's wrong. All of us at the school are worried, 'cause we don't want her marryin' so hasty, maybe somebody who don't deserve her and won't treat her right. Then Miss Theo told me a while back if she married, her husband could take everything she owns. Which would mean the school, too, wouldn't it? So if this bloke didn't like us, he could toss us all out on the street.'

'True, a husband normally controls his wife's wealth,' Dom admitted.

'Her aunt's a great lady, so she'll be marrying Miss Theo off to some grand gentleman. I know how the toffs look at us—and I just bet this husband person would want nothin' to do with us, nor let her run the school neither. And even though she's got Charlie, Miss Theo'd be awful sad if she lost all of us. So we got to find her and talk her out of this.'

'I'd certainly like to know what happened,' Dom admitted. Having half-formed an idea of perhaps courting Theo Branwell himself, the notion of her marrying another man didn't sit very well with him, either.

'So you'll go to London and find out what happened?'

He wasn't sure how he was going to justify inserting himself into so private a matter when he had no claim at all upon the lady…but he knew curiosity alone, not to mention a fierce need to protect and shelter her, wouldn't let him rest until he found out.

He was her landlord, after all. If something about the management of the school were going to change, he needed to know that.

And when had Theo Branwell ever hesitated to insert herself into *his* private affairs?

He was smiling at that thought when Jemmie said, 'Mr Ransleigh? I know I ain't always been too friendly-like, and I'm sorry for that,' he said, his freckled face flushing. 'But I know you like us, or you wouldn't've let Miss Theo

rent your building. She told me you been askin' around for
a trainer to teach me how to manage horses, and someone
to help Georgie learn to farm. You like Miss Theo, too—I
know you do. And she likes you. She comes back smilin'
after she's been with you, happy like I've not seen her since
the colonel died. So I think she'll tell you what's wrong—
and listen when you talk her out of marryin'.'

Could he talk her out of it? Or should he just suggest a
suitable candidate?

He'd already broached to himself the idea of courting
her. But he meant to consider it at leisure—not let circumstances rush him into something with such enormous and
irreversible consequences.

Delectable consequences, his body whispered.

Ignoring his carnal urgings, he told Jemmie, 'I'll leave
for London immediately and see what I can discover.'

Jemmie uttered a sigh of relief. 'I'll be on my way back
to the school, then. Can make a good bit afore nightfall,
if I get a-goin'.'

'Why don't you go post? I'll spot you the fare. It will be
faster than…whatever means you can find on your own.'

'Thank 'ee, Mr Ransleigh. That'd be right nice. But
just a loan, now.'

'Just a loan.' Rooting in his waistcoat for some coins,
he thought that if Theo Branwell were going to be as independent and resistant to taking help as her protégé, trying to straighten whatever fix she'd got herself into was
going to be difficult.

'And, Mr Ransleigh? You will hurry, won't ya?'

'I will.' After ringing for a servant, he handed Jemmie
enough blunt to see him safely back to Suffolk. When the
footman appeared, Dom instructed him to have one of
the grooms carry Jemmie to the nearest posting inn, and
ready his own vehicle.

He walked up to his room, to set Henries packing while

he wrote his host a quick note. With luck, he could follow Jemmie's departure with the hour.

Curiosity, unease, and puzzlement kept chasing each other around his brain. He couldn't imagine what catastrophe could have made calm, capable Theo Branwell look 'agitated' and 'fidgety-like'. Nor change overnight the mind of a woman who'd seemed dead set against marriage.

He wanted to find out, though. And he wanted to get to London before his unusually flustered Theo did something precipitous he'd not be able to undo.

Chapter Fifteen

That same afternoon, Theo and Charles arrived at the London residence of her Aunt Amelia in Jermyn Street. After seeing the boy up to a bedchamber with a maid in attendance, she made herself as presentable as was possible after so much time on the road. Having asked the butler not to announce her, she went to knock at the door of her aunt's private sitting room.

Lady Coghlane, wearing a fetching afternoon gown, was dozing on her sofa when Theo walked in. She was halfway across the room when her drowsy aunt, opening one eye, recognised her and sat up with a start.

'My darling Theo! What a delightful surprise!' she cried.

'Please, sit,' Theo said. 'I didn't mean to disturb your rest, only to tell you I'd arrived.'

Her aunt sank back against the cushions, looking befuddled. 'Did I know you were coming? Not that you aren't welcome to visit whenever, and as often, as you like!'

'No, this trip was…rather sudden.' Now that the moment for explanation—and confession—had come, Theo wasn't sure how to begin, the numerous speeches she'd rehearsed in the coach deserting her. Too unsettled to sit, she took a turn about the room.

Inspecting her closely, Lady Coghlane frowned. 'You look distressed, my dear. What is wrong? And how can I help?'

Theo turned to face her aunt, twisting her gloved fingers together. 'The truth is, I'm in a devil of a coil, and I only hope you can help me! Or will still want to, once I've told you the whole.'

'Still want to? Don't be silly! Of course I'll want to, my dearest, darling niece! With Richard gone, you're my nearest blood, save my own children. I'll always love you, regardless of what you've done. Though, with that orphanage you were determined to thrust into the midst of Suffolk gentry...' She paused with a shudder. 'Regardless of what's happened, we'll deal with it!'

The idea of Lady Coghlane swooping up to Suffolk like a fairy godmother, applying the magic wand of her society position to buttress Theo's position, brought Theo a temporary respite from her anxiety.

'It has nothing to do with the orphanage—at least not directly.'

'Whatever it is, let me first ring for some tea. Every situation looks better after a warm, soothing drink.' After tugging at the bell pull, she said, 'Where did you break your journey? Did you get any rest?'

Not sure whether she felt relieved or more anxious at the delay, Theo said, 'We travelled pretty much straight through, except at night, so Charles could have a bed to sleep. I brought him with me.'

'And the others?'

'They're at school. Which is up and running now, by the way. Renovations of the building went splendidly, I found a lovely girl, Miss Andrews, to teach, and an older couple to live in as cook and general handyman. I was in the process of considering applications for a tutor for Charles— before he gets too accustomed to being at the school, too.'

'That wouldn't be wise,' her aunt agreed. 'You can't expect him to act like a gentleman later if he's raised like a foundling. And—what of Mr Ransleigh?'

Theo swallowed hard, Dominic Ransleigh being the one topic she'd forbidden herself to think about since the nightmare of Lady Hazlett's visit.

'He's been an exemplary neighbour. His grandfather amassed quite a magnificent library at Bildenstone, which he is allowing me access to. I…enjoy his company. He's very easy to talk to.' *Oh, and so much more,* Theo thought distractedly.

A knock at the door was followed by the entry of the butler with the tea tray. Once they'd settled themselves in with full cups, Lady Coghlane said, 'So, tell me what's troubling you.'

Her stomach, half-settled by the warming tea, twisted into knots again. 'I suppose it started with me falling in love with Marshall, supremely confident that we would live together the rest of our lives.'

Her aunt gave her a sympathetic glance. 'I'm sure you did believe in for ever…ill advised as that was, with him being a serving officer during a bloody conflict.'

'You'll remember that, almost five years ago now, I was going to accompany Lord Everly's wife back to London for the birth of her child.'

'Of course I remember! You were going to stay with me.'

'Only she became ill on the journey, and we ended up at a convent until after the birth of her child.'

'Yes. Also that she didn't long survive his birth.'

Theo took a deep breath. 'What you didn't know is that she wasn't the only one taken ill. After I learned that Marshall had been killed, I was distraught. Even more so because I'd only just discovered I was…increasing. You see, Alicia wasn't the only one who gave birth at that convent.

She died in childbed, and her child with her. Charles, the infant I brought back with me, wasn't her son—he is mine.'

Theo waited miserably while her aunt's eyes widened. Dropping her teacup with a clatter, she gasped, '*Your* child? You mean Charles is *your* son?'

Theo nodded. 'Mine and Marshall's. Oh, I was "ill advised" indeed! So confident of our future, I begged Marshall to make me his before I left with Alicia for London. Never dreaming he would not be there that winter to marry me.'

'Oh, my poor dear! What a predicament! Did Richard know?'

'No. I intended to confess the whole to him upon my return, even as I dreaded losing his good opinion—as I dread losing yours, now. But when I arrived back in camp and informed Everly's commander of his wife's death, the colonel assumed the infant I'd brought back with me was their son. Before I could get another word out, he went off into a diatribe about the perfidy of the nobility, with the Marquess of Wareton refusing to acknowledge either the marriage or the child. He asked if I could continue to look after the boy, at least temporarily. I barely had time to agree before he shooed me out to deal with an important dispatch. Then, with the news spreading through camp that Everly's wife had died and I'd brought back her son, it seemed wiser—for Charles's sake and Papa's, more than for my own—to let it be thought he was the legitimate—if unrecognised—grandson of a marquess. Rather than the illegitimate son of a colonel's daughter.'

Theo faced her aunt, the churning in her stomach intensifying. 'I'm so ashamed I let you and Papa down.'

The remorse and guilt she usually suppressed swept through her in a staggering wave. Swamped by it, she needed every bit of strength to hold the sobs at bay, only a single tear escaping to trickle down her cheek.

Her aunt rushed over to embrace her. 'There, now, my poor dear!' she crooned, rubbing Theo's trembling back as she tried to regain control. 'You needn't apologise to me for doing what girls in love have done from time immemorial. If the gods were female, you wouldn't have conceived—or if you had, your beloved would have stayed alive to marry you!'

After a few moments, when Theo regained her composure, Lady Coghlane released her and resumed her seat. 'To tell the truth, of late I'd suspected as much—especially when you were so adamant about keeping Charles, even after Richard's death.'

'You suspected?' Theo cried, horrified. 'Do you think anyone else might?'

'Calm yourself, my dear. I doubt anyone who doesn't know you well would suspect a thing. If the account of Charles's birth was to be challenged, it would have happened when you first brought him back to camp. It's just that I know you truly want the best for him, and knowing that, it seemed…odd for you to hold on to the child after your father's death, when you could no longer ensure he would be raised *by* a gentleman *as* a gentleman. Unless he meant more to you than a chance-met orphan.'

'He does,' Theo acknowledged.

'Why did you feel the need to reveal the secret of Charles's birth now?'

Smiling grimly, Theo recounted her confrontation with Audley Tremaine—and the subsequent visit from Lady Hazlett.

'Wonderful that the viscount and his lady want a relationship with the boy,' her aunt said, after listening thoughtfully. 'But…to take him from you, now, after more than four years? That would be very hard.'

'Impossible. So I proposed a bargain: I marry a well-positioned gentleman, who can provide the advantages of upbringing and access to the gentlemen of society the viscount would, let them develop a relationship with Charles, and I get to keep him with me. Which is why I came: to have you work your magic, and find me someone suitable to marry. Do…do you really think you can find someone?'

Lady Coghlane steepled her fingers, pondering. 'Nothing has changed since we last discussed you marrying. You'd insisted then that you must keep Charles. I assume, if you reached an understanding with a gentleman, you would reveal his parentage?'

'Of course. It's a delicate balancing—I don't want the information to become common knowledge, but I'd never marry anyone who wasn't fully aware of my circumstances.'

Lady Coghlane nodded. 'Wise to proceed that way. As for who you might marry, I must give the matter some thought.'

'Lady Hazlett seemed to think it would be difficult to find someone elevated enough to be suitable who'd also be amenable to marrying me. I'd need a "paragon", she said.'

'I wouldn't have you marry anything else!' Lady Coghlane said roundly. 'Let me put my mind to it and see who I come up with. By the way, I'm promised to dine with the Stauntons tonight. Why don't you come with me? As it happens, I have the gowns my daughter-in-law Lissa commissioned this spring, before she learned she was increasing. You're much of a size; I think my maid could alter them to fit you. She'll certainly be able to do something with that hair!'

'Tonight?' Panic swirled in her stomach. 'I thought I'd have some time to…get acclimated before going into company. I knew you wouldn't let me out of the house in my current wardrobe.'

'Given your circumstances, I don't think you should waste a minute,' her aunt said frankly. 'It's fortunate Lissa's gowns are to hand. It would be best for society to discover you're in town immediately, so I can set my friends listening for the interest it generates. After all, my dear, you *are* an earl's granddaughter, and very rich! After you've had an hour to rest, I'll have Marston bring those gowns to your bedchamber. Choose some you'd like to wear until we can get you to my mantua-maker. Then, after I've spoken with my friends tonight, I'll be better able to advise you on the likely candidates.'

Rising, her aunt came over to give her another hug. 'Don't worry, my dear. We shall find the right gentleman to make you happy—and keep Charles with you.'

'As long as I can keep Charles with me, I will be happy,' Theo said fervently.

As her aunt walked her out, Theo hoped her fairy-godmother aunt could make both circumstances come true.

Though Aunt Amelia had allotted her an hour to rest, Theo found she couldn't. After ten minutes reclining on the bed, her mind ticking fiercely through various scenarios like an overwound clock, she bounced back up.

Driven by the imperative to marry, feeling helpless at knowing the resolution of her dilemma depended on the good will of someone she'd not even met, and writhing with frustration at that helplessness, her stomach churned and head throbbed. How could she attract a potential suitor with the correct qualifications, someone who would be so taken with her that he wouldn't mind the added burden of another man's child?

Until now, the idea of marriage had been only a vague proposition put forward by Aunt Amelia, no more real than a mirage. Since having to make her bow on the censorious stage of the Marriage Mart seemed so unlikely, she'd been able to dismiss the prospect. Now that taking that step was imminent, its outcome so important and the result of failure so disastrous, dread and doubt assailed her like footpads setting on a drunken dandy.

She was too old, she'd never been a beauty, and she was certainly not docile. Aunt Amelia's maid could pretty her up, fix her hair, and dress her in more fashionable gowns. But would it be enough?

Could she learn to hold her tongue, be meek and attentive, defer to the gentlemen? Was it even fair for her to do so, when she'd be unable to sustain such behaviour for the rest of her life?

And what would she converse about, if she dared open her mouth? She knew very little of English politics, nothing of fashion or *ton* gossip. Would she be reduced to murmuring polite 'As you say's, or smiling inanely?

Prepared or not, she had to begin this very night.

Panic bubbled up, adding to the already caustic mix of urgency and uncertainty. She wasn't at all sure she could do this.

But she *had* to do it. Maybe she'd better remind herself of the reason she was doing it.

She'd go see Charles.

Theo walked into the bedchamber to find Charles chatting away to Constancia. As she looked at him, her breath stopped and her chest squeezed painfully.

Now that the toddler roundness of his face had given way to a boy's more sculpted shape, the outline of Marshall's chin and cheekbones was readily apparent. Add to that the curling blond hair and bright green eyes, and for anyone who'd known Marshall well, the resemblance was striking. Much as she resented the dilemma Tremaine had thrust her into, she couldn't fault him for recognising it, especially since Charles's purported parents had both been notably dark.

Dear enough to her in his own right, Charles was also

the living embodiment of a time of hopes and dreams when life awaited, a blank slate for she and Marshall to write upon it whatever they wished, their love a shining beacon lighting the way into their future.

A beacon that had kept her from succumbing to despair after her father's death, that had forced her to move past her loss and plan a future, for all of them.

Despite the anguish of losing Marshall, the anxiety over the shame and scandal she might visit upon her family, the ever-present worry over the secret becoming known, she wouldn't give up a day, even a second of life with Charles. If there was an ache in her heart that he would never call her Mama, as long as she had him with her, she could live with that.

He turned and saw her. 'Miss Theo!' he cried with delight, running over to her.

Theo buried her face in the soft golden locks and hugged him so tightly, he squirmed away in protest.

'London is so big!' he announced. 'I've been looking out the window with Constancia, and the buildings just keep going and going and going! The streets are so skinny, and there's no open fields. Where are you going to ride Firefly? Or me my pony?'

'One doesn't ride very much in the city, except at the park. The streets are so crowded and noisy, horses don't like it.'

'Can we go to the park, then?' Charles asked, picking up immediately on the one place riding was permitted.

'I'll take you tomorrow morning, I promise. It's already too late today; I'm told the fashionable gather to ride and walk in the park in late afternoon.'

'Will we get my pony then?'

Theo laughed ruefully, wishing Lady Hazlett to perdition; once promised such a treat, as tenacious as she—and his father—Charles would keep asking until it appeared.

'We can't get your pony at the park. I'll have to see where we can find one in London. But I will start looking.'

'What are we going to do in London, then? It's too far to go to the school. I miss Jemmie and Georgie.'

Theo felt a pang; her aunt and his grandmother were right. Having had children his own age to play with since birth, now that the excitement of the journey was over, Charles missed their company. He needed to interact with others—particularly those with whom he would continue to associate after he was grown.

Avoiding the question, she said, 'I hope we won't be in London long. Then we can get back to Thornfield and the school. You'll have your pony, and a tutor, so there will be many things to do.'

'But what will we do here?' he persisted, too intelligent to be fobbed off. 'If there's lots of wagons and carriages in the park, there will be lots of horses. I like to look at horses.'

'We can do that. There should be soldiers here, too, and we can go watch them on parade.'

His face lit up. 'I'd love to watch the soldiers march!'

Mad for the military, like his papa, she thought. Marshall had told her how, even as a second son, he'd had to fight for his father's permission to join the army. Recalling the desolated look on Lady Hazlett's face, she could understand why. Praise God, there would be no Napoleon waging war when *her* son grew up!

'There are many activities in London, you need only decide what you'd like to try. Later, I'll have you come to her room and say hello again to my aunt. For now, you can play with your soldiers until dinner.'

'What are you going to do until dinner?'

'I have to try on dresses,' she said in a disgusted tone, making a face.

Charles giggled. 'I'd rather play with my soldiers.'

'So would I. How about you try on dresses and I play with the soldiers?'

'I'm a boy, I can't wear dresses,' he replied in the serious tones of a child not yet old enough to recognise the facetious.

Theo pretended to study him up and down. 'I don't know, I think you'd look lovely in a gown. Don't you, Constancia?'

'Oh, yes, *senhora*, most beautiful in a gown,' the maid agreed, grinning.

'Let's just see, shall we?' Theo said, grabbing him. 'Come, the dressmaker is waiting.'

'No!' he protested, squealing with glee as Theo pulled him towards the door. 'No dresses, no dresses!' he cried between shrieks of laughter.

Laughing herself now, Theo halted at the doorframe. Kneeling down to surround him with her arms, she said, 'No dresses? Are you sure you don't want any?'

He pulled free within the circle of her arms and straightened his shirt. 'No, Miss Theo. You know boys don't wear dresses.'

Theo gave an elaborate sigh. 'I guess you're right. But it's not fair. I'd so much rather play with soldiers.'

'You can come and play later, after you're done with the dresses. I'll let you have General Blücher,' he volunteered, naming his favourite toy soldier.

'What a handsome offer! I shall take you up on it,' she said, rising. 'Now I have to go, before Aunt Amelia comes hunting for me.'

Charles gave her a measuring glance and looked around the room. 'You could hide under my bed.'

Already a tactician, she thought. 'No, when duty calls, one must answer. But I'll remember I have General Blücher to look forward to once I've finished.'

She leaned over to plant a kiss on his head, determination renewed. *There was nothing she would not do to keep him with her.* 'I'll save you some lace.'

Chuckling at his grimace of revulsion, she walked back to her room.

Chapter Sixteen

Later that evening in her bedchamber, Theo gazed at her reflection in the glass, while Marston peered over her shoulder, smiling. 'You look quite a treat, miss, if I do say so myself!'

The figure staring back at her was certainly an improvement, she admitted. Her hair, cut under protest, had been washed and curled and pinned up in a seemingly careless assortment of waves. The gown, in a becoming shade of gold that picked up the shimmer of her brown eyes, was mercifully free of excessive lace and furbelows.

It did, however, feature a form-enhancing silhouette, tiny puffed sleeves, and a bodice cut so low she'd probably contract a congestion of the lungs before the night was out. 'Are you sure you can't add a ruffle of lace here?' she asked, pointing to the low neckline.

'Heavens, no!' the maid replied in scandalised tones. 'Half the girls in London have to pad their corsets to achieve such a full, rounded bosom. You should be proud to display it.'

'It's certainly "displayed",' Theo muttered. 'I feel as naked as an army jolly-bag strutting her wares on a Lisbon street.'

At that moment, Aunt Amelia walked in. 'How lovely!' she exclaimed. 'Marston, you've outdone yourself!'

'So I'll do?' Theo asked, making a pirouette.

'Splendidly! I knew you'd be enchanting, once I got you out of those old gowns and that musty habit!'

'Are you sure it's not an imposition to bring me when I've not been invited?' Theo asked, grasping at the last available straw to delay her inevitable society début.

'I sent a note to Jane Staunton this afternoon, telling her you'd arrived unexpectedly, and asking if she'd mind if you came along. She replied that she'd be delighted— especially since she had an unexpected visitor, too. Her nephew, in from the country.'

'Don't tell me,' Theo said drily. 'He's a bachelor of good reputation and fortune.'

'Quite. A widower, with three children a little older than Charles.'

'On the prowl for a new wife to oversee his brood?'

'Jane wasn't sure, but Lord Sayle isn't fond of London, so she couldn't see any other reason for him making the journey—especially after he told her he planned to stay for some time.'

Theo tried to summon up some enthusiasm. 'Charles would like having other children about. What does Lord Sayle do? What could I talk to him about?'

'Well, he was never in the army.' Theo's hopes of finding a congenial conversationalist faded as her aunt continued, 'He did attend Eton and then Oxford—the New School, not Richard's college. The barony is very old; his estate is in Kent, and I understand he raises some lovely horses.'

'Oxford. Horses,' Theo repeated a bit desperately.

'Besides, you needn't worry about conversing. Ask him about his estate; after that, you'll probably only need to nod and smile.'

Inanely? Theo wondered. *Would there be opportunity to add an 'as you say'?*

Reading the anxiety on Theo's face, her aunt said again, 'You mustn't worry! Just be yourself, and the company can't help but admire you.'

'Spoken like a true loving aunt,' Theo said, giving that lady a kiss. 'But thank you for trying to raise my spirits.'

Lady Coghlane shook her head. 'Silly girl! Why someone who lived between two armies, survived advances and retreats and poor food and sleeping who knows where, could be in such a panic over a simple dinner party, I can't imagine!'

'I knew what to expect in those retreats and advances and billets. I don't know anything about surviving the London *ton*.'

'Just look and listen! You'll soon find how to get on.'

Taking a deep breath, Theo nodded. She certainly hoped she'd 'find how'. The consequences of failing to catch an eligible gentleman's eye were so dire, she couldn't bear to think about them.

A short time later, her aunt's carriage deposited them before a handsome town house in Grosvenor Square. Her heart beat faster as they ascended a wide marble staircase to be announced by the butler to a drawing room full of people.

The room glittered with an array of chattering women whose beautiful gowns in a rainbow of hues were set off against the black coats and pristine white neckcloths of the gentlemen.

How different, the sober attire of civilians, compared to army uniforms in vivid colours with their flashes of gold braid and frogging, she thought, feeling even more out of place.

Then Aunt Amelia was introducing her to her hostess,

Lady Staunton, who in turn introduced her to other guests. One of them, Lord Sayle, was the nephew in question, a distinguished-looking man greying at the temples whom Theo judged to be in his late thirties. After murmuring the proper polite phrases, she followed her aunt to a group by the fireplace. Before any further conversation was necessary, the meal was announced and their hostess led them into the dining room.

Theo dreaded the moment she would lose her aunt's support. As one of the highest-ranking ladies present, Lady Coghlane would be seated beside their host, while the unmarried daughter of an earl's younger son ranked far down the table.

She hoped their hostess would regale them with some of the delicacies for which she'd heard London was famed, so she might apply herself to her dinner and salvage something enjoyable from the evening. Feeling like a rank recruit who'd stumbled into one of General Wellington's staff meetings, she couldn't wait to escape back to Jermyn Street.

Wine was poured, and Theo took a thankful sip, returning the nodded greeting of her dinner partner. Who, wonder of wonders, turned out to be Lord Sayle.

After a few moments of silence, he murmured, 'I won't bite, you know.'

Theo started, then laughed. 'Excuse me, I didn't mean to be uncivil. I suppose I look as awkward as I feel,' she admitted—before remembering that candour was not a virtue prized by society.

Her dinner partner didn't seem offended. 'You look lovely, as I'm sure you know.'

'Oh, d-dear,' she stammered, colouring. 'I really wasn't trolling for a compliment.'

'That's not at all what I thought. But I'm very happy to give one so well deserved. You're Miss Branwell, aren't you? Lady Coghlane's niece?'

'Yes. And you're Lord Sayle, Lady Staunton's nephew.'

'Yes. Now that we've sorted out the family, what shall we discuss?'

How best to safely answer that? 'Why not tell me about your estate?' she answered cautiously.

'Let's not talk about something so ordinary!' He must have read alarm on her face, for he smiled. 'I shouldn't tease you. My aunt told me you've only recently come to England, having lived your entire life abroad, first in India, then following the drum with your father in Spain, Portugal, and Belgium. Also that he fell at Waterloo. My sincere condolences.'

The reminder brought a sharp pang of loss, no matter how many times it was mentioned. 'Thank you. I understand you've recently lost your wife as well. My sincere sympathies.'

He nodded, his expression turning sad. 'It was…very distressing. But one soldiers on, as I'm sure you know.'

'Yes,' she affirmed, liking him the better for this plain evidence of how fond he'd been of his wife.

Though it was nothing to her attachment to Marshall— or he wouldn't be in London looking for a replacement, a mere year after her death.

'Tell me more about your life,' he was saying. 'It's been so much more exciting than mine.'

Dangerous territory, she thought. Struggling for some socially appropriate opening, she finally shrugged. 'My aunt would say there's little about it fit to discuss at a dinner party. I've recently settled at a manor in Suffolk, and have never visited Kent. I understand you raise horses. Won't you tell me about your estate?'

Tacitly accepting her reticence, he nodded. 'Horses, yes. But more cattle and crops.'

'Some of the land at the estate bordering my house has

been much neglected, and the owner is now anxious to improve it.' *Maybe she could learn something of use to Dom.*

Dom. A sudden yearning for him filled her, so strong it almost made her dizzy. How she wished she were back at Bildenstone, riding through the meadows with him! How immensely different, the ease and comfort she felt with him, compared to the stiff awkwardness of this dinner party!

Since her searing conversation with Lady Hazlett, she'd deliberately kept herself from thinking about him—and the fact that her marriage would put an end to the friendship between them for good.

Which, of course, was for the best.

She was only uncomfortable because she was not yet well acquainted with *this* man, she told herself stoutly. Once she got to know Lord Sayle better, it would be easier.

She hoped.

In any event, he seemed pleasant enough as he obligingly described his home and acreage, requiring her only to add that polite nod at intervals.

'I understand you have three children,' she said when, inevitably, he fell silent and looked to her for a conversational contribution.

'Yes. My eldest son is preparing to leave for Eton. I shall sorely miss him, but alas, it's time. My lovely daughter I trust I shall not have to part from any time soon, since I spoil her so thoroughly no suitor will have her,' he admitted with a laugh. 'My younger son is just out of short coats. Rascals all, but I dote on them.'

'I have a little boy, too, that I've cared for since his birth,' she inserted. *If keeping Charles were going to dissuade a prospective suitor, she might as well find out immediately.*

'So my aunt told me,' he replied. 'I think it very noble of you, to insist on supporting the poor orphan, even after your father's death. Infamous that his father's family refused to recognise him!'

Theo smiled fondly. 'Had Lord Wareton ever visited Charles, he would not have been able to turn him away. Since I'm completely attached to him, I'm very glad his grandfather never made the effort.'

'You enjoy children, then.'

Was she being tested? 'Yes. Travelling with the army, there were always some running about. My father and I became attached to several, particularly the son of Father's sergeant-major. Jemmie foraged for us, watched out for Papa's horses, and generally made himself useful.' *A prospective suitor needed to know about Charles, but it was probably best not to fully reveal her connection to the other orphans just yet.*

'It shows broadness of character, to appreciate even children of that class.'

Theo had to keep herself from stiffening. He was, after all, repeating what most of his peers would say. Only someone like Dominic Ransleigh, who'd been with army, could understand what these children had been through and how dear they were to her.

How was she to safeguard them, though, if her eventual husband wanted her to have nothing further to do with them?

Her chest tightened and for a moment, it was difficult to breathe. *One problem at a time,* she told herself. First, she needed to find prospects who'd accept Charles. Whatever happened afterward, she'd make sure her other charges were protected.

Lord Sayle seemed to have cleared that first hurdle.

Smiling determinedly, she prodded him for more details about his land and children, which he willingly supplied. Respecting her reticence, he made no further enquiries about her own upbringing and circumstances.

Unlike herself, who'd stuck her nose immediately into Dominic Ransleigh's affairs.

He'd not slapped her down for it. Would Lord Sayle, were she to let her true 'colonel's daughter' nature show?

She suppressed a sigh. If matters between them progressed, she'd find that out in due time.

Conversation became more general, several other ladies vying to secure Sayle's attention—one of them, a dazzling blonde with a scandalously low *décolletage*, giving her an angry glance for having monopolised it thus far.

So it begins, navigating the ton's *fields of fire,* Theo realised ruefully.

When, some hours later, she met her aunt to gather their cloaks and depart, she had to admit dinner had not been as dismal as she'd feared.

As soon as they were enclosed within the privacy of their carriage, Aunt Amelia said, 'What did you think of Lord Sayle? He seemed quite attentive.'

'He was…pleasant. When asked, he told me about his estate and fields and his children, just as you assured me. I promise you, though *he* asked, I evaded giving any details about my own upbringing and experiences, so I don't think I shocked him.'

'Thank heavens for that!' Lady Coghlane said with a chuckle. 'I believe you made quite a favourable impression.'

'How could you tell? We talked for a time, it's true, but before long his attention was claimed—almost forcibly—by other ladies, especially the blonde on his right.'

'Lady Serena—Mrs Maxwell,' her aunt said with a sniff. 'Thinks she's entitled to the admiration of any gentleman within sight of her lovely face or dulcet voice.'

Theo grinned at her tone. 'Not a favourite of yours.'

'No. She's a shameless flirt, who may or may not be

collecting lovers while her poor husband languishes in the country. But having already provided him with the requisite heir and two more, he lets her go her own way.'

To be married and yet alone...that would be worse than losing Marshall, she thought. 'Sad.'

'Perhaps, but not uncommon. Few couples find what you and Marshall shared. I'm pleased you liked Sayle, and even more pleased *he* liked *you*, but he's hardly the only champion! I've planned a little tête-à-tête with a friend tomorrow, to examine other possibilities. But you won yourself one suitor tonight, which is useful in making other gentlemen more attentive.'

'What makes you so sure? We hardly spoke after the beginning of dinner, and Lady Serena hung on his arm all during tea, once the gentlemen rejoined us.'

'Perhaps, but though his attention might be drawn away by that annoying Lady Serena or someone else, his gaze always turned back to you.'

Her aunt's words brought to mind the man to whom *her* gaze always returned. *Dom.*

A *frisson* of desire and longing rippled through her. Damnation, that prudence and propriety had forced her to forgo tasting in full measure the bountiful passion that always simmered between them.

Then, as she recalled Lord Sayle's kissing her hand as he bid her goodbye, the observation struck her.

Not once around *him* had she felt that heated anticipation in the pit of the stomach she felt always when she was near Dominic Ransleigh.

The next afternoon, Theo returned to her aunt's house, refreshed after a long walk in Hyde Park with Charles and Constancia. There'd been ducks to feed on the Serpentine, a vendor selling meat pasties, and some beautiful high-stepping bays being exercised by a groom. Trotting back to the waiting carriage after the excursion, her son declared London not so bad a place after all.

After seeing him to his room, Theo returned to her own chamber. She'd just tidied her windblown hair when the butler came up to inform her that Lady Coghlane would like the pleasure of Theo's company for tea.

Knowing her aunt had conferred with a friend earlier that day, Theo returned the expected acceptance and walked to her aunt's sitting room, a sense of dread in her belly.

'Come in, my dear,' her aunt called, her smile brightening as she took in Theo's new gown in Prussian blue, done up with frogged fasteners, *à la* Hussar. 'Very fetching! Marston has done good work—although we must also visit the modiste tomorrow and let you choose some fashionable gowns of your own!'

'I do like the military style of this one. Although, if the evening gown I wore last night is an example of what's "fashionable", I'm going to go about feeling like I've joined the *demi-monde*!'

'Nonsense! Lady Serena's gown was lower in the bust than yours by a good two inches. But I didn't ask you here to discuss gowns, but something more important.'

'More important than gowns? Isn't that statement a sacrilege?'

'Almost,' her aunt agreed with a chuckle. 'But discussing your prospects *is* more important.'

Theo's humour evaporated instantly. Annoyed at the response, she told herself that since marriage was inevitable, she might as well begin looking on it more optimistically. *Think of the prize.* A whole childhood's worth of time to walk in the park, skip stones, eat meat pasties and watch high-stepping horses with her son.

'Very well,' she said with determined cheerfulness. 'What do your spies report?'

'I called on an old friend from our come-out days, Sally Jersey. She's one of the patronesses of Almack's, very well connected, and knows everyone. She'd already heard about your appearance at Jane's dinner, and confirmed that Lord Sayle is definitely interested.'

'Really, Aunt, how could she possibly know?'

'Oh, a comment to a friend at his club, overheard by a servant, who mentioned it to one of hers—she has her little informants all over town. Anyway, I think we can include him on the list.'

'There's a list?'

'Of course. I'd already begun compiling one, but wanted to get Sally's opinion.'

Theo shook her head. 'Sounds like preparation for a military campaign.'

'It is a campaign, of a sort. Finding the proper marriage partner always is, for a girl of your station.'

'No one just falls in love?' she asked, only half in jest.

Her aunt looked up, sympathy in her eyes. 'It does happen—but why not carefully cultivate the prospects, so if you *do* fall in love, the gentleman in question is suitable?'

'I suppose you're right,' Theo admitted. Not just anyone would do—she needed a husband with the same power and standing in the polite world as Lord Hazlett, if she hoped to keep Charles out of the hands of his grandparents. 'Very well, who's on the list?'

'Two widowers, Mr James Lloyd, very wealthy and well connected—his father was the Duke of Ingleston's youngest son. Lord Terrington, another baron with extensive property and a large motherless family, and Jeremy Carleton. He's not much older than you, an amusing rattle always welcome in company, much sought after for his charm and wit, but always evasive of marriage.'

'So why would he be interested in me?'

'All the loveliest, most accomplished girls have been

paraded before him—and he's shown not a bit of interest. When she twigged him about his elusiveness, Sally said he replied that all the girls were beautiful, sang and played delightfully—and were as boringly similar as if produced by the same sausage press. Sally thinks he'd be intrigued by someone different and unexpected.'

'I'm certainly that,' Theo said ruefully. 'Though if rather ungraciously comparing young ladies, who were doing their best to be pleasant company, to ground meat is a comment typical of his wit, we might end up at daggers drawn.'

'He probably said it to amuse Sally, that being the sort of naughty comment she likes.'

'Well, I wouldn't,' Theo said flatly.

'I suspect he'd soon figure that out, and accommodate his wit to your tastes.'

'Then I'd have to wonder whether he possessed any strong convictions of his own.'

Lady Coghlane raised an eyebrow. 'You'll certainly charm him if he prefers ladies being difficult.'

Theo blew out a sigh. 'I'm sorry, Aunt Amelia. I shall try to be more accommodating, and look for the positives in each proposed match. So, how do we begin the campaign? Ask them all to dinner and parade me around, like a horse at Tattersall's?'

'Since I know you're only funning, I'll not dignify that with a reply. Sally is giving a musicale tomorrow evening, and they should all be present—no one turns down an invitation from Lady Jersey! Having heard how unusual you are, I suspect she's as eager to meet you—and see how the gentlemen react to you—as I am for you to meet the gentlemen.'

'Wonderful,' Theo muttered. 'Now I get to perform under the eye of one of the most discriminating arbiters of the *ton*. Even in Portugal, everyone had heard of Lady Jersey.'

'Just be yourself, child. She will enjoy your natural wit. We'll have Marston prepare another gown for the musicale, but in the morning, we must definitely call on the modiste. After Sally's party, I expect you'll be engaged for some entertainment every night.'

Theo tried not to shudder at the prospect of spending every evening for the foreseeable future being trailed through the *ton* like a fat minnow on a hook until some acceptable gentleman bit. But Aunt Amelia was doing everything she could to assist her, and much as she yearned to flee back to Thornfield Place and don her well-worn habit, she should be grateful. 'Thank you, Aunt Amelia. My responses may not have reflected it, but I appreciate all your help.'

Lady Coghlane's gaze softened. 'I know it's hard for you, leaving your familiar world for one so foreign to you. I'll try to make entering this one as easy as I can.'

'I know you will,' Theo said, tears pricking at her eyes.

Her aunt patted her hand. 'Don't worry, child. I promise, you'll feel more confident once we get you properly outfitted and gowned.'

The awful vista rose before her of being measured and probed and pinned, then having to look at fabric and trimming and lace until her eyes glazed over. Reminding herself this was all for Charles, Theo swallowed hard and said, 'The dressmaker, tomorrow morning, whenever you are ready.'

She was sipping the last of her tea when the butler came in. 'A gentleman has called, Lady Coghlane. I told him it wasn't your usual day to receive visitors, but he insisted I inform you of his presence.'

Aunt Amelia turned to her with a triumphant expression. 'See! It begins already.' Looking back at the butler, she said, 'Which impatient gentleman has called, Foster?'

'Mr Dominic Ransleigh, my lady.'

Theo gasped, and Aunt Amelia gave her a significant look.

His doubtful gaze going from his mistress to her guest, the butler said, 'I hope I was correct in admitting him.'

'Yes, indeed, Foster,' Lady Coghlane said. 'The gentleman is Miss Branwell's neighbour in Suffolk. Tell him we'll join him directly.'

Chapter Seventeen

Impatient to see Miss Branwell, Dom paced the drawing room. Knowing it was impossible for his still-recovering body to ride as far as London, he'd been forced to hire post chaises, and the longer the trip dragged on, the more concerned and anxious he became. When the last hired carriage cracked a bow, delaying his arrival for hours, he'd been ready to grind his teeth in frustration. He'd finally reached London the previous night, far too late to call.

During the interminable journey, he'd had plenty of time to ponder the conundrum of Miss Branwell's unexpected decision to marry and consider what he might do about it. Though he'd not planned on taking so giant a step this soon, he *had* been toying for some time with the idea of courting her in earnest.

She was lovely, intelligent, unusual, and would never bore him. She'd infused him with a desire to do something important and exhibited total confidence that he would find such a calling—at a time when his own confidence in the future had been at a low ebb. It was thanks in large part to her avid interest in Bildenstone and her probing questions about the land and the estate that he'd started driving out, leading him to the idea of establishing a draught-horse-breeding operation.

And he'd never, ever, desired a woman with the intensity that he wanted her.

After interminable days of waiting, ready to explode with the urgency to discover the truth—and find out whether or not he'd be radically altering his future—Dom hadn't been about to let some starched shirt of a butler deny him entry. He was reasonably sure Miss Branwell, never one to fuss about dress, would join him immediately, even if not properly attired for receiving calls. Though if she didn't appear in the next few minutes, he'd quit the room and go looking for her.

Then he heard the whisper of moving hinges and looked towards the doorway. Miss Branwell entered, stopping him in mid-stride.

She looked radiant in a dark-blue gown with military trim, and she'd done something new to her hair. The glossy brown locks twisted and curled and framed her face in little ringlets that made those luminous brown eyes seem enormous. His mouth dried and for a long moment he could not take his gaze from her face.

She stared back just as fixedly, seeming to drink him in. That ever-present, instantaneous *something* sizzled in the air between them.

'Mr Ransleigh, how nice to see you again.' Lady Coghlane, whom in his total absorption with Miss Branwell, he'd not even noticed, walked over to extend her hand. 'I'm so pleased you decided to take me up on my offer of hospitality, though I didn't expect to see you in London this soon!'

He pulled himself together and retrieved his manners from wherever they'd gone missing. 'I came to town unexpectedly. Thank you for letting me in—even though your butler said you weren't receiving today.'

'We're always available to friends and neighbours, aren't we, my dear? As it happens, though, you've caught me at some correspondence I must finish. Theo, might I impose on you to entertain our guest? Perhaps a walk in the garden? It's such a fair afternoon.'

Throwing Lady Coghlane a look of gratitude, Dom said, 'A walk in the garden would be delightful. If you would indulge me, Miss Branwell?'

'Of c-course,' she stuttered, still looking unsettled.

As soon as he'd bowed Lady Coghlane out, she turned to him. 'What is it? Is something wrong at the school? Are any of the children hurt?'

'No, nothing like that,' he assured her, forgetting until that moment how concerned he'd been about *her* welfare when Jemmie turned up unannounced. 'Shall we walk?'

She exhaled a long breath. 'Now that my heart has commenced beating again, I think I can manage it. I'll even be able to contain my curiosity over what brought you to London until we get outside, out of earshot.'

He offered his arm and she took it. *Ah,* he thought, closing his eyes to savour the delicious thrill that tingled through him at the touch of her hand. She must have felt it, too, for she inhaled sharply and looked up at him, her dark eyes wide.

Realising she was staring, she blushed a little and said, 'It's good to see you again, Mr Ransleigh. Even better, now that I know none of the children are in danger.'

He was the one in danger, Dom thought as he led her to the town-house garden. Thank goodness servants lurked behind every overlooking window, else the minute he got her out the door, he might have succumbed to the ever-present urge to kiss her.

'How was your journey?' she was asking him. 'You didn't ride, did you?'

'Can't quite manage that yet,' he replied. 'I came post.'

'You appear refreshed. Your arm didn't pain you overmuch?'

'No more than always. I have to admit, I made rather liberal use of the laudanum last night.'

'Now, since you're well accustomed to my directness, may I skip further pleasantries and ask why you've come to London? You mentioned nothing before you left Bildenstone beyond a trip to Newmarket and a visit to Holkham.'

'I hadn't planned on coming. Until I was told the rather astonishing news that you'd suddenly conceived an urgent desire to marry. So urgent, you abandoned the school and headed for your aunt's house with hardly a word to anyone. Jemmie was most upset.'

'You've visited the school,' she guessed, colouring.

'Why the sudden wish to marry? I've no claim upon you that would make such a personal matter my business, but you are my tenant, a condition which would certainly be altered by your marriage. Besides, I seem to recall when we discussed wedlock, you declared yourself firmly against it, saying something like "only desperation would drive you to it"? Have you just lost your fortune on the 'Change? Do you need me to spot you a loan to secure the school?'

She smiled a little, but her eyes had gone bleak.

'No, my fortune is intact.' She dropped his arm and took a step away, then halted, looking back at him. 'I was going to try to fob you off with some plausible excuse, but I'm a terrible liar. You already know some of the worst about me, so I might as well tell you the rest.'

'I would very much like to know why you've had such a radical change of heart. There's always been honesty between us, which I prize, just as I admire your frankness and ability to face facts as they are, free of wishful imagining. And I think it goes without saying that whatever you tell me will be held in strictest confidence.'

'Only one thing I must insist on before I tell you,' she said, her expression almost...defensive. 'I believe you've developed a fondness for the school and the children. Despite what you may think of me, will you pledge to help safeguard them?'

'Nothing you reveal could alter my regard and admiration—but if you insist, yes, you have my promise.'

'Very well,' she said, and took a deep breath. 'You remember Audley Tremaine, who visited me at the school?'

Distaste and irritation stirred. 'The man you wouldn't let me pummel. How could I forget?'

'After I refused his…disreputable offer, he threatened to reveal something he'd just discovered. I tried to mask my concern by asserting no one ever believed what he said. Well, I was wrong.'

She looked suddenly weary and heartsick. Dom had the strongest urge to wrap his arm around her and enfold her against his chest. Resisting it, he said, 'What had he discovered?'

'Tremaine was acquainted with Lord Everly and his wife, Alicia, and knew them both to be dark-haired and dark-eyed. That day at the school, he got a close look at Charles, who is, obviously, blond and green-eyed. As was my fiancé, Marshall. Putting two and two together, Tremaine concluded that Charles wasn't Lord Everly's son, he was Marshall's. And mine. He must have gone straight from Suffolk to Viscount Hazlett's estate, for the day you left for Newmarket, I had an unexpected visitor. Lady Hazlett arrived, wanting to meet Charles. And telling me she intended to take him away with her.'

Dom felt like he'd just been dealt a roundhouse blow to the chest. 'Charles is…*your* son?'

Miss Branwell lifted her chin and turned back to face him squarely. 'Yes. I had made it known that Alicia became too ill to finish the journey to Lisbon, so we had to stay at the convent until the birth of her child. But I was ill, too, having only just discovered I was increasing when I got the news that Marshall had been killed. We both gave birth there. Her child died; mine survived. When I brought Charles back with me, intending to confess my shame, Everly's commander assumed the infant was Everly's. Seeing a way to keep Charles from being branded a bastard, I didn't correct him.'

Dom shook his head, still trying to wrap his mind around the astounding fact. 'No one else knew, or suspected? Not even your father?'

'Constancia knew, of course. Widowed by the war, she'd taken shelter at the convent with an ailing child who later died. She agreed to accompany me as Charles's nurse. But no one else knew.'

She paced away from the house, away from him, down the small *allée* of trees. As he followed, the full horror of the situation she'd found herself in slowly registered: her fiancé dying…finding herself unwed…increasing…the prospect of the shame, scandal, and the inevitable banishment from polite society she would endure once the truth became known. The child of the man she loved branded a bastard for ever—and nothing she could do to prevent it.

Heaven have mercy, how alone and frightened and desperate she must have been!

Reaching the back garden wall, unable to go further, Miss Branwell halted. Turning to him, anguish in her eyes, she said, 'I wish now that I had followed the dictates of conscience and revealed Charles's true parentage from the first. Papa would have been shamed and embarrassed, but he was a soldier, and had faced worse. Forfeiting his respect and good opinion would have been terribly painful, but my conduct deserved his disdain. Now, unless I take some immediate remedy to prevent it, my irresponsible behaviour threatens me not just with the loss of my son, but the possibility of incurring such censure I might have to close the school, or risk making it impossible for my orphans to find respectable positions when they leave it.

Ruining a number of lives, instead of just two. Only one remedy can prevent all that. Marriage.'

Dom tried to quell the thousand questions running through his head and concentrate only on the important one. 'Why is marriage the remedy?'

'I induced Lady Hazlett to agree that, if I wed a man of substance who can provide the same social advantages for Charles the viscount would—a man of discernment to model himself after, one with the proper connections to introduce Charles at university, in his clubs, and those masculine domains necessary to a gentleman's life—she would allow me keep Charles and uphold the lie that he is Everly's. If the Hazletts support the story of Charles's parentage I have always put forth, Tremaine's version won't be given any credence.'

'What of Lord Everly's father, the Marquess? What if he should change his mind and decide to recognise the boy?'

'Lady Hazlett thinks it unlikely. As do I, at this late date. The Marquess has an heir, several other sons and a number of grandchildren. Lady Hazlett's are the only conditions that matter. And so I must marry. I cannot lose Charles. '

Dom stood silent for a long moment, mulling over what she'd told him. Though Jemmie's alarm had been sincere, he'd discounted the boy's account as over-dramatic, thinking there was probably some more rational explanation for Theo's sudden departure.

But analysing the dilemma after knowing the truth, he had to admit he could not come up with any better remedy than an immediate marriage. 'With the grandparents insisting the boy must be raised as a gentleman *by* a gentleman, there doesn't appear to be any alternative.'

Then he girded himself to ask the only other question that had bedevilled him on the long journey to London.

'Had you someone in mind to marry when you left for London?'

'No. I'm trusting Aunt Amelia to help me find someone suitable. I'll take any gentleman who will accept Charles, serve as his mentor and keep our secret. Most likely some widower needing a new mother for his brood, or an older man wanting a nursemaid.'

Huge relief filled Dom. *So there was no secret admirer waiting in the wings; he could take centre stage himself.* 'Someone who seeks only a governess or a nurse? You'd be bored and miserable within six months.'

'What I feel doesn't matter, as long as I can have Charles and keep the school safe. Which brings me to that favour I mentioned. Even if Aunt Amelia works her miracle and finds a gentleman who'll accept me, it's quite possible he will not allow me to continue running the school. If that happens, would you watch over it for me until I can make other arrangements?'

She gazed imploringly up at him, looking taut as an overstrung bow ready to snap. Incorrectly interpreting his continued silence as disapproval, she continued. 'Think what it would mean if you were threatened with losing one of your cousins—like Will, who nursed you for months after you were wounded. Wouldn't you do whatever you had to, in order to prevent that? What is boredom and dissatisfaction compared to losing someone so dear to you?'

She was trembling, tears hovering in corners of her eyes. 'Please?' she added in a whisper.

No longer able to restrain himself, Dom took her hand and kissed it, the decision already made somewhere on the road to London. 'I can do that, and more. Why not marry me? My family and connections pass muster, you can keep Charles and manage the school. You won't be bored, and—' he ran a finger over her lips '—I can guarantee you won't be miserable. In fact, I think I can quite confidently promise…delight.'

'Oh, Dom,' she whispered, a few tears spilling over to slip down her cheek. To his joy and relief, she closed her eyes and leaned into him. He pulled her against him, wrapping her in his warmth and strength, cradling her as he breathed in her delicate violet scent.

Just as he was about to tell her not to worry, he would always be there to take care of her, she gave a little gasp and pushed him away.

'Oh, no, I couldn't marry you!'

Taken aback, he said, 'Why not? I haven't a title, but I have a large and well-connected family. My uncle's an earl; in fact, I seem to recall that Viscount Hazlett is part of my uncle's coalition in the Lords. I can guarantee to raise Charles as befits a gentleman and assure him entry into whatever career he wants.'

'No, no, it isn't that! Your background is perfect, and I know you care for the children.' She looked up at him, a few more tears dripping down, distress on her face. 'You're—you're too nice, and I like you too much!'

He stared back at her. 'I've heard of unions between parties who cordially detest each other, but I'd never heard of *liking* being a barrier to marriage.'

'It's not that. Oh, I'm making a muddle of this.' She took a deep breath, obviously trying to recover her composure. 'When you like someone, you want the best for them. So I couldn't allow you to be dragged into a marriage, just because I'm caught in a predicament of my own making.'

Relieved, he smiled at her. Dear Theo, trying to 'protect' him as she did her orphans. 'Don't you think I have presence of mind enough to make that decision myself?'

'I think you are brave, and compassionate, and wonderfully generous! But you've only recently ended an engagement—too recently to be pressed into making another. And you yourself admit you haven't yet figured out what you mean to do with your life. How could I let you tie yourself to something and someone who will be of no help to you in whatever endeavour you finally decide to pursue?'

'Just because you will be running the school doesn't mean I can't pursue other options,' he argued. 'In fact, if the breeding operation I'm envisioning comes to fruition, the focus of my business will be in Suffolk, headquartered at Bildenstone Hall. Besides, don't you always quote your father, something about nothing being certain and having to make the best choice as the battle rages? Adapt to conquer?'

She looked at him reprovingly. 'It's not fair to use my father against me.'

He'd not been anticipating resistance—swift and grateful acceptance, really. At the shock of realising she might actually refuse him, feelings of protest and dismay welled up, along with a desire to make her his wife that was much stronger than he'd expected.

'Besides,' she was continuing, 'what if you fall in love? I have loved someone completely, utterly, madly. It's wonderful and magical and I wouldn't want you to miss that.' She grimaced. 'Nor would I want to be your wife when you fell in love with someone else.'

'How long did it take you to recover from losing your fiancé?'

A shadow crossed her eyes. 'One never completely gets over it.'

'Just so.' He nodded. 'My cousin Alastair was completely, utterly, madly in love with a woman who jilted him practically at the altar. Devastated, he joined the army, determined to die gloriously in battle, or some such rot. He survived the war, but he's never truly got over her. So if that's what being madly in love is, I'd just as soon not experience it. Why can we not be *sanely* in love? Isn't friendship and shared interests and compatibility of mind a much sounder basis for a union meant to be happy over a lifetime? And what of this?'

Stepping forward, he drew her to him and feathered kisses from her ear down her throat to the neckline of her gown. 'This,' he murmured as she sagged against him, 'is also unique, this connection between us.'

'C-can't base a marriage on that,' she whispered disjointedly.

'I think it an excellent basis,' he said, gratified that he had to steady her on her feet. 'We've tried to ignore the attraction—but it burns between us whenever we're together. You feel it, too, don't you?'

'Yes,' she admitted.

'I've never experienced anything stronger. I think it will last a long, long time, binding us together. Making us one.'

He kissed her then, a soft, glancing brush of his lips against hers. Then exulted, desire coursing through him, when she immediately opened her mouth, sought his tongue, and wrapped her arms around his neck. Kissing him back with passion and also, he thought, anxiety and fear and relief.

After a few moments, breathing hard, he broke the kiss. 'So marry me, Theo.'

She shook her head dazedly. 'I can't think when you kiss me like that.'

'Thinking is highly overrated.'

'But marriage would be for ever! There'd be no trial period, like I proposed for the school, during which you could reconsider and toss me and the children out. You shouldn't make such an important decision so hastily.'

'I've had time to consider it.'

'How could you? I've only just explained the situation!'

'Jemmie found me at Holkham. In fact,' he added with

a smile, 'he practically ordered me to come to London and sort this out.'

'Jemmie ordered you!' she gasped, her cheeks flaming red. 'Oh, the…the rascal! I'll strangle him for this!'

'It was enlightened self-interest. He knows I like the children and the school, and if you married, a new husband might not.'

'I'm still going to strangle him.'

'He also said he knew I liked you—and that after we'd been together, you seemed happier than he'd seen you since your father died. I'd like to go on making you happy. Won't you let me? Not to mention, we don't want to let Jemmie and the others down.'

The struggle played out over her expressive face. Attraction, affection, and the strong connection that went beyond the physical pulling them together; opposing that, her fierce sense of honour insisting she not allow him to make such an important decision so precipitously, badly as she needed his help.

Had he ever met a woman so brave—or so stubborn? Then a niggle of doubt crept in.

'Am *I* pressing *you* too hard? Would you truly prefer to marry one of the prospects your aunt lines up?'

'There's no one I'd rather marry,' she blurted, sending another flurry of relief through him. 'But,' she added, biting her lip, 'my wishes are not important.'

'Why?' He looked at her curiously. A disquieting notion occurred, and he frowned. 'You don't really think you should marry a man you don't love or even like and be miserable for the rest of life as some sort of penance for the mistake of conceiving a child out of wedlock?' At the slight alteration of her expression, he said, 'Great Heaven, I'm afraid you might! Not that I can speak for the Almighty, but surely God forgave you for that sin long ago. You need to forgive yourself, and think seriously about what would make you, not just stoically endure, not just be content, but happy.' He drew her back against him. 'Delirious, even.'

He kissed her again, harder, deeper this time, until they were both dizzy and gasping for breath.

'Marry me, Theo,' he urged, brushing his mouth over hers.

She nuzzled into him, whimpering.

'Was that a "yes"?'

'I—I don't know! My senses are swimming and my mind doesn't know up from down. C-come back tomorrow, and I'll answer you then.'

He set her on her feet. 'I'll come back tomorrow. And ask you again. And kiss you again. Count on it.' With that, he bowed and walked away, his heart pounding, desire pulsing through his veins.

That he wanted her more than ever was no surprise. That he wanted so badly for her to marry him was.

After that last kiss, however, he was feeling pretty confident that he was going to be satisfied on both counts.

Chapter Eighteen

Theo watched her erstwhile fiancé stride down the garden path until he was lost from sight. Her senses still tingling from his kisses, she tottered to a bench and sat down hard.

She ought to pinch herself. Dominic Ransleigh—'Dandy Dom', formerly society's darling who had snagged a duke's daughter for a bride—couldn't have just asked *her* to marry him.

Could he?

She took long, slow breaths, trying to settle her agitated body and calm her disordered mind. What, exactly, had he told her?

That Jemmie had tracked him down to inform him about her abrupt departure from Thornfield. She really should strangle the boy when she got back, she thought with a sigh.

That Jemmie knew she liked Dom, and Dom liked her. She felt a flush of embarrassment heat her cheeks.

Obviously they hadn't masked their mutual attraction as well as she'd thought.

After the acute discomfort of Lady Staunton's dinner, and with the prospect of a series of equally uncomfortable evenings to come, she'd had to resist the urge to throw herself on Dom and accept him immediately. But she'd paid a high price once for making a decision of enormous consequence without careful reflection, and she'd not do so again.

Still, how great a contrast between the excitement and sense of safety she'd felt, just seeing Dom standing in her aunt's drawing room, and the dread with which she viewed having to entertain other potential suitors—even the accommodating Lord Sayle.

She was far more comfortable around him than she'd been with any other man since Marshall, and had been from their first meeting. Feeling *at home* in the heart of one's home was a valuable thing. Plus, they shared a love of books, horses, and a common interest in the children and their futures.

Marrying him would certainly meet the criteria required by Lady Hazlett. She'd gain an incomparable role model for her son and the support of Dom's well-connected family when it came time for Charles to attend university and choose a vocation.

She could return to the countryside she much preferred, get back to running her school—and have Dominic Ransleigh at her side and in her bed.

Ah, how often had images of heated encounters between them invaded her dreams! Accept him, and she'd no longer have to resist the desire he aroused so effortlessly. After awakening many nights in the dark, afire with longing, she'd be able to follow through on all her erotic imaginings, with the right to explore every glorious inch of his body and discover every possible way to bring them delight.

It was several moments before she could drag her mind from those enticing possibilities back to cold, hard reality.

He didn't love her, and in marrying him, she'd deprive him of the chance to fall in love—or risk turning into the duty wife of a man smitten with another woman. Wincing at the unpleasant possibility, she concluded that boredom or outright misery would be preferable.

Plus, marriage should be an equal bargain. He offered her salvation from an untenable situation, but what did she bring him, save a school full of problems and the possibility that an unsavoury old scandal might one day pop up out of the box into which her lies had crammed it and shock his world, like some evil grinning jack-in-the-box?

Was she, on some unconscious level, pushing herself towards an unhappy marriage as a penance for her sins, as he'd alleged? There might be more truth to that charge than she'd like to admit.

Or was her reluctance, as she hoped, based more on high principle—not allowing him to sacrifice himself in a cause not his own. Though, as he'd argued, he was a man grown, making this choice of his own free will. She had no right to keep him from making it.

Though she had every right to refuse, if after sober analysis she deemed the benefits he offered did not outweigh the risks of marrying a man she could all too easily fall in love with.

For she had to admit—if only to herself—that she more than *liked* Dominic Ransleigh. All the reasons that made it so attractive to accept his hand, made it far too easy to go from liking to *loving* him. Hadn't she promised herself, after the total devastation of Marshall's death, she would never, ever put herself at risk for that kind of desolation again?

The possibilities of loss were more than just having him fall for another woman. True, with the war over, she needn't fear losing him in battle. But there were still fevers and carriage accidents and any manner of dangers that could snatch away one's beloved.

Then she had to laugh at herself. Had the girl who once had been sublimely unconcerned about sending a soldier off to battle now become prey to such alarm she must worry about every ghostie, goblin, and terror that whispered in the dark?

All she knew for sure was she very much wanted to marry Dominic Ransleigh—and that she very much feared doing so would be a huge mistake.

Unable to resolve the matter, she jumped up in disgust and headed back to the house.

Aunt Amelia would want to know what they had discussed, and she'd have to come up with something glib to fob her off. She could not bear revealing her conflicted feelings for Dominic Ransleigh to anyone, even her sympathetic aunt. Who, in any event, would be certain to dismiss any reservations she might have and urge her to get Dom leg-shackled before he changed his mind.

First, she had to make up hers.

Mercifully, she had the rest of the evening and all night to wrestle with it.

Next morning, in the wake of a mostly sleepless night, Theo could hardly recall what tale she'd spun for her aunt or how they'd spent the rest of the evening. Pleading a very real headache, she'd taken herself off to bed early, only to toss and turn as the clock struck through the hours. *Marry or not, marry or not,* its steady tick seemed to taunt her.

It wasn't fair, she thought, sitting in bed in the pale morning light, clutching a cooling cup of chocolate she would gag on if she tried to sip it. Wanting him too much couldn't be good, could it? It would be so easy to fall in love with him—and therein lay disaster.

She knew he'd be here soon, expecting the answer she'd promised. The butterflies in her stomach turned to swallows, swooping and diving against her ribs.

Would she be giving in to her sensual self against her better judgement if she accepted?

Yet, accepting him would solve her problem immediately, making it much less likely that Tremaine could cause any more damage. Thereby safeguarding the school, and giving Charles the most wonderful mentor she could ask for.

Shouldn't protecting herself from the dangers of falling in love be her own task—her peace of mind in avoiding that possibility less important than the security of Charles and her orphans?

Susan arrived with her gown, and had just helped her into it when a knock sounded at the door.

'Mr Ransleigh is here again,' the butler informed her with a frown. 'I told him it was much too early to call upon a lady, but he insisted.'

The swallows swooped through another circuit. Placing a hand on her stomach, she said, 'Yes, I was expecting him.'

His disapproving glance now settling on her for having encouraged such a breach of decorum, he said, 'Very well. I shall inform him you'll be down directly.'

A few minutes later, Theo slipped quietly into the room. Dom stood by the window, gazing into the garden, tapping one booted foot impatiently. She took in the tousled blond locks, the noble profile, the tall, broad-shouldered torso, no longer so thin. *This man may soon be my husband,* she thought with a sense of wonder.

Then he turned and spied her, and every nerve in her body vibrated with awareness. 'Good morning, Mr Ransleigh,' she said, hardly able to get the words out of her tight throat.

He paced over, pulled her against him, and kissed her fiercely. Fuelled by lust and terror, she kissed him back just as hard.

Finally he broke away, still binding her against him with his one good arm. Gazing at her intently, he said, 'Was that a yes?'

She hesitated, still unsure of her answer. She truly hadn't decided before she walked into the room what she was going to do, her thoughts and emotions having yawed wildly back and forth from 'yes' to 'no' since he'd left her yesterday.

His fierce gaze softening, he cupped her cheek with his good hand. 'Do you trust me, Theo? To watch out for you, and protect you, and cherish you?'

That question, she had no trouble answering. 'Yes, I trust you.'

'As I trust you, to watch out for and protect and cherish me. Is there anything else more important than that?'

Her lips trembling, she shook her head.

'Then, Theo, will you marry me?'

With his touch gentle and his voice tender and his bright blue gaze fixed on her face with affection and concern, she said the only thing possible.

'Yes, Dom, I will marry you.'

With a cry of triumph, he hauled her close and kissed her again. Finally releasing her, he said, 'We *will* be happy, Theo, I promise you! Now, shall I go and inform your aunt?'

Having now committed herself, Theo felt a succession of conflicting emotions rush through her—excitement, elation, anticipation, desire, doubt, fear. It was all she could do to say, 'Not now. She'll be abed for hours yet.'

'When and where do you wish to wed? With the need to resolve Charles's position, it's probably best to make it soon. I can ride to Doctors' Commons and procure a special licence, and we could marry whenever you wish. Here, at your aunt's house, or back in Suffolk. Unless you'd prefer to wait to establish residency so we could wed at St George's in Hanover Square?'

'Soon, in this house, would be best,' she confirmed.

'I'll be off, then, and call on your aunt later.' Gently he

took her chin again and angled her head up, his good eye searching her face. 'Are you sure? You won't change your mind later, feeling you were coerced into this?'

She laughed feebly. 'Shouldn't I be asking you that?'

He grinned, the eye patch making him look positively piratical. 'I'm getting what I want. Or I will be soon. Ah, what a wedding night I anticipate!' He drew one finger across her lips.

Yearning ignited in its wake. 'How long do we have to wait?'

His grin broadened. 'I'll try to make it as short as possible.' He gave her another quick kiss. 'I'll see you this afternoon.'

With a purposeful stride, he went out…leaving Theo frozen, a hand to her trembling lips, torn between elation and terror.

Exultant, Dom practically danced out of the parlour. Until the very last minute, he wasn't sure Theo was actually going to accept him—and somewhere over the course of the last few days, it had become terribly important to him that she did. Strangely enough for so important a step, and one he'd not seriously considered until very recently, the idea of marrying her seemed so natural and right, he'd had not a single second thought from the moment he decided to propose.

He'd make sure she never regretted accepting him, either, he vowed. Living with and loving Theo—ah, especially making love to Theo—was going to be an entertaining life's business. He couldn't wait to begin.

Ticking off in his mind all he needed to do to put together a wedding with the least possible delay, Dom paced towards the entry door. He had little doubt Theo's aunt would enthusiastically approve their plans, especially given the delicacy of her niece's position.

Then it suddenly occurred to him that for his marriage with Theo to be a success, one other important person must approve their union. Stopping short so quickly the footman escorting him out nearly ran into him, he turned to the servant and said, 'Before I go, I'd like to speak to Master Charles. Would you show me to his room, please?'

Whatever the footman thought about escorting a visitor who'd arrived far too early up to the room of a person who generally did not receive guests, he merely blinked and motioned Dom to follow him. A few minutes later, he gestured towards the open doorway of a third-floor bedchamber. 'He's in there, sir.'

'Thank you. I can find my own way out.'

As the servant retreated down the hallway, Dom moved to the doorway.

Peeking in, he noted the maid, Constancia, in a wing chair, bent over some sewing, and Charles by the window, sunlight glowing on his fair curls as he repositioned an array of toy soldiers in rows before him.

Dom watched for a moment, curious about this child who meant so much, his mother had been ready to sacrifice her own happiness to keep him. *What would you do if you were threatened with losing one of your cousins...wouldn't you do whatever you had to, in order to prevent that?*

That argument he could understand—losing Will or Max or Alastair would be unthinkable.

Tapping on the doorframe, he said, 'May I come in?'

Charles looked over to the newcomer, his face brightening. 'Mr Ransleigh!' he cried. 'Have you come to take us home?'

Clever boy, Dom thought. Nodding a greeting to the maid as he entered, he replied, 'I thought I might. Would you like that?'

'Oh, yes! London is big and noisy and there are some very nice horses in the park, but I like Thornfield better.

And I miss Georgie and Jemmie and even stupid Maria. Will we go soon?'

Dom walked over and knelt down, so his face was level with the boy's. 'It should be very soon. Before we go, though, Charles, I wish to ask you something. I want to marry Miss Theo.' Ignoring a gasp from the maid, he continued. 'When we get back, you'd both come and live with me at Bildenstone Hall. Would that be all right with you?'

The child paused, considering him. 'Could we still go to the school?'

'Every day, probably.'

'Will I still get my pony?'

Ah, the things of importance to a child. 'Did Miss Theo promise you a pony?'

'After my papa's friend visited us at Thornfield, she did.'

'You mean Lady Hazlett?'

Charles considered the matter for a moment before giving an affirmative shake of the head. 'She said it was time for me to have a pony, like my papa did at my age.'

So the grandmother's blackmail began immediately, he thought. 'Of course you may have a pony. But you will have to learn to ride him properly.'

'Oh, I will!' he exclaimed, his eyes wide with excitement. 'Will you teach me? Jemmie says you are a s'perior horseman. I think it means you ride well.'

'Yes, I'll teach you,' he said, agreeing upon the instant—his first obligation as mentor to Theo's son. Oddly enough, he found himself looking forward to the task. 'Riding well is an important skill for a gentleman.'

Charles nodded. 'Miss Theo says I have to learn to be a proper gentleman, like her papa and mine. They both died in the war.'

'I'm sorry.'

The boy studied him again. 'Jemmie says Miss Theo

likes you, and Jemmie knows everything. Maybe if you marry her, she'll smile more. I like it when she smiles.'

The memory swooped in: Theo after their gallop, laughing in delight, impulsively embracing him. 'I like it, too.'

'Do you like to play soldiers?' the boy asked, gesturing towards the lead figures arranged before him.

'Mr Ransleigh was a soldier,' Constancia inserted. 'He fought in the same war as Miss Theo's papa.'

Charles's interest intensified. 'You were a soldier, too? Will you tell me about it?'

A sudden flurry of images filled his head: smoke, flame, the cacophony of rifle, musket and artillery fire, the yells of the charge, the screams of the wounded. With a shudder, he shook them off. 'Some of it.'

'Can you show me the battles, where the soldiers were? I have General Wellington, General Blücher, and lots of cavalrymen!'

'I could help you arrange the men and explain tactics. Battles are all about tactics, you know.' *As is life,* he thought.

'You can marry Miss Theo, then. Can it be quick? I'm ready to go home.'

'It's a bargain.' Dom held out a hand, and the boy extended his, taking Dom's and shaking it firmly. 'When we get back to Bildenstone, I'll show you the battles. I must go now, but I'll see you later, Charles.'

''Bye, Mr Ransleigh,' the boy said, turning back to his soldiers.

'You are truly to be wed, Senhor Ransleigh?' the maid asked softly as Dom turned to walk out.

'Yes, Constancia. As soon as it can be arranged.'

'Good.' She nodded approvingly. 'You will be kind to Miss Theo, yes? She has suffered much.' She made an oblique glance towards the child. 'She needs a man who will treat her as she deserves.'

'I hope to make her very happy.'

Constancia regarded him steadily. 'See that you do.'

Feeling that he was going to be watched on several fronts, Dom quit the room. How amused his cousins would be, he thought with a smile as he paced down the stairs, when he told them he owed the winning of approval for his suit to his knowledge of the battles they'd fought and his ability to teach riding.

Chapter Nineteen

Four days later, Theo nervously smoothed the skirt of her new Pomona-green gown, watching the clock on the mantel tick closer to the time when she must go down to her aunt's parlour and be married.

Married. The idea still made her stomach clench, sending eddies of trepidation and excitement through her.

She wasn't where she'd expected to be, or feeling how she'd expected to feel when about to plight her troth. It should have been at the English embassy in Lisbon, the wedding breakfast afterwards thronged with army friends and their families who'd relocated to Portugal for the duration of the war. Awaiting her should have been Marshall in his dashing cavalry tunic, attended by his squadron mates, and her father, solemn in full dress uniform, ready to give her away.

All that seemed like a hazy dream from a faraway world. That younger Theo, so completely in love and absolutely confident of the future, was gone too, lost somewhere along the rocky trail from an isolated convent in the Portuguese hills.

The man waiting downstairs, though, was no less worthy of her faith, affection and trust than Marshall. How many women were lucky enough to find two such paragons? If it came to it, she probably knew Dom better than she'd known Marshall, given a whirlwind courtship in the middle of a war. She and Dom had ridden together, walked together, sharing their interests and discussing problems at a length and leisure not possible in an army on the march. Marriage might be the fearful unknown, but she had no doubt whatsoever of the sterling character of the man she was about to marry—even if she still harboured unsettling doubts about the wisdom of marrying him.

Aunt Amelia, though, had been unabashedly delighted when Dom had called, soliciting her permission to wed her niece. He'd set her laughing, telling her he was relieved she'd agreed, else he'd just wasted a great deal of blunt on a special licence.

Her thrilled aunt, insisting Theo must have a new gown of her very own in which to be married, had carried her off to the modiste that very afternoon. A half-finished dress of green shot through with gold caught her eye and was fitted to her immediately. She thought it flattering, and Aunt Amelia, Susan and Constancia all agreed.

She hoped Dom would think so.

Constancia and Charles walked in, startling her out of her reverie. 'Your new dress is pretty, Miss Theo!' Charles said. 'Why did I have to get new nankeens? They're scratchy, and I like my old ones better.'

'A special occasion calls for festive clothes, and the trousers will soften,' Theo said. 'I will only be married once.' *Dear Lord, may this not be a mistake!*

While Charles wandered to the window, eager to inspect the horses traversing the lane, Constancia took her hand. 'Senhor Ransleigh is a good man, Miss Theo. He will take care of you and the boy. This have I prayed for since we left Mary Santo das Montanhas.'

Dom *was* a good man. It made loving him harder to resist, but at the same time quelled that part of her nervousness which stemmed from putting herself in the hands of a man not her father.

A husband held so many rights over a wife, including ownership of all her wealth. Sensitive to that, the day after she accepted his proposal, Dom insisted they consult her father's solicitor and have papers prepared *before* the wedding that would place in trust for Charles all the properties she wanted him to have and set aside a good portion of her inheritance in separate funds for Charles, the school, and her own personal use—all of it untouchable by a husband.

When she protested that made it sound like she didn't trust him, he reminded her that once married, the law gave her no further control over her property—and if anything happened to him, those assets would go to *his* heirs, administered by a solicitor who would look to *their* interests—not those of her or Charles.

Though there wouldn't be time to complete the complicated process before the wedding, he'd also insisted the solicitor begin setting up the jointure and settlement agreements she would receive out of his own funds in the event he predeceased her.

'Not that I have any plans of shuffling off this mortal coil,' he assured her. 'I didn't live through all that pain and suffering to trade this for a halo yet—not when the best part of surviving is about to begin.'

Waggling his eyebrow roguishly, he placed tickling little kisses on her hand that made her laugh and relax, for the moment, the tension within her that coiled tighter and tighter as the wedding approached.

No, she had no qualms about the character of man she was marrying. Just the institution itself—and the difficulties of keeping her emotions in check when living so close to the mesmerising Dominic Ransleigh.

One problem at a time, she told herself. First, she needed to formally settle her arrangement with the Hazletts.

Though too anxious about the school to want to delay their return to Suffolk by taking a wedding journey, she had agreed to remain in London a few days by themselves to settle into their new relationship. The best way not to worry about the ramifications of that relationship, she figured, was to spend that time enjoying the sensual freedom marriage would give them.

Now, *that* prospect she could view with enthusiasm.

After another knock, a beaming Aunt Amelia swept in. 'It's time, Theo, dear. How lovely you look!'

'I'll never be the beauteous daughter of a duke, but I hope I'll do,' she replied ruefully.

'You'll be yourself, and that's what Dominic Ransleigh wanted,' Aunt Amelia assured her.

I hope so, she thought as the small group descended the stairs.

As she entered the parlour, her eyes went immediately to Dom, who stood next to the priest and a gentleman in a Dragoon's uniform she didn't recognise. Dom, too, had the erect bearing of a soldier. But instead of colourful regimentals, he wore a black jacket over a cream waistcoat and black trousers, the jacket perfectly fitted, the sheen of the fabric elegant, and all of it looking spanking new, as if he'd just returned from his tailor. *'Dandy Dom' indeed,* she thought, awe and attraction rippling through her.

Then he saw her. A smile lighting his face, he murmured something to the priest, his gaze never leaving hers as he walked over to take her hand and kiss it. 'How lovely you look! Is that a new gown? I like it.'

'You're looking rather fine yourself. Did you fit in a visit to Bond Street?'

Dom laughed. 'I'm not sure whether my tailor was more gratified to receive a new order or horrified at trying to make a garment for a man with one arm that still fit to his standards of perfection.'

'He succeeded. Though you look equally splendid in an old hunting jacket.'

'You didn't seem so impressed when you met me that first day in the lane.'

'You were thinner then, and tired. Now you're…not.'

'I can't wait to show you how much I'm…not,' he murmured, before turning her towards the soldier who'd followed him. 'Who'd have thought I'd come to such an important day with all my cousins scattered who knows where? Even my uncle, who practically lives at the Lords, is out of town. I had to scour the clubs to find a friend to stand up with me. Miss Branwell, may I present Lieutenant Tom Wetherby, another stout member of the Royals.'

'Delighted, ma'am,' the Dragoon said, bowing. 'I'd kiss your hand, but Dom would skewer me with my sabre.'

Before she could reply, the priest waved to them. 'Time to take our places,' the lieutenant said, and ushered them back to the prelate.

Dom squeezed her suddenly trembling hand in his warm one. 'Trust me, Theo?' he murmured as he led her over.

'Y-yes.'

'Smile, then. You're supposed to be the happy bride— not a prisoner on the way to the guillotine. You'll have our guests think you don't really want to marry me.'

'I must smile, then. I can't have them thinking you anything but the most compassionate, understanding, helpful gentleman I've ever known,' she added, annoyingly close to tears.

'And wise. You could add wise. Witty, well read, liberal-minded.' He lowered his voice to a mock-seductive range and bent to whisper at her ear, 'And devastatingly attractive.'

'Modest, too,' she added with a chuckle, her nerves settling, as surely he'd meant them to. 'And altogether wonderful.'

And he was. She must do all she could to see he never

regretted taking up the cudgels in defence of his too-tall, too-opinionated, problem-encumbered spinster tenant.

Over the next few moments, they intoned the ancient words of the wedding service, Dom placed a plain band on her finger, and the priest pronounced them man and wife. When her perplexed expression afterward protested the kiss of the new bride that was practically chaste, he murmured, 'Wait until later.'

Then it was off to sign the parish register and into the dining room, where Aunt Amelia had assembled a bountiful repast for a small group of family and a few of her closest friends.

One of those turned out to be the formidable Lady Jersey, who cut her from the crowd and drew her away with the expertise of a Lake country sheepdog managing his herd. Leaning close, she murmured, 'I shall congratulate you, even though you cheated me of the amusement of watching you lead the suitors Amelia and I had chosen a merry dance! But I can't complain; you've pulled off a coup. Only a man as high in the instep as the Duke of Dunham would think his daughter could do better than a Ransleigh. No matter; I've invited the duke and the daughter to dine next week. I can't wait to share the details of your nuptials.'

She swept away to attach herself to the Dragoon, leaving Theo immensely relieved she'd got herself married before she was pulled into that lady's web of intrigue.

Still, as the afternoon wore on, she became increasingly anxious for the party to end. Her cheeks ached from smiling, her head ached from giving polite replies to congratulations and turning evasive answers to those brash enough to enquire about the brevity of their courtship. Dom had abandoned her to play the perfect bridegroom, circulating among the society ladies Aunt Amelia had invited, parcelling out attention equally, keeping them all nodding and laughing with his wit. It was the first time Theo had seen him work his charm in public, and his skill was impressive.

When he finally came back to claim her arm, she said, 'Now I'm sure the wedding was a mistake.'

His smile faded instantly. 'What do you mean?'

'The way you've bedazzled all Aunt Amelia's friends, you should have been a politician. I can see you now on the hustings, charming the masses.'

'All the Ransleigh men are bedazzling,' he tossed back. 'And I think we've been sociable long enough. Shall we leave? The staff at Alastair's town house has a cold supper ready for us whenever we like. If we get to it. I anticipate the meal we share first may last a very long time. I'm ravenous, and I've been waiting for it for ever.'

Desire spiralled though her. 'No more ravenous than I.' As he clasped her hand and led her over to Aunt Amelia to say their farewells, Theo hid a secret smile.

Oh, was she ravenous! And she couldn't wait to start proving it.

Less than an hour later, the carriage deposited them a short distance away at Dom's cousin Alastair's town house in Upper Brook Street. The travelling case with some of her clothes and toiletries had been sent over earlier, and Susan waited to attend her.

As Dom took her arm and walked her up the entry stairs, she was finally able to cast aside all her fears and embrace the one thing about this marriage she knew would be an unqualified success.

'You're trembling,' Dom murmured as they reached the floor where the bedchambers were located. 'You're not afraid, are you?'

Now, when the time had finally come to make all her imaginings real? 'Oh, no! I'm eager.'

She halted, making him stop beside her in the hallway.

She ran a finger over his lips, then slid it down his shirt to draw a line from his waistcoat down his trouser front, increasing the pressure as she descended. She smiled when she felt his member leap under her tracing finger. 'I think you're eager, too.'

After an inarticulate response, he kissed her. Joyously she tangled tongues with him, laving and retreating, teasing and withdrawing. Dom fumbled behind him for the door handle, walked them in and banged it closed, and kissing still, wrapped his arm around her and backed her towards the bed. When her legs touched the edge, he finally broke the kiss, panting. 'Wine, before I snuff out the candles?' he asked, gesturing towards the decanter on the night stand.

'You needn't snuff out the candles. I'd like to see… everything.'

'Certainly I would,' he said with a wry grin. 'I'm not so sure *you* should, though. Wouldn't want for my bride to faint with horror before I can even make her mine.'

Her teasing smile fading, she wanted nothing so much as to reassure him. 'Oh, Dom,' she said softly, 'don't you know I will see nothing but honour in your scars? And *be* honoured, that you've given me the right to touch them?'

He stood beside her, still looking uncertain. 'If you're sure.'

Snagging his cravat, she untied it and used the freed lengths to pull him down to the bed. Then, still in hat, gloves, gown and pelisse, she went down on her knees before him and wrenched open the buttons of his trouser flap.

His erection sprang free and he groaned as she took him in her gloved hands, smoothing the soft kidskin up and down his hard length before guiding him into her mouth.

She sampled the smooth slick head, nibbled at the ridge, slid him fully into her mouth.

'Theo—no—can't stand much more,' Dom gasped.

She paused, sliding him slowly, slowly, slowly free. 'You want me to stop?' she asked, and drew her tongue by infinitesimal millimetres across the head of his erection. 'Stop this?' She took him within and suckled gently. Withdrawing again, she said, 'Or this?' before plunging him deep.

Since by then he appeared to be beyond words, she took that as permission to begin a rhythmic pattern of sliding him deep, pulling him free then sliding him deep again.

Writhing against her, he tugged off her hat with one frantic hand, raked the pins from her hair and wrapped his fingers in the curly strands. A short time later, the tension in his body released as he reached his peak.

Afterward, he pulled her head against his torso and leaned over, embracing her, while his gasping breath and thundering heartbeat filled her ears.

A few moments later, when he'd regathered strength enough, he levered her up on the bed beside him. She tilted his head down for a long kiss. 'Much better than wine.'

He wrapped his arm around her, kissing the top of her head. 'Theo...merciful heavens...I never dreamed...'

She chuckled. 'I know. You see, I'm wonderfully inventive—' he groaned '—and I have a vivid imagination. Oh, so vivid! The nights I lay awake, dreaming of doing that...'

He smiled then. 'I could tell you something about nights and dreaming and imagining. But I'd rather show you.'

Positioning her at the edge of the bed, he knelt before her. He drew her face down for a soft, sweet kiss, and slipped his hand under her skirts to toy with her ankle.

Already thoroughly aroused by her ravishment of his body, she licked at his lips, seeking entry. He refused to open for her, kissing closed-mouthed as she laved and nuzzled.

Meanwhile, his stroking fingers slowly ascended her

leg, kneading and caressing the muscle of her calf, then cupping and fondling her knee. She gasped when he broke the kiss for a moment to lick his finger and apply its soft wet pressure to the sensitive skin behind her knee.

As he slowly worked his hand higher, her knees fell apart, her legs a boneless conduit of sensation from his stroking fingers down to her toes, up to where her centre throbbed. When he reached the velvety skin of her inner thighs, he finally, finally opened his mouth to her, and she surged within in a frantic slash of tongue and teeth.

By the time his fingers reached the crease where her thigh joined the soft curls of her mound, she was beyond kissing, her breath in gasps, her hands clutching his shoulders. She cried out when at last, at last, he glided one probing finger up and across the flesh of her centre, and moaned when he slid the finger within.

But before she could move her hips against it, desperate to reach completion, he pulled the hand away. She'd barely gasped out an inarticulate protest when he swept her skirts back and let his tongue take the path his fingers had just traced.

A few quick strokes of his tongue, and the tension that had been building through her peaked in an eruption of such intensity that for a moment, there was nothing but blinding light and heat and sensation.

When the cataclysm receded, she sagged and would have fallen flat back on to the bed, had Dom not supported her. Gently he held her up and eased her back against the pillows, then seated himself beside her. 'You're right. Much better than wine. But if we're going to talk about dreams and imaginings…' He grinned at her. 'I haven't yet begun.'

Theo lay her limp head upon his shoulder. 'This has already been the most erotic night of my life—and I'm not even undressed yet.'

With a tender look, Dom pressed a kiss in the centre of her forehead. 'Fear not, dear wife. The night has only begun.'

Some time in the early dawn hours, Dom awoke. In the moonlight drifting in from the window, he looked down at Theo, snuggled by his side, her hair a tangle of curls on the pillow, her bare shoulders showing above the bed linen she'd pulled up over her breasts.

Ah, her glorious breasts! Tasting and nibbling and teasing them had been one fantasy he'd been able to turn into reality this night. Also, the one of slowly undressing her, one piece of clothing at a time—and for this game, ladies had such a delightfully large number of garments to remove—tasting each bit of skin as he revealed it. Then another, of having them both naked and slick, kissing slowly as they explored each other with hands and mouths before she pulled him over her and urged him within and wrapped her legs around him to draw him deeper as he thrust again and again.

He'd expected Theo to be passionate, and the reality more than lived up to the dream.

Thank heavens for Jemmie! He must hire the best trainer in England to school the lad. But for the sergeant-major's son, he might have been halfway across England when Theo had been driven to marry in haste to secure her son and her orphans. Some other gentleman might have seen her, appreciated her, felt called to save and protect her.

The very idea of any other man marrying her, holding her, touching any bit of her, even to solve her problems, brought a fierce indignation welling up.

Theo was *his.*

He must be the luckiest man in England.

How wise he'd been on that journey to London, deciding to marry her straight away, with no delays for courting or manoeuvring around other gentlemen or second and third thinking. Marrying her felt right then, and felt even more absolutely right now.

The realisation settled over him then, not in a *coup de foudre* or a lightning strike, but with a calm sense of absolutely certainty.

He was *in love* with Theo Branwell. That was why deciding to marry her had been so easy and done with such confidence in its absolute rightness.

He looked down at her, shaken by the revelation, but filled with the sweetest sense of peace and delight. He wasn't sure when love had begun to curl its tendrils around his heart, growing so quietly he hadn't noticed, until now, when the mature length and strength of it covered his heart and soul completely.

He only knew, with same certainty he'd felt when he decided to marry her, that he loved her, and always would.

And she…liked him?

He frowned and shook his head. No, that would never do. He was almost certain she felt more strongly than that. But for some reason, she was afraid. He'd seen that nervous anxiety on her face a number of times since she accepted his proposal.

Why? Surely she knew he'd never hurt her, that he meant to cherish her. She'd several times affirmed that she trusted him.

Then he recalled the off-hand remark he'd made about marrying someone she did not love to 'punish' herself. Did she still think some sort of retribution for her mistake meant she had no right to be happy? Or, having been devastated by loss before, was she afraid of claiming a happiness she might lose again?

The death of a fiancé that placed her in such horrific circumstances would make anyone afraid to chance loving again. As for any lingering notion of punishment, constant affirmation of her worthiness from someone who knew of her past, and admired her for surviving it, might finally free her from any lingering hold it had upon her.

He should woo her, until she was assured of his love and secure enough to let go of the past and love again without fear. Until she believed in the depths of her soul that she was deserving of happiness. That he would always support her. That she would never again be left alone and desperate and in danger.

How best to reach her?

Beside him, Theo stirred. Opening groggy eyes to smile at him, she slid a hand up over his bare leg. As his member leapt in response, Dom knew he had his answer.

His Theo had no fear at all of love*making*. If he wooed her with words and bedazzled her with kisses, until she trusted the affection they shared was as deep and unending as their passion, he could bring her to acknowledge and eventually revel in loving him.

Then he truly would be the luckiest man in England.

He'd just have to think of ways to seduce her.

Ah, now *that* was a challenge he could embrace with enthusiasm!

Chapter Twenty

Two days later, Theo sat at the table in the breakfast room sharing a light repast with her husband.

Her *husband*…the fact of being wed still amazed her every time she thought of it.

Though they'd spent so much of their marriage thus far in the bedchamber, she felt her face flush every time one of the servants looked at her, as a footman did now before refilling her cup.

'That's all, Thomas, you may go,' Dom said. Grinning as he looked at her no doubt rosy cheeks, after the footman left the room, he said, 'It's all right, Theo, we're married now.'

'I could scarcely face Susan when I finally got back to my room yesterday at noon, when we'd arrived so early the previous evening! I apologised for having her wait so long to help me change. And I still feel…odd, knowing they all know what we've been doing. '

'They expect it. Maybe not so much of it…'

She felt her face heat further, and his grin turned into a chuckle before he took her hand and kissed it. 'My Theo. So calm and matter of fact in public—and such a siren in the bedchamber. Who dreamed I would be lucky enough to marry every man's secret fantasy? I'd be the envy of London, did anyone suspect.'

'Well, I trust you're not going to go announcing it in your clubs,' she said tartly, still feeling embarrassed.

'Certainly not! It's my secret—and my good fortune. I hope the last two days have made you as happy as they've made me.'

She smiled and squeezed his fingers before releasing them. 'I've been wonderfully…content.'

His smile wavered, as if that wasn't the answer he'd hoped for. Before she could figure out what else to say, he said, 'This will be our last day before we rejoin the others at your aunt's and prepare to leave London. Lady Coghlane urged me, and I think it wise, to complete purchasing a wardrobe for you before we go back to the country.'

'"Dandy Dom's" wife, after all, should look the part?' She made a face. 'Must we? I thought you didn't mind me riding about in my comfortable old habit.'

He laughed. 'I've wanted to have the dressing of you since the day we met. And the *un*dressing. Since I've managed that last several times, quite skilfully I thought, it's time to proceed to the former.'

'My old habit being a challenge—or an affront, as it is to Aunt Amelia?'

'A bit of both.'

'Sure you don't want to do more of the "undressing" first?' she asked, leaning over to give him a lingering kiss.

He reached up to hold her chin, prolonging the kiss, which now lacked the urgency of passion long denied, but was sweeter for the promise of passion to come—wherever and as often as they chose.

When he finally broke the kiss, Theo noted with gratification that Dom looked as flushed as she felt.

'Now, where were we?' he asked unsteadily. 'Ah, yes. Commissioning some new gowns and a new habit.'

Theo groaned. 'You *do* have a mind like a poacher's trap.'

'Did you think to distract me? Remember, I have a reputation to maintain.'

'Very well. But only if you promise me a ride in the park this afternoon.'

'It will have to be tomorrow. I've already made an important appointment for today—visiting Tattersall's to find a pony for a little boy.'

She drew back a little, surprised. 'A pony? When did Charles ask you about that?'

'The day I proposed, I asked his permission to marry you, and he said he would agree, as long as he got his pony—and I showed him how to arrange his soldiers in line of battle.'

Something softened and twisted in her heart as Theo realised Dom had thought to include her son in his vision for their marriage. *He really would be the protector and champion she and Charles both needed.* 'That was so kind of you. Even if he did take shameless advantage of the opportunity, the little rascal.'

'Enlightened self-interest, like Jemmie. I've got no suitable ponies at Bildenstone, so it would be best to find one for him here. We'll have a groom bring it back, while we take the carriage.'

Impulsively, she rose and went to hug him, gratitude and affection intensifying the connection she'd always felt to him. 'Thank you for accepting my son,' she whispered.

He caught one hand and kissed it. 'You and your son are one blood. I could no more marry one without embracing the other than you could marry me without inheriting my cousins as well—though, to your relief, none of them are yet near enough to irritate you. But be warned! Eventually, Max, Will and Alastair will be tripping over our threshold and taking over our sitting room.'

'I shall love to welcome them.'

'So, before Tattersall's—which, sadly, admits gentle-men only—we shall visit the modiste.'

'Very well—but I can't imagine anything more of a dead bore.'

'Oh, no, it will be tantalising. I can imagine you in—and out—of each gown. Then there are chemises, and stays, and stockings, and garters…'

'Chemises and stays and garters!' she echoed, scandal-ised. 'You cannot accompany me to buy those!'

'Why not? Because I'll be looking at you lasciviously the whole time?' he asked, grinning again—obviously en-joying her discomfort.

'It would be too intimate to view such apparel together, in front of total strangers,' she said stiffly, her face heat-ing again at the thought.

'Very well.' He relented. 'Gowns only.'

'That *will* be a dead bore,' she muttered.

He caught her chin again. 'What will be the forfeit, if I prove you wrong?'

'You can have your wicked way with me—when we re-turn, of course, not in the modiste's dressing room.'

'And here I thought you had imagination.' He sighed. 'I'll take your bargain, though. Did you bring with you the gown of Prussian blue *à la* Hussar?'

She looked at him blankly for a moment. 'You mean the dark-blue one with the double buttons and frogging on the front? Yes, Susan packed it.'

'Wear that one,' he said drily. 'While you're chang-ing at the modiste's, I can imagine undoing all those little buttons.'

Chafing at having to waste their last morning together at a dressmaker's, Theo dutifully presented herself a half-hour later in the requested gown, and a short time after that, the hackney deposited them before the elegant shop of 'Madame Emilie'.

To Theo's chagrin, the shop girl who greeted them must have recognised Dom, for a moment later, the modiste herself hurried over in a flurry of curtsies. Welcoming him by name, she enquired about his injuries, expressed her joy at his recovery and her delight to see him back in her shop. After telling her what they were seeking—Theo mute through the whole exchange—Madame Emilie hurried off in pursuit of the latest copies of *La Belle Assemblée* and the materials Dom had requested.

'She greeted you like an unexpected bequest from a distant relation,' Theo murmured. 'Just how many mistresses have you dressed here?'

Dom laughed. 'Just one former fiancée—even wealthier than you, and much more interested in acquiring a wardrobe.'

'Madame must have been devastated when she heard you'd broken the engagement and gone off into the country.'

Merriment in his eye, Dom nodded. 'Probably saw half her projected yearly earnings disappear in the dust of my departing coach. We'll have to make it up to her.'

At that moment, the modiste returned. '*Eh, bien*, so we begin, yes? First, I must take your lady's measure.'

To Theo's embarrassment, Dom accompanied them to the dressing room, despite her motioning him out when the shopkeeper's back was turned.

Settling himself in the corner, he watched avidly as the dressmaker's assistant removed her garments, until she was standing before him clad only in chemise and stays. Her body grew tight and prickly as Dom's gaze followed every movement of the tape being drawn against her body, his eye darkening with desire.

It was almost as if it were his own fingers tracing over her skin, rather than a strip of numbered cloth.

By the time the measuring was completed, she was feeling hot and shaky. But there was more.

Seated again with Madame to discuss style, he *did* touch her. Sliding his hand over her shoulder and down her arm to demonstrate a desired cut and length of sleeve…sweeping a palm over her hip to indicate a fit of skirt… And when his fingers made a leisurely transit across her chest, the tips almost but not quite grazing her nipples as he outlined the depth and cut of the *décolletage*, it was all she could do to hold back a gasp.

Desire pulsing through her, relieved to be almost done, she was envisioning what she would do to him once she got him back to the town house when he announced it was time to choose the materials.

Bolts of fabrics were dutifully bought in.

First, he talked of colours—peach, apricot, honey. His voice and the heavy-lidded gaze he fixed on her made her picture biting into rich, ripe fruit, its perfume filling her senses, its juice sweet against her tongue.

Her eyes fixed on his mouth, she jumped when he took her hand and ran it across the subtle texture of the lute string. He unrolled some of the honey silk from its bolt and draped the material over her neck, slowly rubbing its sensual softness against her bare skin, from her chin to the tops of her breasts.

Her nipples hardened, and a moist, urgent throbbing started between her legs.

He moved to a velvet and then a lace, her intensely sensitised skin feeling every nuance of difference between softness and texture, weight and lightness as he drew them across her—as if he were making love to her with fabric.

She thought she would go mad with frustration and impatience.

When at last the assistant finished getting her back into her garments and the modiste left them, looking immensely pleased at the number of gowns they'd commissioned, Theo leaned over to whisper, 'What must she be thinking!?'

Dom shrugged, his heated gaze on her lips. 'She's French. She'll think I was seducing you.'

Her face burned with chagrin—but the idea of him practically making love to her in public was so immensely arousing, her mouth felt dry. 'If you ever shopped like this with anyone else, I'll murder you,' she finally managed to get out.

He grinned at her. 'Only with you. Most females require no assistance to enjoy shopping.'

By the time she was released from the torture of the shop to find a hackney, Theo was almost beyond speech. She scarcely knew what she replied to the idle chat he made during their short drive back to Upper Brook Street.

When they arrived, before Dom could say anything else, Theo took his hand and marched him straight upstairs to their bedchamber, where bright afternoon sun blazed through the windows.

Good; he'd be able to see everything clearly.

Time for the boot to go on the other foot.

'I never thought shopping would take so long,' she said as she closed the door behind them. 'Did you really find this garment so offensive?'

'It's not offensive. I rather like it.'

'But at the shop, you said you preferred something lower cut. To better display my breasts?'

He nuzzled her neck. 'Seeing more of those breasts is always a good thing.'

'Perhaps I should remove the gown, then. Will you help me?'

'Willingly.' To her satisfaction, his breath caught, his fingers fumbling with ties and laces as he freed her from the gown. When he'd helped her out of it, she swept a hand towards her stays. 'Are these too plain, do you think?'

'Absolutely,' he said promptly, obviously catching on to the game.

'Take them off as well.'

He swept a bow. 'As my lady commands.'

He undid them and Theo shrugged them off.

'What of this chemise? You'd prefer a new one, of finest linen, so fine you can see my body beneath it? These—?' She cupped her breasts, thumbing the nipples until they peaked. 'And this?' She slid a hand down to stroke over the dark curls at her mound.

'Yes,' he breathed, his gaze locked on her.

Theo untied the laces, pulled the garment over her head and let it drift to the floor beside her.

Sitting abruptly on the edge of the bed, Dom watched her intently, his chest rising and falling, his lips moist and parted.

Feeling triumphant, powerful, and oh-so-female, Theo kicked off her slippers and walked over to him, naked but for her stockings and garters.

She stopped before him and put one foot up on his knee, opening her most intimate area to his view. She took his limp hand and stroked it over the embroidery of the garter on her unbent leg.

'These, I think are pretty enough. Don't you agree?'

A garbled sound issued from his lips.

Tightening her grip on his hand, she drew it straight up her inner thigh, across the tight curls of her mound, and dipped his index finger into the slickness between her legs. Shuddering as his guided touch further heightened her arousal, she moved his finger to stroke her there, again and again through the increasing wetness.

'You see what you do to me?' she whispered.

Apparently beyond speech, he made no answer.

Guiding his now moist finger, she traced a wet path down the inner thigh of the bent leg until it reached her other garter. 'This, too, I think is…adequate.'

With a growl, Dom grabbed her waist and levered her on to the bed. Sliding her feet up so both legs were fully bent, he parted her knees to open her to him completely, then laved with his tongue where his finger had just been.

Theo gripped the bedclothes, her heartbeat stampeding as he licked and nuzzled. She twisted under him, trying to angle him deeper, inside her, and he murmured at her to be still.

Nibbling and laving gently, he inched closer, until finally, when she thought she could stand it no longer, moving to her pulsing centre. By the time he thrust his tongue deeper, moving in long, hard strokes within, then without to caress the little nub, she was gasping. It took only a few more strokes to bring her to shattering climax.

Afterward, as she lay panting, scarcely conscious, she dimly heard the rustle of him loosening his shirt, unbuttoning his trouser flap. Uttering a long moan of pleasure, she felt the smooth head of his manhood against her slickness. So limp, she was unable to tease him further, she closed her eyes, the waves of pleasure building again as he caressed with his hardness the damp flesh his tongue had just pleasured.

Finally, as she breathed his name, he entered her. She thought he intended to be gradual and slow, but he must have been as transported as she, for after two short strokes, he thrust deep. She wrapped her legs around his back to urge him on, harder, faster, until he cried out and the hot press of his seed spilling deep inside her brought her over the edge again with him.

A long time later, after drifting on a languid cloud of satiation, she came to earth to find herself tucked against his good shoulder.

'I'll never think of shopping the same way again,' she murmured.

'If that is how you pay a forfeit, we should make wagers daily.' After kissing her forehead, he said, 'I thought we should make a short detour before we return to Suffolk.'

She shifted to look up at him. 'I don't really need a wedding trip. Nor do I want to leave the school on its own much longer. I still have some apprenticeships for the boys to set up with the local craftsmen.'

'It would be a brief stop. Before we go back to Bildenstone, we should take Charles to Hazlett Hall to meet the viscount and his lady.'

When Theo gasped, he said, 'Confront the ogres in their den. Or, less melodramatically, forge the agreement for how we mean to go on. You were prepared to bind yourself to a stranger with no hope of future happiness to safeguard your relationship with your son. I think it's important that we hammer out a formal arrangement with the Hazletts now, so you can be easy about his future—and ours.'

'You…you would deal with the viscount for me?'

'Of course. I'm your husband, Theo. I have that right now. And didn't I promise to defend you? I can't think of anything you are more eager to protect than your relationship with your son. So let's accomplish that now.'

She'd known she would have to confront Charles's grandparents again, probably soon. But that Dom would suggest it, and offer to take her there and stand as her champion in dealing with the only people who could threaten to take Charles from her—that, she had never envisioned.

'I don't mean to meddle in what you see as your business,' he continued when she didn't immediately reply, 'but wouldn't settling this now put your mind at ease?'

Relief and gratitude filled her. 'Oh, yes! It would mean a great deal to have it settled. And please, "meddle" all you like!'

He smiled at her, the look so tender her chest grew tight and she had to hold back tears, the affection she struggled against threatening to engulf her.

'Plan on it, then. I don't want you to worry about losing Charles ever again. I promise, I'll make sure that never happens. Trust me, Theo?'

'I trust you,' she whispered. *And I'm very much afraid I love you, too.*

Chapter Twenty-One

A week later, their carriage approached the pastoral vista before the old Tudor manor of Hazlett Hall. Dom watched Theo closely, a curious mixture of jealousy and concern warring in his chest.

For one, he'd like to put to an end for good and all any lingering connection to the man she'd loved so deeply. On the other, he knew that as long as Charles remained of primary concern—and that would be for ever—he would have to deal with her memories of the man who'd sired him. And for her to truly be open to finding happiness again, she would have to be assured of keeping her son.

He'd already displaced Marshall Hazlett in her arms. Though he really didn't begrudge her fond memories of her child's father, he hoped to soon rival the man in her affections. But securing the boy's future he could and would settle today.

Clasping and unclasping her hands, she gazed out the window at the manor house, Charles dozing by her side. Attuned now to signs of her nervousness, he captured one of her restless fingers.

'Steady, Theo. Everything will work out as you wish. I promise you.'

She nodded. 'I'm so very grateful you offered to accompany me. It seems so…strange, coming here, seeing the place where Marshall grew up, where I once thought I'd return as his bride.'

'Forgive me for preferring that you're coming here as mine.'

She smiled, a little forlornly. 'Forgive *me* for letting myself be dragged into the past. I'm not sorry that he was so large a part of it—and I am very, very glad that you are my future.'

'Glad' wasn't exactly what he was hoping for, but under the circumstances, he would have to settle for it. Giving her a kiss to signify his approval of that sentiment, he leaned her back. 'What do you know of Viscount Hazlett's feelings about Charles? I suspect his opinion will have more impact as to how we resolve this than his wife's.'

'I really don't know anything. Lady Hazlett spoke of her own longing to reclaim a part of her blood, but she gave me no sense of how enthusiastic, or resistant, her husband was to that desire.'

Dom could see apprehension in the furrow of her brow. 'We shall soon see. And don't worry, sweeting, regardless of his position, we will agree to nothing that does not guarantee Charles remains with you.'

A few minutes later, the carriage drew up before the entrance, and Dom gave Theo's hand a reassuring squeeze. He'd sent a note ahead to Viscount Hazlett, so he wasn't surprised when the butler, who escorted them through a timbered great hall into a wainscoted withdrawing room, informed him that Lord and Lady Hazlett would receive them shortly.

While Charles delightedly examined the carvings of griffins and gargoyles on the roof beams, Theo paced before the fire. Dom watched her, wishing there was more he could do to ease her anxiety—about the interview to come, and for the heartache she must inevitably feel at knowing her son, but for his father's early death the viscount's rightful heir, had no legal right to the home whose sculptures so fascinated him.

The door opened, admitting a tall, balding man whose grey hair might once have been fair, and a slender, still lovely lady—who had eyes for no one but the boy.

Hearing them enter, Charles halted his inspection and looked over as Lady Hazlett walked towards him, a tremulous smile on her face. 'Welcome to our home, my dear!'

Dom had to admire the lad's manners, for he gave her a proper bow before saying, 'You came to visit us at Thornfield, didn't you?'

'I did,' she affirmed.

'I have my pony now. When you visit again, I'll be able to ride ever so well.'

'I'm sure you shall,' Lady Hazlett said. Holding out her hand, she said, 'May I introduce you to someone? My husband, Lord Hazlett.'

Charles didn't look impressed, but he took her hand and let her walk him over to the gentleman who'd stopped abruptly just inside the room, his gaze locked on his wife and the boy.

The viscount was scrutinising the child as avidly as Charles was inspecting him. Dom watched his face as scepticism gave way to surprise, and as the boy drew closer, he paled and shuddered visibly.

'Lord Hazlett, may I present Charles,' his wife said.

Charles made another bow. 'Pleased to meet you, my lord,' he piped.

Dom turned his attention to Theo, who had been observing the proceedings with anxious eyes. Nothing the highest stickler could find to fault in the boy's manners so far, Dom thought—he was the picture of a well-brought-up gentleman's son.

First hand to Theo.

Lady Hazlett looked back over her shoulder at Dom and Theo. 'Mr and Mrs Ransleigh, forgive my lack of manners. I wished Lord Hazlett to see Charles before we proceeded any further. You both are also very welcome in our home. Now, if you will permit, Mrs Ransleigh, I'd like to take Charles up to the nursery while you speak with Lord Hazlett.'

Getting the child out of the way so he couldn't overhear anything he shouldn't, Dom thought approvingly. It seemed Lady Hazlett had the boy's welfare at heart, then.

Turning back to Charles, Lady Hazlett said, 'We have some very fine toy soldiers in the nursery. And some balls and games and a toy horse that your f—that other children enjoyed very much.'

'Soldiers?' Charles echoed. 'Oh, I would like to see them. May I go, Miss Theo?'

'Of course, Charles. Mind your manners, now.'

'I always do. You know that,' he said calmly before trotting out with Lady Hazlett.

Lord Hazlett stared out the open door until the pair was out of sight. Still pale, he started when he turned back to them, as if surprised there was still someone in the room.

'I'm Hazlett, of course,' he said belatedly, bowing to Theo and holding out a hand to Dom. 'You're Swynford's nephew, aren't you?' Turning to Theo, he said, 'So you're the woman my son meant to wed?' Glancing towards the door through which Charles had just exited, he said, 'A pity you didn't bother to get your marriage lines before you proceeded to that.'

Theo's chin jerked up and her eyes turned cold. 'Yes, isn't it? But since that guarantees the child has no claim on you, we will just collect him and take our leave.'

Before Dom, in a fury, could utter something blighting and lead her away, the viscount held up a hand. 'I'm sorry, that was unkind. I must ask you to forgive an old man's shock…and pain.' He sighed. 'But for a Frenchman's bullet, or a few weeks' delay, I'd not be facing the prospect of turning the home of my ancestors over to a cousin, instead of the son of my son.'

'There's nothing anyone can do to change the laws that prevent Charles from inheriting,' Dom said. 'But if you'd like to salvage some relationship with the son of your son, we're prepared to discuss it—as long as you treat my wife with respect.'

'My apologies, Mrs Ransleigh,' the viscount said. 'There will be no living with my wife if we don't reach some agreement. Won't you take a seat? I'll have Sanders bring wine.'

Giving Theo a reassuring look, Dom led her to the sofa, their host seating himself in the wing chair opposite. 'I have to admit, I didn't really believe all that nonsense Tremaine spouted when he visited here. A nasty piece of work, that one, and his father before him. It angered me to have him lead Emily on—she's never stopped mourning the loss of all her chicks, and to have him setting her up for more heartache! Which is what I thought you'd done, too, young lady, when she visited you. But she's right; the boy is the image of Marshall at that age.'

'Why would I lead her on? Since having anyone question the already accepted story of Charles's parentage would put him at risk, I should probably, by rights, have denied the story and turned her away. But I could see how much it would ease the pain of Marshall's loss for her to know his son—and I couldn't.'

'It's hard for me to forgive you for spinning such a yarn about the boy's father, keeping us in ignorance of his existence for so long. True, I can't pretend to understand what you faced when you found yourself increasing, with Marshall dead and you not yet married. But how convenient for your reputation, to have a dead man's dead son's name to claim for my grandson.'

As Theo flinched under the harsh words, Dom stood up, a hand on her arm. 'Another speech like that,' he said with cold fury, 'and I'll take my wife and the boy and you'll never see or hear from him again.'

The fire died out in the viscount's eyes. 'I beg your pardon—again, Mrs Ransleigh.'

Theo gave a short nod, and Dom sat back down.

'What I did, I did to protect Charles,' Theo said, her eyes going distant, as if she were reliving the events. 'If all I'd cared about was my own good name, I could have left him at the convent, as the sisters urged. I'd confessed my sins and received absolution, they said, but if I took the child back with me, my shame would become known, and society would never forgive it. But right from birth, Charles was so fair. Even if some Portuguese peasant wanting a sturdy son took him in, he'd always look like a foreigner. Always be an outsider. I thought, even as a bastard, he would fare better in his homeland. Stumbling upon an identity as Everely's dead son was never what I'd planned. And he was my *son*, mine and Marshall's! How could I abandon him in a foreign land?'

'Well, that coil can't be unspooled now. But even as a bastard, we would have accepted him, loved him, found a place for him.'

'How could I have known that? I couldn't risk exposing him, only to be rejected—and then have him grow up with a taint on his name.'

'You have your chance now, Lord Hazlett,' Dom interrupted. 'Learning about him today, or four and a half years ago, wouldn't have made any difference; under law, he could never inherit the title or the entailed portion of your estate. You can still leave him whatever you wish that isn't entailed, and when he's old enough, he'll be told of his true lineage. If you do want him, why not just enjoy sharing that?'

'Aye, that's what my wife counselled. Loving him should be easy enough. He's the image of my dear b-boy,' he said, his voice breaking.

'He was dear to me, too,' Theo said, tears glittering in her eyes.

Dom put his hand on her shoulder, wanting her to feel his silent support. 'They are both under my protection now,' he said evenly, but with a warning in his voice. 'Unlike your son, I managed to get a ring on her finger. I'd appreciate your support of the plan my wife and yours agree upon, but if you attempt to harass her, we'll raise the boy without you. You have no legal claim to either of them.'

The viscount met his steady gaze. 'Do you mean to dictate terms to me?'

'Not at all. I'm merely reminding you of our respective positions. Treat my wife with the courtesy and respect owed to her as the woman your son loved and the mother of your grandson. As part of my duty to secure her happiness, I'm prepared to respect her wishes about letting you and your wife see the boy and draw him into your lives. As long as you never attempt to cut Theo out of this. Or disparage her in any way.'

Lord Hazlett looked back at Theo. 'You seem to have found a champion.'

She gave Dom a look of affection and gratitude. 'I have.'

'About time she had one,' Dom muttered.

'Very well. Why don't you stay a few days,' the viscount said, addressing himself once again to Dom, 'while my wife and yours work out the details of sharing Charles? If that is agreeable to you, Mrs Ransleigh?'

Dom looked over at Theo.

'Anxious as I am to get back to Suffolk, I suppose we could spare two days,' she said. 'For Charles.'

She couldn't be more anxious than he was, Dom thought. Anxious to get her away from things that mired her in the past, unable to move into the future. *Their* future. He couldn't wait to get her back to Bildenstone Hall, where he could continue wooing—and seducing—his new wife. Every day he spent with her, it grew more important to him to persuade her to let go of fear and pain and embrace the future, loving only him.

'I should like to join Lady Hazlett and Charles now,' Theo said, breaking into his abstraction.

'I'll have Henry show you up,' Lord Hazlett said. Turning to Dom, he said, 'Would you like a stroll about the grounds? There's a fair vista from the back terrace. I seem to recall you breed hunters. I'd invite you to the stables, but I sold off all mine after…after Edward died.'

His eldest son and heir had been killed in a hunting fall, Dom knew. 'Having been cooped up for hours in a coach, I would enjoy a walk. Perhaps you could tell me about selling your hunters. I have some to dispose of as well.'

As they walked out, Dom felt confident the two ladies who loved Charles the most would quickly come to terms over the logistics of sharing his life.

Then came Bildenhall, and the final conquest of his bride's heart.

Chapter Twenty-Two

A week later, the carriage came to a stop outside the school—Theo, in her eagerness, having begged Dom to let her visit the children before returning to Thornfield.

Smiling, he watched as she sprang out the carriage door almost before the wheels had stopped.

Nor was she the only anxious one. As soon as she descended, Jemmie ran out of the building, followed by the others.

The air rang with choruses of 'Miss Theo! Miss Theo!' Maria, ever silent, raced over and threw her arms around Theo's waist. Soon she was surrounded by a laughing, chattering group of children.

'Yes, I'm back. No, I'll not be leaving again,' she replied to the questions being peppered at her.

'Did you come back married?' Jemmie asked.

Blushing a little, she said, 'Yes, I did.'

Seeing that as his cue, Dom came over to take her hand. 'I asked Miss Theo to marry me, and she did me the honour of accepting my suit. We were wed in London, about two weeks ago now.'

'We had a big party,' Charles inserted.

'Oh, I like parties! Why didn't we get to come?' Anna asked.

'It's a very long coach ride,' Theo explained. 'I thought you'd prefer having a party here. Miss Andrews, could you grant a short holiday, so I may get reacquainted with the children?'

'Of course, Miss—Mrs Ransleigh. My heartiest congratulations to you both!'

While the children closed in around her again, Jemmie approached Dom and held out his hand, which Dom shook solemnly.

'Thank you for helpin' her out.'

'It was my pleasure.' *Oh, if you only knew how much!*

'Guess she don't need to wait for me to grow up no more,' he said wistfully, his eyes on Theo.

The teacher walked up to them. 'Jemmie, could you help me carry some of the books to the cupboard?'

Eagerly, the boy turned to the blonde, blue-eyed, apple-cheeked Miss Andrews—who was only a handful of years older than Jemmie. 'Sure can, miss.' From the flush on his face as he took the books, Dom speculated the lad might soon find another candidate to replace Theo as the lady he wanted to protect and care for.

Before the teacher could lead him inside, Charles came trotting up. 'Can I help, too? I missed you, Jemmie!'

The older boy smiled and tousled his hair. 'Sure, scamp. I missed you, too.'

With the girls still clustered around Theo, Georgie came over to tug at her skirt.

'Farmer Jamison came to the school, Miss Theo. He said I can come work with him. Will you talk with him tomorrow? He said I can help him put wheat seeds in the meadow!'

'Of course, Georgie. I'll ride over tomorrow. Today, I'll be getting resettled at home.'

'Ready?' Dom asked, holding out his hand.

She looked fondly at the children, whom Miss Andrews was calling back into the building. 'Ready.'

He helped her into the coach. Charles having begged to remain at the school with his friends, with Mr Blake to drive him home later, they set off for Thornfield Place.

'I know it sounds ridiculous,' Theo said after she'd snuggled on to the seat beside him, 'but while we were still in London, I was so caught up in the wedding...and what came after, and then completely occupied by the task of settling things with the Hazletts about Charles, and then thinking about the school and the children on the way back to Suffolk, I've only just begun considering what to do about Thornfield. I imagine you'll want your wife to reside at your home.'

Dom smiled. 'That's generally how it's done.'

'I'd thought to keep the staff at Thornfield for the duration of the lease, even though, after the first week or so, we will no longer be living there. Just because my circumstances changed so suddenly, it's not fair to deprive them of jobs they expected to sustain them for at least the next year—'

She halted with a frown. 'Though I suppose you now control any lease written in my name?'

'Under the law, probably. But I assured you from the beginning you were to have a free hand with the school and any of your properties you wish to control, as well as the funds set aside for you.' He grinned. 'Only now, you can spend my funds, too.'

'Careful what you offer,' she warned, her expression teasing. 'I might decide the school needs a stable for Jemmie to train in, or a forge for the boys to learn blacksmithing.'

Dom groaned. 'Which would doubtless prove more expensive than jewellery or gowns. I knew a wife was going to cost me, one way or another.'

'This one will try to cost you as little as possible,' she said, suddenly serious.

He tipped up her chin to give her a kiss. 'This one is worth whatever she costs.'

'I hope you'll always think so,' she said, her voice gruff.

'I will,' he assured her. 'Once we pick up some things at Thornfield, you will join me at Bildenstone tonight, I hope? If you absolutely insist, we can stay at Thornfield, but I'd much prefer to carry my bride across the threshold of her room in the house that will be her home for the rest of her life.'

She nodded. 'I did plan on that, though I think I'll let Charles stay at Thornfield with Constancia for a few days. All his things are there, and it will be less disrupting for him to take the move in stages.'

'He won't stay there long when he realises his pony is in the stables at Bildenstone.'

'You're probably right,' Theo said with a smile. 'I also thought you might like us to have our first few nights in your home to ourselves.'

He gave her a quick kiss. 'I definitely like the sound of that!'

They stopped briefly at Thornfield. While a maid ran up to collect some of her things, Theo spoke with the butler and the housekeeper, who passed along their congratulations and the staff's—with rather anxious looks, Dom thought, until Theo assured them their positions were secure for the duration of the lease. Expressing their relief at that, and their disappointment that they'd no longer be able to personally serve so kind and understanding a mistress, they sent the bridal couple off with their good wishes.

A short time later, the coach finally reached their destination. As Dom gave Theo his arm up the steps, she halted, looking wide-eyed at the ivy-covered brick front. 'I know I've been here before, but it's different, somehow—coming here as if I belong.'

'You do belong now. Here, and with me. Always,' he assured her.

Then Wilton opened the door, his worn face breaking into a rare smile as he ushered them in. 'Welcome back, Mr Ransleigh—and Mrs Ransleigh. Congratulations, sir, on acquiring so lovely and accomplished a bride!'

Mrs Greenlow rushed up then, making Dom suspect the household had been lying in wait for them. 'Welcome back, master and mistress! Mr Blake sent one of the farm boys to let us know you'd returned. I took the liberty of arranging a small feast in honour of your homecoming. And, Mistress, if it pleases you, I'd like to suggest that Nancy, our senior housemaid, act as your lady's maid.'

'With the new wardrobe you commissioned soon to arrive, you'll be needing a maid to keep it in order,' Dom said, eyeing Theo, who made a face at him behind the housekeeper's back.

'Thank you for your thoughtfulness, Mrs Greenlow,' she said to the housekeeper. 'I'm sure Nancy will be exemplary.'

'Shall you proceed to the small dining room?' Wilton asked. 'I believe Cook had the meal ready to serve whenever you returned.'

Dom exchanged a look with Theo. Though he would rather show his wife up to her new rooms and make her at home in the most intimate way possible, he knew they couldn't disappoint their excited retainers.

'A feast?' Theo whispered to him as she took his arm.

'Eat quickly,' he replied with a rueful look.

And so they did, trying to do justice to the multiple courses Cook presented, complete to wine and wedding cake.

* * *

At last they finished, thanked the staff and bid them goodnight, and Dom was able to escort Theo upstairs.

'The wedding celebration they prepared for us was thoughtful, but we'll want to host a larger gathering for all the staff—and the neighbourhood,' he told her as they climbed the stairs.

Theo groaned. 'I hadn't thought of that, but I suppose you're right. At least I'll be able to employ the talents of the Thornfield staff in the preparations. We can make it a large enough affair that the children from the school can attend, too.'

'You can introduce them to Lady Wentworth,' Dom said with a chuckle. 'Now, that's an event I'll look forward to!'

A moment later, they reached his chamber. Dom paused outside his door. 'This will be a little more awkward than it would have been a year ago, but if you wrap your arms around my neck, I think we can manage.'

Smiling tremulously, she obligingly reached up and clasped her hands behind him. Going up on tiptoe to kiss him, she said, 'You've guaranteed my respectability by making me the wife of the most important man in the county, secured the future of my son, and protected my orphans. I'd do anything for you.'

Let yourself love me, then, Dom thought.

Inside the door, he carried her to the bed. Undressing her tenderly, he kissed each bit of flesh revealed, making that erotic journey more slowly than he had the first time, wanting her to feel to the marrow of her bones how much she was cherished.

In the aftermath of loving, he clasped her to his side, both of them panting and spent. His whole heart expanding with peace and joy, he couldn't imagine life without her; couldn't imagine any other woman in her place.

He ached to say the words, but he knew, when he reached the point of confessing his love, she needed to be nearly there, too, or he'd frighten her off, like trying to loop a halter over a colt not yet ready to be led.

Not yet. But soon.

Easing her against the pillows, he said, 'I shall have to rustle out Mother's jewels from whatever vault they were put in after my parents' death. There's a ring that's always given to Ransleigh brides, and then there are the Ransleigh rubies. A magnificent set, Mama always wore them for special occasions.'

Theo shook her head. 'Coming to Bildenstone, a wedding feast, carrying me over the threshold, now your mama's ring and jewels… Somehow, being married seems more real and *permanent* here.'

'It is real and permanent,' he said with a grin. 'No trial period, remember? We're yoked in harness for life now.'

'I hope you'll never regret it. I know I'll never stop being grateful.'

Dom tried not to wince. He wanted so much more than *gratitude* from Theo. 'I won't regret it.'

'Would you like to come with me when I call on Farmer Jamison tomorrow?'

'I would. His holding is known to be so prosperous and it's one of the few farms I haven't yet visited.'

Yawning, she sank back against the pillows. He followed her down to give her a kiss. 'Don't think you're going to sleep just yet.'

'Oh, Dom! It was a very long carriage ride today.'

'I'm thinking of another ride.' He moved his fingers to caress one breast, then the other, while she stirred and murmured under his hand. 'This one's just beginning.'

And it was…the seduction would continue, until he won his heart's desire—all of *her* heart.

* * *

The next morning, Dom sat at ease in the saddle outside the stables at Bildenstone, waiting for Theo to join him. A feeling of joy and well-being suffused him, a contentment that went far beyond the peace of last night's lovemaking. He had a fine home, a lovely wife, good land that, with the projects for improvement he'd read about at Holkham, he looked forward to making better. And an exciting new endeavour to begin, as soon as he completed the sale of his hunters.

For a man who, a few short months ago, wasn't sure he was going to survive, he was surrounded with blessings.

Theo exited the stable and rode up. 'Thank you for having Firefly brought over.'

'I thought you'd prefer your own mount to anything left in my stables—which is not much, now.'

'I see Charles's pony arrived safely, too.' She chuckled. 'You're right, once Charles learns the pony is here, he'll have Constancia hustled out of Thornfield's nursery and on the road to Bildenstone in a flash.'

'Mrs Greenlow already has their rooms prepared.'

'Will you visit any other farms after we meet with Mr Jamison?'

'Just him today. I'm looking forward to meeting with the tenants, seeing if I can persuade them to implement some of the techniques I saw and read about at Holkham. I'll also ask around to see who's best suited to take over Winniston's duties as steward. Though if I can't find anyone, Thomas Coke said he knew of several young men he could recommend. I'll probably consult my cousin Alastair, too. He has a fine estate in Devonshire. I'll have to take you there; it's a beautiful part of England.'

'I'd like that, once the school is fully settled. Which is where I'd like to ride first, to see Charles and check on the children, if you're agreeable.'

'I'm agreeable to anything that pleases my wife.'

She gave him a naughty grin. 'Careful, now! I shall recall that phrase and use it against you.'

They rode in companionable silence, Dom taking the opportunity to admire Theo on horseback. He loved watching her, the smooth line of her figure leaning over her mount, the soft tones as she crooned to her mare, her hands stroking its neck. The horse obviously liked it—and Dom couldn't blame her; he loved that soft voice and those hands touching him, too.

He caught himself before he could drift into reliving their latest love-play—an exercise that would tempt him to abandon plans to meet farmers and look instead for a secluded dell. A sudden memory recurred, and he grinned.

There might be occasion today to fit in both.

Theo looked up then, saw him staring, and coloured. 'What?' she asked, patting at her hat. 'Have I a curl coming loose? A leaf on my skirt?'

'No, your habit is perfection. I just like looking at you.'

Her eyes softened. 'Not half so much as I enjoy looking at you.'

He raised his eyebrow. 'All of me?'

Her look turned wicked. 'Oh, especially *all* of you.'

'I shall keep that in mind for later. You mentioned you wanted to explore the possibility of setting up other apprenticeships? We could ride to see the masters together.'

Her face brightened. 'I'd like that! You provide excellent counsel and advice.'

For the rest of the ride, they discussed which craftsman's skills might enhance the learning experience for the children. Arriving at the school, mindful of the disruption their arrival caused yesterday, they waited quietly until they heard Miss Andrews dismiss the children for a break.

They came running out, exclaiming as they saw their mentor.

While Theo chatted with the girls, Jemmie came up to Dom.

'Mr Jeffers talked with me when he come to school the other day. He told me you might be lookin' into breeding some draught horses. If'n you do, could you let me help you?'

'You'd rather do that than apprentice at a racing stud?' Dom asked curiously.

Jemmie shrugged. 'What do the likes of me have to do with them fast horses and the toffs that own 'em? Some fancy gentlemen winnin' or losin' more blunt than I'll see my whole life on which one comes across a line first! Naw, I'd rather know the horses I bred ploughed Jamison's field faster, or let the neighbours finish their ploughin' with the horses still havin' stamina enough left to do Widow Blackthorn's fields, too.'

'I haven't completed purchasing all the stock yet, but when I do, yes, I'll let you help.'

'Thank you, Mr Ransleigh.' Jemmie grinned. 'I knew I done the right thing when I sent you after Miss Theo.'

After Theo finished her conversation and gave Charles a hug, they remounted and headed through the Home Wood to the northern boundary of Bildenstone estate, where Jamison's fields were located.

They received a warm welcome from the farmer's wife, who invited them to sit and have some cool cider while she sent one of her daughters to tell her husband, out ploughing in the furthest field, that visitors had arrived. The farmer himself hurried up a few minutes later.

'First, may I offer my congratulations to you and your lady,' Jamison said.

'Thank you. We were wed in town, at the home of my

wife's aunt, but we plan a grand party soon so that all of Bildenstone's tenants can celebrate with us.' Dom kissed Theo's hand, making her blush. 'I'm a very lucky gentleman.'

'Aye, so folks say! They admire what you've done fixing up the old barn as a school, Mrs Ransleigh, and offering jobs to the many that need them. Now me, I've the opposite problem—fields to work, and all daughters but for my newborn. So I'd be right pleased to hire young Georgie to help me. Doesn't know a turnip seed from a carrot yet, but he's eager, and he'll learn.'

'He'll continue lessons at the school in the afternoons,' Theo said, 'but I'd see he was driven out to help you in the mornings first. Shall we have him begin next week? Good!' she said as the farmer nodded. 'Thank you, Mr Jamison, for giving him a chance.'

'Be my pleasure, Mrs Ransleigh.'

'Our thanks to your wife for the cider. It was delicious!' Theo said.

'Honoured to have you stop by, ma'am.'

They walked back to collect their horses, grazing in the nearby meadow, and a few minutes later, waved goodbye and set off towards Bildenstone Hall.

'Pleased to have the business with Georgie settled?' Dom asked.

'Yes. If I can find places for the others at positions that interest them, doing useful things, I'll be even more pleased. As Papa would be, too.' She gave him a mischievous look. 'Even if establishing a school for the orphans wasn't exactly his dying wish.'

'He'd be proud of you, Theo. I'm proud of you.'

She flushed at his praise. 'As I am proud of you. I heard you mention to Jemmie that you might start breeding farm horses. Do you think that would hold your interest?'

'The fascination of breeding is in studying characteristics, seeing which will transfer, which will not. If I ended up with an animal that would help more farmers feed themselves and their neighbours, that would be not so bad a result.

'I think it would be a wonderful one!'

'It is good to be well thought of by one's wife.' *Even better to be loved,* he thought. But with admiration, gratitude, and trust, love should soon follow…shouldn't it?

'You said you'll have to go to Newmarket?'

'Yes. On my last trip, I arranged the details of the sale with the stable manager; he'll begin setting it up as soon as the horses arrive from Upton Park. I'll need to go supervise it—and purchase the sorrels and trotters to start the breeding project.'

'Will you be away long?'

'Perhaps a week or so. Will you miss me?'

'Very much.'

'Maybe we should get ahead while we can, then.' *And maybe it was time for another try at seduction…*

Halfway through the Home Woods, Dom pulled up his mount near a small stream that ambled along the east side of the road. 'Shall we let the horses have a drink? We could sit there under one of those trees you so admire.'

She chuckled. 'I'd like that.'

Dismounting under a large oak, they let the horses go to the water. Dom leaned back against the tree trunk, pulling Theo to him for a long, slow kiss.

'Maybe it's time to fetch the horses and get back to Bildenstone,' she suggested, heat in her eyes as she trailed fingers down his chest to his breeches. He groaned when she touched him, already hard and ready. 'It appears you're definitely eager to return.'

'Or we could stay. Isn't there something erotic about the sibilant trickle of water over stone?' he asked, reaching under the jacket of her habit to caress her breasts as he kissed her again.

For a moment, Theo responded, opening her mouth to him. But as he started on the buttons of her jacket, she pulled away.

'No, Dom, not here.' She pushed away from him and crossed her arms over her breasts, creating a distance between them that was like a sudden slap after the intimacy of the previous moment.

'Loving under the stars was what started all the misery. That and Tremaine spying on us,' she whispered.

Dom put out a hand to steady her. 'You're safe here, Theo. Not on foreign soil with threats all around. We're on my land. It's private. No army of reprobates to spy on us.

'There might be a gamekeeper. If he saw me naked, he'd be so shocked, he might shoot himself.'

'No, he'd think he'd seen a vision. A forest nymph. *My* forest nymph. I'll not try to persuade you into this, if it makes you uncomfortable. But it's not just that. These last few weeks, since our wedding, I've seen you smiling, as if almost brimming with happiness, and then you…stop yourself. The smile fades and you…turn inward. As if you think you don't deserve to be happy. Life, love, is a *gift*, Theo. It's too rare and precious to turn away from.'

'I'm…frightened to trust it, Dom,' she whispered. 'If I let myself go and lost again, I'd be desolated. I can't go through that.'

'We can't keep ourselves safe from whatever lies ahead,' he argued. 'Ponsonby was standing right next to Wellington at Waterloo when that cannonball took off his leg—and not a hair on Old Hookey's head was even ruffled. Life is random, unpredictable—and never safe. Isn't it preferable to embrace every joy while you have it, than to shut yourself off for fear of losing it? You're the bravest girl I know. Don't hold yourself back!'

When she shook her head and pulled away, exasperated and driven by need, Dom cried, 'I love you, Theo! Can't you see that? I know you care for me. Why won't you let yourself love me back?'

'Because I…I can't! Not now! Not yet!'

'I seem to remember a girl in a lane telling me "You could if you wanted to".' Angry, frustrated—why did she have to be so stubborn?—Dom continued. 'You told me to look past my limitations, to all that I could still be. I can't believe you don't have the courage to try, after all you've suffered and survived!'

'That's right,' she snapped back, 'I *have* suffered and survived. By protecting myself—and carrying only the burdens I could handle!'

Stung, he said, 'Well, thank you very much. I shall try very hard not to be one more "burden" you are forced to handle.'

Furious, Dom stalked off and threw himself on to his horse. He knew he'd said too much, but her ridiculous resistance made him so angry! And he loved her so much, he'd better take himself away before he said anything more.

Chapter Twenty-Three

Hands on her hips, furious too, Theo watched Dom ride off.

They'd only just settled the matter with Charles. Why did he have to push her to examine her feelings, looking for a declaration she was not yet ready to give?

Then, with a shock, she realised—he'd said he loved her. *Loved her.*

And what did she do after that heartfelt declaration, but push him away!

Idiot.

He'd offered her his heart—shouldn't she have the courage to accept it? She knew she trusted him not to hurt her, and as he'd said, nothing in life was sure. So why was she still so afraid?

Losing Marshall, finding herself alone, pregnant, unwed, had been a horror that had haunted her for years. But she'd faced other difficult situations since then—the loss of her father, the loss of her familiar place in the army, coming to an unknown land where she knew almost no one—without falling to pieces. Wasn't it time for her to move beyond the trauma of that past?

Let it go, and embrace Dom fully?

Still, when she thought of saying words of love out

loud—irrevocable words that couldn't be taken back—a sudden panic made it hard to breathe.

She couldn't do it, not yet. He had to give her a little more time.

She sighed. In any event, she needed to apologise. He'd professed his love, and she, basically, had rebuffed him. It took only a moment's reflection to realise how she would feel, had she confessed *her* love for *him*, and he'd pushed her away, claiming he wasn't prepared to take the risk of loving her.

She felt like she'd been punched in the stomach.

Sick and shaky, she collected her grazing horse and looked around for somewhere to mount.

Once again, she found nothing at all she might use as a mounting block.

It looked like she'd face another long trudge home.

Nearly two hours later, she arrived back at Bildenstone, hot, disgruntled, and more than a little annoyed with herself. She'd call for a bath and refresh herself before she went looking for Dom. Maybe put on something cut low in the bosom, to distract him, while she apologised and before she showed her contrition in a way he would most appreciate.

Maybe if she kept him too exhausted and satiated from lovemaking to think, he'd be content enough not to press her about the other.

Feeling better, she gave her horse to a groom outside the stables and proceeded on to the Hall.

'Wilton, where is your master?' she asked as he opened the door for her.

'I expect he's halfway to Hadwell by now, mistress.'

Theo stopped short. 'Hadwell?' she echoed.

'Yes, he told me he hoped to be well on the way to Bury

St Edmunds by nightfall, and from thence to Newmarket soon after.'

'He…he already left for Newmarket?'

'Yes, ma'am. He did tell me to beg your pardon on his behalf for leaving so suddenly. A messenger came from his stable manager at Newmarket this afternoon, saying all the stock had arrived and requesting his presence there as soon as he could manage it.'

'I see,' she replied, her recently revived spirits taking a sharp downward spiral.

'Shall I send Nancy up to you?'

'Yes, please,' she murmured distractedly.

Up in her room, she stood, looking out the window. Towards Newmarket.

She knew he was angry when he'd left her by the stream. But she still couldn't believe he'd left without waiting to speak with her, or attempting to repair their quarrel.

She must have wounded him even more than she'd thought.

She never thought she *could* wound him that badly. He must care very deeply.

She'd wanted to bathe, apologise, and make it all up to him.

It appeared all she'd be getting was a bath.

Five days later, Theo still had no word from Dom. She busied herself completing the transfer of her belongings from Thornfield, and checking in at the school, but always with a sense of looking over her shoulder, listening for hoofbeats.

She'd thought she was self-sufficient, but suddenly there seemed to be a tremendous gap yawning around her where, a very little time ago, there'd been none. She'd expected to miss Dom, especially after parting on such an ill note, but she found herself missing him much more than she'd dreamed possible.

When had he become so important to her well-being?

Wilton wanted to know when she wished to schedule the party for the tenants—and she wanted to consult him. She needed to set up a training program with the blacksmith for Jemmie—and she wished to ask his advice. Miss Andrews had a question about some stories she might read to the children—and she automatically thought about asking him for recommendations.

Dinners, sitting at the small formal table alone, were wretched, and even evenings spent exploring the magnificent library didn't cheer her.

Nights, of course, were the worst. A few weeks of anticipating the unparallelled bliss she'd found in his embrace quickly made her entirely resentful of having to sleep alone. Nor had she ever slept as well as she did after his sweet and thorough loving.

After not resting well at night and missing him continually by day, she soon became short-tempered even with Charles.

To travel as far as Newmarket, he'd be gone at least a week, she thought disconsolately.

All she knew for sure, was when he got home, she meant to give him a welcome, and an apology, he would never forget.

Later that same day, Dom rode towards Bildenstone. He should have remained at Newmarket another day or two; there were still horses from Upton Park not yet disposed of, but once he set up the purchase of several Norfolk trotters and Suffolk sorrels, so anxious was he to return to Bildenstone, he turned the rest of the hunters over to his stable manager and set out.

He'd hated to leave Bildenstone without speaking with

Theo—who delayed so long coming home after their quarrel by the brook, Dom knew she must have been even angrier than he'd thought.

His fault, all of it. He'd pushed her too hard, too soon. So what if it took another month, or two, or a year, until she trusted him and trusted their life together enough to admit she loved him? He *knew* she did, on a deep level that connected them in spirit as passionately as the union they made between their bodies.

He shouldn't yearn so much to hear her say the words, when her tender touch showed how much she cherished him every time they came together. And in the meantime, he should be thankful for the blessing of having claimed her as his wife, when, but for divine intervention in the form of Jemmie, he might have lost her to someone else before he could begin to woo her.

He hoped, despite his abrupt departure, that she'd not still be angry when he returned.

He *was* bringing her a gift, which might help him redeem himself. He smiled. At the least, it would give her a new project to work on.

Never again, he promised himself, would he be impatient with her.

It was mid-afternoon by the time he turned down the lane to Bildenstone. Finally reaching the manor, he left the horse to find its own way to the stables, too impatient to wait any longer.

'Wilton, where is your mistress?' he asked as the butler admitted him.

'Welcome home, sir! The mistress rode over to the school today.'

'Is Master Charles with her?'

'He and his nurse were going to Thornfield to gather

up the rest of the young master's things. Shall I bring you some refreshment?'

'Later,' he said. He'd go clean up a bit, then ride out to meet Theo. 'Would you tell Cook I'd like something special for dinner tonight?'

''I'll let her know, sir,' Wilton said, bowing.

Though nearly writhing with impatience to see Theo again, he thought it best not to meet her all covered in mud. Trotting up the stairs, he called for a footman to bring him hot water.

A half-hour later, cleaned and changed, Dom had a fresh horse brought round and rode off towards the school. It would be better to meet her in private to apologise, so he might gauge her mood, he thought as he urged his gelding to a canter, but he was too impatient to wait until she returned and they could have some guarantee of privacy.

Then, with a leap in his heart, he heard the clip-clop of approaching hoofbeats. As he looked over the next rise, he saw the familiar bay mare in the distance. Thrilled beyond measure that it was Theo, he pulled up, waiting for her to meet him.

'Dom!' she cried, making his heart exult at the unmistakable joy on her face. 'I'm so glad to see you! Was your Newmarket trip successful? If you'd let me know you were coming back today, I would have been at Bildenhall to meet you!'

'When we finished early, I came at once; I didn't want to wait long enough to send a note. It was bad enough that I had to ride off without seeing you after my hasty and ill-advised speech by the brook!'

Her face flushed. 'I thought I'd made you angry, and I was heartsick, for the quarrel was just as much my fault as yours.'

'No, I pushed too hard, Theo. I love you, will always love you, and I'm willing to take whatever you can give me. Having you as my wife is the most important thing to me.'

With a huff of frustration, she said, 'How dare you declare all that to me on horseback, where there is nothing I can do about it! We're not far from the stream. Shall we ride there and let the horses drink while we finish this conversation?'

'Lead on.' He gestured.

Continuing without further speech, they soon reached the old oak. Dom dismounted and hurried over to catch Theo as she slid from the saddle. He pulled her to him, their kiss of greeting long, slow and sweet.

Dom held her against him, savouring her violet scent, her warmth and nearness, the reassuring thud of her heartbeat against his chest. 'How I missed you, Theo. I'm so sorry we parted after angry words. Will you forgive me?'

'Of course. I missed you too, oh, so much! Your absence showed me how vital you've become to me, for I felt I'd lost a piece of myself with you gone. I suppose it crept upon me so slowly, I didn't notice—until you weren't there beside me. The man who makes me laugh and understands how important my orphans and my son are to me and stimulates my mind and eases my anxieties and has supported me through every obstacle I've faced since we met. Who gives me the most exquisite pleasure I've ever known or dreamed of. What an empty shell my life would be without you!'

After that stirring speech, he just had to kiss her again. 'My darling Theo, how could I exist without you? The girl who challenged me in the lane to be more than I thought I could be, who sat on my wall in the rain until I was forced to deal with her, who believed I could accomplish whatever I chose to do, even as I now am—and is making me believe it, too. I thank God every night that my father built a stone barn in the south pasture.'

Then her mouth was on his, demanding, her hands at his chest, untying his neckcloth, seeking skin beneath, her torso rubbing against his erection. She broke the kiss to ease him out of his jacket, free the buttons of his trouser flap, and moved his hand to tug at the jacket of her riding habit.

He stopped her fingers and broke the kiss. 'Are you sure, Theo? I don't want to force you into anything you don't want.'

'I want this now.' She breathed against his lips. 'This land belongs to you. I belong to you. I know you won't let either of us come to harm.'

She could do it, Theo told herself. The episode beside the dry creek in Portugal had led to shame, and the threat of losing her good name and being cast out of polite society that had hung over her for years. But like one of those storms that blew up over those dusty plains, sudden, furious and violent, it had spent itself and moved on. It was over now, over for ever. She could dare believe in a future— with the ardent man beside her.

Fingers hot, shaky, he helped strip off her habit, stays and chemise, laughing as his hand tangled with hers trying to wrest him out of his garments. He laid her down on their jackets, and she pulled him down over her, his skin warming hers, a sense of peace and coming home sweeping through her as he slid into her. After being apart for days, their lovemaking was fast, urgent, and just a short time later, she found bliss in his embrace.

Afterwards, they lay panting, listening to the rush and gurgle of the stream, the breeze ruffling the oak leaves above them. Through layers of contentment, Theo felt a subtle shift as the wind picked up, then a sprinkle of droplets.

'I think it's beginning to rain,' she said, eying the clouds.

Dom rolled to her side and drew her to him. 'I believe you're right.'

As the wind increased in speed and volume, the sprinkle turned into a shower. Laughing, Dom sprang up, then grabbed her hand to pull her to her feet.

'Dance with me!' he cried, his face joyous. 'We'll waltz in the rain.'

'Here?' she asked, half-amused, half-incredulous.

He gestured around them. 'We have a strip of mossy ground as a ballroom floor, the swaying candelabra of oak branches above us, the music of the wind through the trees, and a heart full of melody because you're back in my embrace again. How can I not want to dance, and shout my happiness to the world?'

'Madman!' she laughed. 'Someone might see.'

'They shouldn't look. Come, let's dance.'

He stood gazing down at her, such unrestrained joy on his face, she couldn't help smiling back. He was so uninhibited, so comfortable in himself. She wanted that assurance, that sense of liberation. She wanted *him*.

An answering joy bubbling up, she threw her arms around him and let him waltz her around the bank, while the wind whistled and the stream burbled a melody. The precipitation increased, and she threw her head back, letting warm summer rain course down her face, washing away the dust of the ride.

As she danced with him, drawing on his unconditional support and boundless optimism, Theo felt the burden she'd carried within for so many years rinsing away like that dust before the rain, until she felt so light, buoyed by his love, she thought she might float right up into the clouds.

Dom had given her this, the gift of seeing herself through his eyes: without shame, without guilt, no longer waiting for a reckoning that was surely coming to punish her someday. Freeing her from fear of loss, bringing her to believe in a future.

Marshall would always be dear to her, but the man who'd helped her do all that deserved her love, given unreservedly, just as she'd given him her body.

Finally, laughing again, he halted, mopping his wet hair off his forehead. 'I suppose we need to stop and dress.' He bowed. 'Thank you for the dance, my lady.'

'Thank *you* for the dance, though it's only just begun, my lord. My life. My love.'

Bent halfway over, retrieving his jacket, he halted abruptly and looked back over his shoulder at her. 'What did you say?'

'I love you, Dom. I've known it a long time, but been too frightened to admit it. Until you freed me of that fear, as our marriage has freed me from the past. I only wish I'd struggled out of it sooner.'

Dropping the jacket, he came to her and drew her close. Trailing his fingers down her cheek in a caress, his gaze tender, he said, 'It's all right, beloved. We have the rest of our lives. Which, I promise you, will be a long, long time.'

He placed a kiss on her forehead. 'Now, we'd better get my bride dressed and home before we both contract an inflammation of the lungs. Besides, I brought you a gift which, by now, should be waiting at Bildenstone for you.'

'A gift? You shouldn't have! What is it?'

'You'll see soon enough. Now, help me with these wet ties.'

She assisted him into his soggy garments and he helped

her. Finished haphazardly dressing each other, she stood back to examine him and burst out laughing.

'I can't imagine what Wilton will think when we get back! We look like we've been kidnapped by gypsies, rolled through a hay meadow and then dunked in a stream.'

'Or making love in the rain on a mossy bank?'

She would be brave, as he was. 'Or making love in the rain on your mossy bank beside your stream. My fearless lord.'

Almost giddy with happiness, Dom rode beside Theo back to Bildenstone, where they turned their horses over at the entrance and walked hand in hand up the stairs.

Wilton opened the door to usher them inside. 'The, ah… item you sent from Newmarket has arrived, sir, and has for the time being been installed—under much protest—in the small blue bedchamber.'

'Very good. And don't worry, Wilton. It won't be there long.'

'That is my present?' she asked as they mounted stairs.

'Yes. Let me show it to you before we wash and change. Ordinarily, for a lovely lady, I'd think of gems. But my Theo is hardly ordinary, and if the prospect of wearing the Ransleigh rubies didn't tempt you, I knew no paltry diamonds would. But this—this I thought you might truly appreciate.'

They reached the blue bedchamber, Dom opened the door and waved her in.

The small figure standing by the window whirled to face them. Thin and grimy, his bony shoulders were encased in a ragged jacket that dwarfed his frame, the garment so old and dirty only the frogging and the few remaining buttons identified it as having once graced the back of a Ninety-Fifth Rifleman. Apparently awed and intimidated by his surroundings, he stared at them, fear and defiance in his eyes.

'Theo, meet Tommy of No-Last-Name. He came out of the shadows of the stables in Newmarket, offering to hold my horse for a penny. Before I knew you, I might have tossed him a coin and passed him by with barely a glance. But one lucky day, I met a girl who showed me every one of God's creatures is precious, even the abandoned and the maimed. That every one of us should have a chance to become more.'

Blinking back tears, Theo pressed his hand. 'You were right. This is the best present you could give me.'

Smiling, Dom watched her walk over to kneel in front of the boy. 'Hello, Tommy. Was your father a rifleman?'

'Yes'm,' the boy spoke at last. 'No matter what summun said, he were me da. Me mum give me his jacket afore she died. I never stole it.'

'I'm sure you didn't. How did you get to Newmarket?'

As Theo talked with the child, the trepidation on his face gradually faded, his defensive posture relaxed, and he took her hand.

'Ring the bell, Dom, would you?' she asked a few minutes later. 'Tommy's agreed to let Mrs Greenlow give him a bath before we drive him over to the school to meet the other children.'

'Letting Mrs Greenlow do it? Wise woman,' he teased. 'Looks like he could bite and scratch.'

'Nonsense. He'll enjoy a bath. Won't you, Tommy?'

The boy looked up dubiously, leaving Dom confident he had no notion of what a bath actually entailed. But, with more reassurances from Theo that she would rejoin him as soon as she found him a shirt and breeches, he trotted off with the footman who answered Dom's summons.

She came dancing over to him, gratitude and delight

on her face. 'Thank you for my present! You are the hand-somest, kindest, wisest man I've ever met!'

'And I'm your dearest love, for ever,' he said, hungry to hear the words again from her lips.

She looked up, her eyes tender, her expression radiating affection and joy. 'You are my dearest love, and I will love you for ever.'

With that, she leaned up into his kiss.

* * * * *

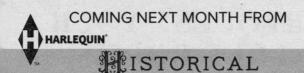

REQUEST YOUR FREE BOOKS!

☰ HARLEQUIN®

ℍISTORICAL

Where love is timeless

2 FREE NOVELS PLUS 2 **FREE GIFTS!**

YES! Please send me 2 FREE Harlequin® Historical novels and my 2 FREE gifts (gifts are worth about $10). After receiving them, if I don't wish to receive any more books, I can return the shipping statement marked "cancel." If I don't cancel, I will receive 6 brand-new novels every month and be billed just $5.69 per book in the U.S. or $5.99 per book in Canada. That's a savings of at least 12% off the cover price! It's quite a bargain! Shipping and handling is just 50¢ per book in the U.S. and 75¢ per book in Canada.* I understand that accepting the 2 free books and gifts places me under no obligation to buy anything. I can always return a shipment and cancel at any time. Even if I never buy another book, the two free books and gifts are mine to keep forever.

246/349 HDN GH2Z

Name	(PLEASE PRINT)	
Address		Apt. #
City	State/Prov.	Zip/Postal Code

Signature (if under 18, a parent or guardian must sign)

Mail to the **Reader Service:**
IN U.S.A.: P.O. Box 1867, Buffalo, NY 14240-1867
IN CANADA: P.O. Box 609, Fort Erie, Ontario L2A 5X3

Want to try two free books from another line?
Call 1-800-873-8635 or visit www.ReaderService.com.

* Terms and prices subject to change without notice. Prices do not include applicable taxes. Sales tax applicable in N.Y. Canadian residents will be charged applicable taxes. Offer not valid in Quebec. This offer is limited to one order per household. Not valid for current subscribers to Harlequin Historical books. All orders subject to credit approval. Credit or debit balances in a customer's account(s) may be offset by any other outstanding balance owed by or to the customer. Please allow 4 to 6 weeks for delivery. Offer available while quantities last.

Your Privacy—The Reader Service is committed to protecting your privacy. Our Privacy Policy is available online at www.ReaderService.com or upon request from the Reader Service.

We make a portion of our mailing list available to reputable third parties that offer products we believe may interest you. If you prefer that we not exchange your name with third parties, or if you wish to clarify or modify your communication preferences, please visit us at www.ReaderService.com/consumerchoice or write to us at Reader Service Preference Service, P.O. Box 9062, Buffalo, NY 14240-9062. Include your complete name and address.

HH15

SPECIAL EXCERPT FROM

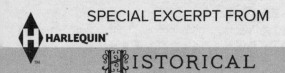

HARLEQUIN®

ℋISTORICAL

*Viscount Amersham has come to Paris on his
Grand Tour to prove his expert skill with the blade.
Yet feisty Alyssandra Leodegrance is* not *the opponent
he was expecting…*

Read on for a sneak preview of
RAKE MOST LIKELY TO REBEL
an exciting new offering from
Bronwyn Scott
and the first in her new quartet
RAKES ON TOUR.

It was darker now. There were fewer lanterns and even
fewer guests in this remote corner of the garden. Her pulse
began to leap. They'd reached their destination—somewhere
private.

"It seems we have reached the perimeter of the garden,"
North commented, his eyes full of mischief. "What do you
suppose we do now?"

Alyssandra wet her lips and turned toward him so they
were no longer side by side but face-to-face. "I've talked
for far too long. You could tell me about yourself. What
brings you to Paris?" She stepped closer, drawing a long line
down the white linen of his chest with her fan. She would
genuinely like to know. She'd spent the past three weeks
making up stories in her mind about what he was doing in
France.

But she'd not come out to the garden to acquire a thorough history of the Viscount Amersham. That would come in time, as those layers came off. Tonight was about making first impressions, ones that would eventually lead to…more. Even so, she rather doubted her brother had expected "more" to involve stealing away to the dark corners of Madame Aguillard's garden with somewhat illicit intentions.

"I *could* tell you my life story," he drawled, his eyes darkening to a deep sapphire. "Or perhaps we might do something more interesting." Those sapphire eyes dropped to her mouth, signaling his definition of *interesting*, and her breath caught. *Something more interesting, please.*

It was hard to say who kissed whom. *His* head had angled toward her in initiation, but *she* had stepped into him, welcoming the advance of his mouth on hers, the meeting of their bodies; gentian blue skirts pressed against black-clad thighs, corseted breasts met the muscled firmness of his chest beneath white linen.

Her mouth opened for him, letting his tongue tangle with hers in a sensual duel. She met his boldness with boldness of her own, tasting the fruity sweetness of champagne where it lingered on his tongue. Life pulsed through her as she nipped his lip and he growled low in his throat, his arm pressing her to the hard contours of him. She moved against his hips, challenging him, knowing full well this bordered on madness; desire was rising between them, hot and heady.

Don't miss
RAKE MOST LIKELY TO REBEL
by Bronwyn Scott
available June 2015 wherever
Harlequin® Historical books and ebooks are sold.

www.Harlequin.com

HHEXP0515

Love the Harlequin book
you just read?

Your opinion matters.

Review this book on your favorite
book site, review site, blog or your own
social media properties and share
your opinion with other readers!

THE WORLD IS BETTER WITH

Romance

Harlequin has everything from contemporary, passionate and heartwarming to suspenseful and inspirational stories.

Whatever your mood,
we have a romance just for you!

Connect with us to find your next great read,
special offers and more.

f /HarlequinBooks

🐦 @HarlequinBooks

www.HarlequinBlog.com

www.Harlequin.com/Newsletters

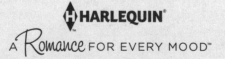

H HARLEQUIN®

A *Romance* FOR EVERY MOOD™

www.Harlequin.com